Outline for Murder

A Michael Bishop Mystery

5/11/19

Mary,
You have a great friend in Bonnie Flynn.
All the best,
Anthony J. Pucci

by

Anthony J. Pucci

Copyright © 2015 Anthony J. Pucci

All rights reserved.

This book is a work of fiction. Names, characters, places, and incidents are a product of the author's imagination or are used fictitiously. Any resemblance to actual events, locales, or persons, living or dead, is coincidental.

Epigraph

"But in the end truth will out."

William Shakespeare, *The Merchant of Venice, II, ii.*

Chapter 1

The last thing he needed was to get pulled over by a cop on the way to school. He could almost hear his students peppering him with their desire for details. "Were you texting?" "Did you get a ticket?" His colleagues would be no better. Their comforting words, "Don't worry, Mike," would be followed by offers to visit him in jail.

Michael Bishop wasn't going to chance a ticket by answering his cell phone while driving down Pleasant Hill Road. Who could be calling him this early in the morning? With his curiosity trumping his annoyance, he put on his right turn signal and pulled in to a Stop N Go. With the engine still running, he pulled out his cell and saw that the incoming call was from someone at school. Why would anyone bother to call him when they knew that he always arrived before 8:00 a.m.? He took the call just before it went to voice mail.

"Mike? It's Sister Ann. I'm glad I caught you." Sister Ann was the middle-aged Sister of The Holy Rosary who was the principal at Holy Trinity High School. Behind her unassuming exterior was a sharp intellect and a steely determination to get what she wanted. Her detractors, of whom there were many, said that she lacked people skills and that she relied too much on the advice of Sister Pat, one of the assistant principals. There was an edge to her voice this Monday morning.

Bishop didn't know what was coming. "Hi, Sister. I've already left for school. Anything wrong?"

"I'll tell you what's wrong," as the edge to her voice became decidedly sharper. "Al Zappala was supposed to be here at seven sharp this morning to have a conference with the Delaneys. He's late and I'm not dealing with them without *him* in this office."

Zappala was in his third year as the school's football coach and gym teacher. No one knew really knew him all that well. He was loud, abrasive, and crude. As long as his teams were winning, he knew that he could do whatever he wanted. "How can I help, Sister?"

"I want you to go over to that man's house and get him over here *now*. I've called, but he's not picking up. Since you seem to get along with him better than most, I thought if I caught you before you got here, you could get over there fast. He probably had too much to drink again last night and is sleeping it off."

Sister and Bishop both knew that Zappala had a problem. Even the kids knew. He recently had told a PE class to go out and "toss the ball around" while he caught up on some paper work. One of the students who had been late to class found him in his office stretched out between two chairs, dead to the world.

"Okay, I'm on my way right now. Will you have someone cover my homeroom?"

"Don't worry about that." Her voice snapped like a whip. "Just get that s.o.b. here. And he better have a damn good reason for making me and the Delaneys wait." She hung up without saying thank you or goodbye. Sister Ann was definitely not having a good Monday morning. The "damn" and "s.o.b" coming from a nun didn't surprise him. He'd learned through the years that most nuns weren't much different than everybody else.

As he made his way back across town, Bishop thought about the coach. Does he realize what kind of trouble he's in? Why would he blow off this meeting? Did he really think that he could get away with his "I'm-the-coach-and-I-can-do-whatever-I-want" attitude? Albert Zappala did have an impressive coaching record. He was the only coach in the area to have more than two hundred career football victories. His teams had won three state titles. That was during his time at Madison High about one hundred and eighty miles west of Groveland. After coaching there for twenty-five years, he had stunned the Madison community when he resigned and took a job as PE teacher and head football coach at Trinity for half the salary. That was a little more than two years ago. Since then, he hadn't made too many friends, but he didn't seem to care. He lived for football. His teams won. No one asked too many questions. Bishop thought about what Sister had said. He didn't consider Zappala a friend, but he did try to get along with everyone on the faculty.

Bishop passed his own house on his way up Pleasant Hill Road. He owned an old farmhouse out in the country. After spending his day with so many people, he appreciated the quiet this place afforded him. Maybe Zappala lived up this way for the same reason. He had never thought to ask him. For Bishop, the solitude was more pronounced since he had lost his wife, Grace, eight years ago. Teaching was now his saving "grace." That was the reason that when he turned sixty-five, he didn't retire. His students kept him young.

It was strange to be driving in this direction at this time of the day. Now that the days were getting shorter, he appreciated the sunlight even more. In the short time since he had driven down this road, the sky had brightened considerably. Bishop was looking forward to getting into the routine of the school day. Trying to put thoughts of confronting Zappala out of his mind, he began to anticipate his day, going over what he planned to do in each of his classes.

As he approached Zappala's house, he slowed down. He'd never been in the house, although he had given the coach a ride to school on several occasions. A black Lincoln Town Car had been backed into the stone driveway and was facing the road. What was he thinking driving a car like that? More than a few teachers had muttered something about him showing off. "Gonna give people the wrong idea about us Catholic school teachers," Steve Marshall had joked in the faculty room one day. Steve, who had a wife, four kids, and Dodge minivan with 157,000 miles on it, was only half joking.

He pulled his Toyota Corolla up to the Lincoln, took the keys from the ignition, and walked up to the front door. If Zappala were "sick," Bishop would call Sister and tell her that the meeting with the Delaneys would have to be rescheduled. He suspected that the meeting had been prompted by Zappala's decision to bench their son, Chris, for the second half of Friday night's win over Central. Trinity was ahead 28-0 at the half so it wasn't as if the coach was risking a team win. He must have wanted to make a point with Chris, and he made it the only way he knew how. The Delaneys were counting on Chris getting a football scholarship, and he wasn't going to impress the college scouts sitting on the bench.

As Bishop approached the house, he saw his reflection in the glass panels on either side of the front door. He was wearing what he typically wore for school – a button down dress shirt mostly obscured by a crew neck sweater, Dockers pants, and a pair of comfortable Rockport shoes. Fortunately, he had never developed the paunch that most men did, nor did he have wrinkles or jowls. One of the more prominent features of his face was the thick salt and pepper moustache that he had worn for years. Overall, he didn't think that he looked all of his seventy years. Most days, he certainly didn't feel that old.

Through the glass panel, he could see that the front door opened into the living room. There was a sofa to the right of the door where newspapers had been tossed, but his view in that direction was partially obscured. A large flat screen TV mounted on the wall was on. ESPN was showing highlights of yesterday's NFL action. A recliner was positioned opposite the screen. To its right was a small table with a glass, a couple of beer cans, and a half-empty bowl of chips. If he had had too much to drink last night, he was, at least, up and about, and catching up on the scores. Bishop figured that it would take only a couple of minutes to pop in, remind him of his meeting with the Delaneys, tell him about Sister Ann's call, and then head back down to Trinity. He hoped that he wouldn't miss too much of his first period class. He wanted to hand back those *Romeo and Juliet* essays to his honors freshmen. Grading papers had consumed so much of his weekend. He was pleased that most of the kids had really seemed to take a liking to the Bard.

    Other than the muffled sounds from the TV, all was quiet. Maybe Zappala was taking a shower. He tried the doorbell this time. Nothing. It probably was broken, and the coach wouldn't have bothered to do anything about it. Although money never seemed to be a problem for him, he certainly didn't spend much on the maintenance of his home or yard. The old wooden exterior was in need of a new coat of paint, overgrown shrubs crept above the window frames, and his riding mower was sitting in the middle of his half-mowed lawn. Growing impatient, Bishop dispensed with etiquette and pounded on the door this time. This guy was going to make him late for class. Still there was no response. Since Zappala could be belligerent and obnoxious even when he was sober, Bishop prepared himself for an unpleasant encounter and banged on the door with both fists. Still nothing. He tried the handle, expecting it to be locked. He was surprised when the door actually opened.

    "Al? Coach? It's me, Mike Bishop. May I come in?"

    The only response was "Just Do It." It was a Nike commercial on ESPN.

Bishop closed the door behind him, walked farther into the living room where the television was showing a replay of a controversial call made by an official in one of yesterday's games. Zappala wasn't taking a shower. He wasn't having breakfast. He was lying face down on the shag carpet in front of the sofa.

Asleep? Passed out?

"Coach! Coach! Are you okay? What happened?"

Bishop bent over the stocky man who probably outweighed him by a hundred pounds, wondering if he would have the strength to lift him up. The maroon sweatshirt he was wearing was likely one with a Holy Trinity logo on the front. His jeans were cinched at the waist with a black belt. He had white crew socks on and no shoes. Instead of the scent of beer that he expected to notice, Bishop was aware of a strange odor that he couldn't quite identify when he was close to the body. He felt his left wrist and his neck for a pulse. His skin was cold. Zappala was dead.

Involuntarily, Bishop's entire body jerked backward, and as he tried to regain his footing, he tumbled into the small table, knocking it over. The cans were empty, and the glass must have been mostly empty as not much beer actually spilled onto the rug. He tossed the cans in a small wastebasket on the other side of the recliner and quickly picked up the glass and the chips as well as his shaking hands would allow. The reality of his colleague's death was sinking in. Poor guy. He must have had a heart attack. He was a prime candidate. Mid-fifties. Overweight. Heavy drinker. Lots of stress. Two hundred wins and three titles don't come without stress.

***

Bishop grabbed his cell phone, and went outside. He thought that some fresh air might help. He made the call to 911 although this was not an emergency. His next call was more difficult.

"Good morning. Holy Trinity High School. May I help you?" It was the bubbly voice of Terry Mortenson, the school's office secretary who had been a true friend to Bishop over the years, especially in those dark weeks and months after Grace died. Of the office staff, only Terry could be that bubbly on a Monday morning.

"Terry, this is Mike. I need to talk to Sister Ann right away."

"How late are you going to be? I already got someone to cover your first period class."

"I don't know. That's not why I'm calling. Just get Sister, please."

"Mike, I'm sorry. She's in a meeting with the Delaneys, and she isn't in a very good mood because Zappala hasn't shown up."

"I know, Terry. That's why I'm calling. Al isn't going to show up. I'm at his house right now. He's dead, Terry."

"What! Oh my God! How awful! What happened? Are you okay?"

"Yeah, I'm all right, I guess. Shaking a little, but I'll be fine. I called 911 and help should be here soon. You need to get Sister Ann on the phone."

"Right. Let me put you on hold. I can't believe this has happened." The bubbly quality of her voice had been replaced by a noticeable quavering.

He was on hold for no more than thirty seconds when he heard the voice of Sister Ann for the second time that morning.

"Mike. What's happened?"

"I went up to his house to give him your message, and there was no answer when I knocked on the door. I could see that the television was on, so I thought he was either hung over or taking a shower. The door was unlocked. I didn't see him until I walked in. Must have been quick. Probably happened last night when he was watching television."

"Mike, you stay there. Do you want me to send Ron up there?" Ron Jennings was one of the assistant principals and a good friend.

"No. There's no need. Nothing he can do. I'll be fine. What will you tell the kids?"

"Good question. The only family that he had lived in Connecticut as far as I know. I'll let the police notify them, but I need to tell the kids. They'll want the truth. I've been through this before. When I was at Pope Pius in Brooklyn, one of the teachers dropped dead during cafeteria duty. We're in for a rough few days. I'll alert the people in guidance and Father Mahoney. I'll wait until the end of first period to make an announcement. I'll lead them in a prayer." She added, "Mike, I'm sorry that you had to be the one to find him." It wasn't often that she said she was sorry about anything.

"Thanks, Sister. I'll be down as soon as I can. Good luck with the announcement."

"Right."

Sister's comment about the truth stayed with him. Yes, kids do want the truth. So does everyone else for that matter, but the truth was not always what the Holy Trinity community got from her. She ran the school as if it were her own little kingdom, dispensing the truth, or her version of it, when and how she saw fit.

As he re-entered the house, he heard the ESPN host still discussing that controversial call with two analysts on a split screen. He picked up the remote to turn off the chatter. Coach would certainly have had an opinion on the matter, one that he would have shared with others whether they wanted to hear it or not. That was one of the things that put people off about him. When he put the remote down, he realized that the last person to touch it was now dead. He took another look at the body. His left arm was extended above his torso as if he was reaching for something. His right arm was underneath his body. The man who had been such an intimidating presence was gone. The Delaneys wouldn't have the chance to vent their anger. Sister Ann would have to come up with some nice things to say about that s.o.b.

Chapter 2

The 911 response team had yet to arrive. In the interim, Bishop faced the prospect of being in the presence of a dead man, a man who worked where he worked and lived on the same street. The realization that his colleague's life had been so quickly taken left him shaken. At seventy, he was easily fifteen years older than the coach. He tried to suppress thoughts of his own mortality. His legs were still shaky, his stomach queasy, and his mouth dry. He decided to find the bathroom. As he walked through the kitchen with its clutter of dishes in the sink and an empty pizza box on the counter, he heard the faint sounds of music. As he walked down the hallway, he recognized the voice of Mama Cass singing, "Monday, Monday." The music was coming from the clock/radio in Zappala's bedroom. He pressed the off button and took a quick look around the room. There were a few sports magazines on his dresser, another television on a stand opposite his bed, and a basket of clean clothes that hadn't been put away. There were no photos of himself or his family. The bed had not been slept in. Bishop found the room cold and depressing.

    He walked by another bedroom that was obviously used as an office/trophy room. A metal desk like the ones at school stood against one wall, its top littered with papers and file folders. On a small table next to the desk, there was a small television, a DVD player, and stacks of disks in their jewel cases. He had probably used that to watch film of opposing teams. Another larger table held so many trophies that it looked like it would collapse under its own weight. The walls were covered with sports photos. The partially opened closet door revealed cardboard boxes stacked to the ceiling. Clearly, the coach had been something of a pack rat.

    Entering the bathroom across the hall, he ran cold water from the sink and splashed some on his face. He looked at himself in the mirror above the sink. The shock he had just experienced was clearly written on his face. As he dried his hands, he noticed a bottle of Grecian hair conditioner on the counter. Most people figured that Zappala had used something, but no one really knew why he would bother. Now they would never know that or much else about this man. Bishop took a couple of slow, deep breaths and steeled himself for the rest of his morning. It was anything but "just another Monday."

***

Two burly young men arrived in an ambulance to transport the body to the morgue, a somber but routine task for them. As they got out of their vehicle, Bishop was there to meet them.

"Mr. Bishop, I'm Tom Nelson and this is my partner, Jerry Milone. I had you for English 9." He extended his beefy hand.

"Oh, yes, of course. Nice to see you, Tom. Nice to meet you, Jerry." Jerry's hand was beefy, too. One of the occupational hazards of teaching in a small town for a number of years was that he frequently bumped into former students. Most of the time, he really didn't mind at all, especially if he remembered the student's name.

"Thanks for getting here so quickly."

"I understand we have a deceased male inside," said Jerry, as they pulled a stretcher from the back of their vehicle.

"Yes, he's lying beside the sofa in the living room. That's where I found him when I came in. The door had been unlocked." Then he added, "You know, it's Coach Zappala."

"Really?" Although Tom had graduated long before Zappala had arrived, in a small town like Groveland, a high school football coach, especially a successful one, was something of a celebrity. "It's such a shame. I bet it'll be hard on the kids at school."

"Yes, I'm sure it will be."

Just then a police cruiser pulled into the driveway and onto the grass. Two officers emerged from the car, neither bothering to close the door. One of them shouted to the EMTs as they were about to enter the house. "Hold on a minute! We need to get in there first. You ought to know that."

"Sure, no problem," said Tom. "We weren't going to touch anything," he added defensively.

The other officer approached Bishop. He was clearly near retirement age. Heavy jowls were the most prominent feature of his face, and his belt was partially obscured by his considerable belly. If there was any chasing of criminals to be done, this was not the man to do it. "I'm Lieutenant Hodge. I take it you're the one who called this in."

"Yes, Lieutenant. My name is Michael Bishop. I found the body near the sofa. I felt for a pulse, but he was gone. I accidentally bumped into the table next to the recliner, and some snacks fell on the floor. I cleaned that up as best I could. Other than that, nothing has been disturbed."

If that information bothered Hodge, he didn't let it show. He seemed to ignore the small speaker attached to the shoulder of his uniform that was squawking intermittently. He introduced Bishop to his partner, Officer Williams, a much younger and trimmer man. The three men went into the house together. "Mr. Bishop, what were you doing here this morning?" asked Hodge.

Bishop recounted the phone call that he had received from Sister Ann. Although that seemed hours ago, only about twenty minutes had passed.

"How did you get in the house?"

"I knocked on the door several times, but then I realized that it was unlocked."

"Really?"

Williams, who had been checking the door and windows, said that there was no sign of a forced entry.

After checking the body for any wounds or visible signs of a struggle, Hodge gave the okay for Nelson and Milone to remove the body. "Take him to the coroner's office. Under the circumstances, an autopsy will be required."

Bishop didn't want to stay there any longer than he had to. "Lieutenant, would it be all right if I go now? I've got classes to teach," although as he said it, he wondered just how much teaching he would get done that day. The kids were bound to be upset. They'd probably want to talk. What he really wanted to do was go back in time to that moment before he had taken Sister Ann's call.

"Sure, no problem. I can contact you at school if I have any questions." The perfunctory manner in which he spoke these words led Bishop to believe that the likelihood of receiving such a call was minimal. Then Hodge added, "Say, do you remember Wendy Hodge?"

Bishop hesitated for a moment. Over his forty-five years at Trinity, he had taught literally thousands of students. Not all of them stood out. Some were quite memorable. In fact, scores of former students kept in touch. Others that he would sooner forget were memorable as well. Wendy Hodge didn't fall into either category. "The name sounds familiar. I take it that she attended Trinity?"

"Sure did. Damn near put me in the poor house sending that girl there. Groveland High is a perfectly good school. Went there myself, but all of her friends were going to Trinity so that was that."

"What year did she graduate?"

"'87? '88? Somewhere in there," he said as he removed his hat to reveal a military-style buzz cut.

Bishop laughed. "Well, that is quite a few years ago." He didn't feel quite so bad about not remembering Hodge's daughter. "I'll have to look her up in the yearbook. Once I see a face, I usually remember the person."

"Me, too," Hodge said, "although in my case I'm looking at mugshots."

"What's Wendy doing these days?"

Hodge smiled for the first time since he had arrived on the scene. "She's married, with three little ones, and a fourth on the way." It seemed as though he was going to pull out some photos, but he just tugged at his gadget-laden belt.

"Well, congratulations! Please give her my best."

"I will. Thanks." Hodge headed back into the house, and Bishop turned toward his car.

Just as Bishop realized that his car was blocked in the driveway by the ambulance, Ron Jennings pulled up. He left his car on the side of the road, and sprinted up to Bishop. He was a tall man, in his mid-thirties and athletic. He was wearing a white shirt, striped tie, and khakis. Ron was an easy-going guy who enjoyed his job and got along well with the kids. He was always there to help out a teacher or a student when needed. No one had to ask; he always seemed to know what to say or do. Except now.

"I got here as fast as I could. How are you doing?"

"Me? I'm fine, I guess. It's just a shock, you know? To come in and find him lying there…" His voice trailed off a bit. The next word would have been, "dead."

"No kidding! I'm just glad that I wasn't the one to find him. Not too sure how well I would have handled that." He ran his fingers through his light brown hair as if that would somehow erase those doubts from his mind.

"I'm sure you would have risen to the occasion just as you have so many times at school," replied Bishop as he thought of how deftly Jennings had navigated some difficult situations at school in the five years since he had become an assistant principal.

"Are you thinking of going to school?"

"Yes, I am." Going to school was what he had done for most of his life. He hadn't planned on retiring just yet, but this sudden reminder of life's uncertainties might force him to reconsider exactly what he wanted to do in his golden years. Putting these thoughts aside for the moment, he said, "I just need to wait until I can get my car out." As he said that, the two first responders were wheeling out the stretcher with the body of Coach Zappala covered by white sheets strapped to it.

"Mike, I don't think that's a good idea." Ron had his hand on Bishop's shoulder as he offered his advice. "You've just been through a very disturbing experience. The kids won't be up for any literature discussions today anyway. I really think that you should take the day off. I'll get your classes covered. No problem. Get home and try to relax a little bit."

"Well," said Bishop, "I guess you might be right. I hate to miss class, but considering the circumstances, I think I will take you up on that offer." He began looking forward to settling down in his favorite chair in the sunroom with a good book, some classical music playing in the background, and a cup of hot tea.

Bishop drove the short distance back to his own place. As far as he was concerned, the worst of it was over. As it turned out, he was wrong.

***

After Sister Ann interrupted classes just before the end of the period to make the announcement about the unexpected death of Coach Zappala, the student body fell into an eerie silence. It was suddenly as quiet as if all of the students were taking a final examination. When the announcement ended, students went out into the halls to get their books for the next class. Sister had said that anyone who wanted to talk with one of the guidance counselors or with Fr. Mahoney, the chaplain, would be allowed to do so.

Stephanie Harris, a first-year teacher at Trinity, was in the break room when the announcement was made. Her interests in running and in nutrition made her a model of physical fitness. Although she had only been teaching for a matter of weeks, she carried herself like a veteran. Her youthful enthusiasm and caring personality had made her an instant favorite with both her colleagues and her students.

"Oh my, how sad!" she muttered, more to herself than to Mary Nickerson, a math teacher who had the same prep period. She was about ten years older than Stephanie and about fifty pounds heavier. Her weakness for junk food made controlling her weight a constant challenge.

Mary grabbed a few napkins to wipe her hands of the residue from the bag of corn curls she had just polished off. She started weeping softly. "How can I teach next period, Steph? What will I say to the kids?"

"You'll be fine. Just remember what Sister Ann said. If some students need to talk, there are people available to help. A lot of them might actually prefer to simply carry on with the day's lessons. Just see how it goes. I wouldn't give a test or anything, but we'll get through this."

If it was embarrassing for a veteran to receive advice from a rookie, Mary didn't seem to care.

"I guess you're right. Well, I better get a move on. You too. I don't want you to be late because of me. I'm fine now. Thanks, Steph."

"What lunch do you have today?"

"Second."

"Me too," said Stephanie. "I'll see you then."

Mary gathered her papers and headed off to class. Jack Slater, the school's custodian, had observed the exchange between Stephanie and Mary. A veteran of the Vietnam War, Jack split his school day between doing his job and doing his best to know everyone else's business. As soon as Mary left, Jack remarked, "That one sure is a drama queen." As he spoke, his prominent Adam's apple bobbed up and down.

Refusing to take the bait, Steph looked at the clock on the wall, picked up her belongings, and said, "Well, I have a class waiting for me."

The halls that were normally so full of youthful exuberance were understandably subdued. Some students were crying. Others were asking their friends if they thought that a Chemistry test scheduled for later that day would be postponed. Some wondered whether they would get a day out of school for the funeral. One of the football players asked a teacher if he knew whether practice was still on.

A number of students went to the chapel to pray and to comfort each other. Some faculty members were there as well. In the office, Terry fielded a number of calls as word began to spread. Among them were calls from Russ Chandler and Doug Sanders, two of the assistant football coaches. Each wanted to know if Friday's game would be postponed. No decision on that or much of anything else had been made yet. Each of the coaches also wanted to let the principal know that he was interested in the now vacant position of head football coach. So much for mourning the dead.

Chapter 3

As soon as Bishop got home, he went into his bedroom and changed out of his school clothes and into a long-sleeved shirt, jeans, and sneakers. Since there was a chill in the house, he also put on a hooded fleece with a full zipper down the front.

He was still feeling a bit shaky, so he decided to make himself a cup of hot tea. While the Earl Grey was steeping, he selected Bach's "The Well-Tempered Clavier" from his sizable collection of classical CDs and placed it in the player in the sunroom.

With cup in hand, he sat in his favorite chair, put his feet up on the ottoman, and looked out on his backyard. There was a time after his wife died when he had thought seriously about selling the home that they had shared for over thirty years. Grace was only fifty-eight when she passed away. He relived that painful memory less often than he did eight years ago, but it was no less painful to recall it now.

Grace had been a very successful real estate agent. She enjoyed the flexibility in her schedule, and her outgoing personality made her a natural. She sometimes teased him about the fact that she earned twice the income than he did while working about half the time. Teaching in a Catholic school, his income in the early days was one step above eligibility for food stamps. However, with two incomes and no children, they managed quite nicely. Never ones to live beyond their means, they had even managed to save for a comfortable retirement. It was a retirement that she would never get to enjoy and one that he had so far stubbornly refused to begin.

Grace was so successful in her work that she often earned bonuses and other gifts. That year, she won an all-expenses-paid trip for two to Las Vegas for five nights. Bishop had no interest in Vegas and hated the thought of taking a week off from school. Since the tickets had to be used by the end of October, she decided to ask one of her coworkers, Kim Reynolds, to accompany her. Not long after she arrived in Vegas, Grace became violently ill. She thought she had food poisoning, so she stayed in her room while Kim hit the slots. When Kim returned to their room, she found Grace unconscious on the bathroom floor. She was taken immediately to a local hospital where she died of peritonitis. Although it was rare at her age, her appendix had burst. Had she not ignored the early symptoms, she would still be alive.

The death of Albert Zappala had brought back the nightmarish days that followed receiving the news of the death of his wife. He had some sense of what the Zappala family was experiencing.

***

That belief turned out to be incorrect. Apparently, Zappala had been estranged from his family. His funeral and burial were to take place in Groveland. Only his nephew, Rocco Santorini, planned on attending the service. At Holy Trinity, the rest of the week was a bit surreal. After the initial shock and tears, the kids were ready to get back to their normal routines. Although that seemed cold in a way, Bishop thought that perhaps it was best after all. It reminded him of the family response to the unexpected loss of a boy in "'Out, Out'" by Robert Frost. They, too, had no choice but to get on with their lives. The funeral was held that Friday. Sister Ann had decided to cancel classes for the day so that the all those who wanted to would be able to attend the service. Friday night's football game was rescheduled for the following day.

As he thought more about it, Bishop realized that he knew absolutely nothing about his family. Zappala never said much about his personal life. To some of the male faculty, he had expressed no regrets about never having married. "I get what I want when I want it," was the way he had phrased it to Bishop not long after he had taken the job at Trinity. Sister Ann's policy was that a teacher's personal life was just that, personal, as long as it didn't interfere with job performance. It also helped that Zappala had quickly earned a place on Sister's "A" list. No one knew how he had done that, but it was clear that being on that list had its perks.

Bishop wondered if she had known about his drinking problem from the outset. Would she have been reluctant to hire him or would she have felt that he could change his ways? Despite having worked for her since she had become the principal about twenty years earlier, Bishop often was at a loss to explain some of her decisions. As a coach known throughout the state, she probably hadn't asked too many questions. She would have been thrilled that he was willing to teach and coach at Trinity for far less money than he was making at Madison. There was an expectation at Trinity that teachers try to live by Christian values, represent the school favorably, and set a good example for the students. Of course, there were occasions when staff members fell short of these expectations, not unlike Sister Ann herself and some of her cohorts living in a convent just a few blocks from the school. As Bishop saw it, the problem was that many of Sister Ann's judgments seemed to be governed more by who the individual transgressor was rather than by the transgression itself. All the teachers knew who was on the "A" list and who wasn't.

A line of mourners gathered outside the Langone Funeral Home for a brief service before the funeral mass held at the Church of the Redeemer. As people milled around before the service, no one knew quite what to say so the conversations were awkwardly brief. Bishop did a double take when he caught a glimpse of Russ Chandler wearing a white shirt, necktie, and sport coat as opposed to his usual sweatshirt, sweatpants, sneakers, and baseball cap. He looked uncomfortable. The tie was already loosened and his shirt unbuttoned at the top. Zappala's misfortune had been Chandler's good fortune. Russ, who had occasionally subbed for the coach, had agreed to work as a long-term sub until a search for a permanent replacement could be completed. Russ was clearly a leading candidate in the search for head football coach since he knew the kids and the program.

Sister Ann and Sister Patricia were standing at the entrance as if taking mental notes of attendance. Their constant companionship made for some whispered speculation in the school and in the community. In Sister Ann's view, the day might be a day off from school, but all teachers and staff were expected to attend. The pair had arrived early, determined to be in control of events. While Sister Ann knew well enough how to play the game, Sister Pat, whom some of the students had given an unkind soubriquet, was living proof that the order of the Sisters of The Holy Rosary did not have an entrance exam.

Bishop greeted both sisters as he prepared himself for this solemn occasion. It was Sister Ann who initiated further conversation with him.

"That poor man," Sister Ann began. "We were in a very real sense the only family that he had. I can see why we knew so little about his family. His sister is a pill." Sister Ann had contacted Zappala's family in Connecticut to get details on the funeral that she had assumed would be held there.

"What do you mean by that?" Bishop asked.

"I really shouldn't say. I'm sure the woman was in shock. She apparently is considerably older than Al and not in good health. Her exact words were, 'Maybe now we'll get the money we need to save the bakery.' Can you imagine that?"

"No love lost there, I guess," Bishop responded. "I wonder what she meant by that."

"I certainly was not going to ask her that, Mike, but she went on and on about his money for a while. It was as if the news was a match that ignited a fuse. Her tone became increasing hateful as she told her story."

"What story?"

"Well, I couldn't follow everything that she was saying because when she got going she would occasionally lapse into Italian, but the gist of it is that her family has run a bakery in Hartford for many years. The Santorinis were very successful for many years. When they made a decision to expand, they took on a lot of debt. Shortly thereafter, her husband died, people's eating habits turned away from rich Italian pastries, and she and her son, Rocco, were about to lose the business."

"How does Al fit into that?"

"Maria, that's Al's sister, told me that she had repeatedly contacted her brother for assistance but that he refused to help and didn't seem to care what happened to them or the business."

"What would make her think that Al could help if he wanted to?" Bishop wondered. "Most of us at Trinity aren't making the big bucks," he grinned. Sister Patricia simply snorted her disapproval at the mere mention of the school's non-competitive salary scale.

"I'm well aware of that, Michael. As you know, our rewards are not all monetary. However, you seem to be forgetting that Al worked for many years in the public school system."

"Yes, that's true, and he lived alone in a modest house. His only extravagance seems to have been his love of big cars and a penchant for gambling. He couldn't have had the resources to save a failing business."

"True and not true," said Sister Ann.

"What do you mean?"

Sister was about to answer but was stopped as several teachers came over to greet her. Among them was Stephanie Harris, the rookie French teacher. She was dressed conservatively with a calf-length black coat, black pumps, and a dark leather handbag with one strap slung over her shoulder. Her dark brown hair was pulled back into a ponytail that swayed as she walked.

"I wondered if we might sit together at the mass," she asked.

"That would be fine with me," replied Bishop with a warm smile. Stephanie was the only new teacher on the staff at Trinity this year, and he had taken on the role of a mentor as he had done for a number of the new teachers who had passed through the halls of Trinity over the years.

"I'm so sorry that you were the one to find him. That must have been awful." She took out a tissue to dab at her nose and eyes. Her obvious sadness could not mar her equally obvious beauty. Previously, Bishop had seen her dressed in the practical clothing required of teaching and in jeans and a pullover at games. However, dressed for this more formal occasion, she drew the attention of others without trying.

Bishop knew that she had worked as a paralegal for several years after college before deciding to go back to school for her teacher's certificate. According to Sarah Humphries, one of the gossipy guidance counselors, at least a dozen students had come in during the first week of school to request a transfer out of Spanish and into French. She had made an instant impression on Bishop as well. She was bright, energetic, and funny. She had common sense and a good way with the kids. She had the makings of a good teacher. Over the years, he had seen many young teachers crash and burn. Steph would do well.

They didn't share the same prep period, but their homerooms were across the hall from each other. Occasionally, she would come in at the end of the day to ask a quick question, and as a veteran teacher, he was always more than happy to explain the protocol or offer some friendly advice.

Bishop downplayed the emotional impact that finding the body had had on him. The days following his unhappy discovery had been mostly a blur. He thought changing the topic might be helpful for both of them.

"By the way, Steph, we missed you at the game last week." A number of the teachers sat together in the stands, hoping to discourage disgruntled parents from approaching one of them with a complaint about grades.

"I know. I couldn't shake a headache and decided to go to bed early." That sounded like a polite brush-off to him. Grace would have reminded him that it was wrong of him to try to pump that young girl for personal information that was none of his business whatsoever. How he missed Grace!

His work as an English teacher consumed most of his time. After his wife passed away, his job was his escape. His workload never diminished from the beginning of September to the end of June. Even in the summer, he spent hours planning new material. His social life other than meeting up with faculty at games was mostly non-existent. He had always been more of a loner and a thinker. He was well aware that in a small town such as Groveland rumors spread quickly, and he sometimes worried that people like Sarah Humphries would try to trump up something that wasn't there.

They walked into the church without exchanging another word. As the Beatles had put it, "Let it be," thought Bishop.

***

The funeral mass was designed to be a celebration of Coach Zappala's life, but it depressed Bishop nonetheless. The only member of his family who showed up was Maria's son, Rocco. He was an imposing figure who could have passed as a bouncer at a bar. He was mostly bald, and what hair he did have was closely cropped. Although his face was clean-shaven, the dark stubble gave the opposite impression. The sport coat he was wearing didn't fit very well, as if he had gained some weight since the last time he had worn it. When Bishop was introduced as the man who found his uncle, Rocco showed no particular interest. Sarah, the gossip queen, later told everyone that she had overheard Rocco asking Mr. Langone about the funeral expenses. According to her, Rocco seemed relieved to hear that Al's lawyer was taking care of everything. He was very anxious to meet with the lawyer right after the funeral before he headed back to Connecticut.

The church was crowded with mourners, almost all of them connected to Holy Trinity in one way or another. Most of the faculty were there as well as a good number of students. The Delaneys were among the parents who attended. Members of the football team, all wearing their football jerseys over their dress shirts, sat together as a sign of unity. When it was time for Sister Ann to say a few words, Sister Pat's eyes darted around the pews, looking for anyone who might not be paying rapt attention. She was especially focused on the football team, knowing that they were probably more interested in the new plays that Coach Chandler had put in for Saturday's game than they were in what the principal had to say.

Bishop wasn't very impressed by her remarks that were filled with generalities about the mystery of death and the need to believe in God's plan. Her voice had about the same amount of emotion in it that she used to deliver morning announcements. The only comment that got much of a response was at the end. "I'm sure that Coach Zappala would have not wanted us to unduly grieve for him. Life must go on. Therefore, our football team will be on the field tomorrow, and we will win that game for him." Sister Pat started to clap, and then stopped herself when she realized that no one else was so inclined.

After saying a few quick goodbyes, Bishop slipped out of the church and headed for the comfort of his country home. The sun was shining, but it didn't do much to warm his spirits. He was looking forward to a chance to decompress, maybe even grade a few papers, but when he checked his cell phone for messages, those thoughts faded. He had a message from attorney Andy White's secretary asking him to be at White's office at 4:00 p.m. that afternoon for a reading of Zappala's will. Why on earth would he have to be there for that? He wanted to call and say that he had another appointment and wouldn't be able to attend, but that wasn't true. He would just have to go. He wondered who else had been invited.

Chapter 4

The office of H. Andrew White was located in his Victorian home on Spruce Street. With its wraparound veranda and meticulously manicured yard, it was the type of home that Bishop and his wife, Grace, had dreamed of one day owning. When she died, she took those dreams with her. When he arrived a few minutes early, he met Rocco Santorini for the second time. If Rocco had appeared uninterested at their first meeting, he more than made up for it now.

"What are you doin' here, mista?" The shirt, tie, and ill-fitting sport coat had been replaced with a sweatshirt, jeans, and boat shoes. He hadn't bothered to shave.

"I received a message from Mr. White's secretary asking me to meet him here." Bishop felt as if he was about to have a parent-teacher conference with a very irate parent. But this time, instead of being fully prepared, he had no idea of what to expect.

"Well, there's goin' to be a readin' of the will and I don't see's that has anything to do with you," scowled Rocco. Bishop had visions of Rocco the Baker twirling him in the air like pizza dough and then slamming him onto the floor.

"I guess we'll soon find out," countered Bishop as Andy White came out to greet them both. He was in his mid-forties, with wavy brown hair, and a deep tan. His suit was perfectly tailored. He gave each man a firm handshake.

No one in town really knew much about Zappala's finances. His house was unpretentious although his Lincoln Town Car was certainly the only one to be found in the faculty parking lot. None of the teachers at Trinity made a lot of money; that wasn't what they wanted from the teaching profession. Zappala did take off on weekend flings or binges, but that didn't mean he had money. Bishop considered the fact that Zappala had taught for many years at Madison and had probably accumulated a nice pension from the state. Still, that wouldn't provide the kind of money that would save the family business, so why had they asked him for help as Sister Ann had mentioned? And why had he been asked to be present at the reading of the will?

Both men were led into White's office. Someone was already seated at the large mahogany desk facing the oversized window that overlooked Spruce Street. As the three men entered, a woman turned to meet them. Bishop was surprised.

"Sister Ann! What are you doing here?"

Sister maintained her perfect posture in one of three high-backed executive chairs that had been positioned across from White's desk. Her hands were folded as if in prayer, with the plain silver band on the fourth finger of her left hand symbolizing her marriage to God still visible. She had placed a small black handbag next to her chair.

"I guess I'm here for the same reason that you are. I received a call from Mr. White asking if I could attend a reading of the will this afternoon." There was a distinct chill in her voice. She was already in a defensive mode. With Sister Ann occupying one of the end seats, Bishop sat in the other end chair, leaving Rocco no choice but to take the middle seat.

Rocco was none too pleased with this development. "What's goin' on here, White? Why are these people here? If this is about the will, I'm the only one that's family. They don't belong here."

"I'm afraid they do, Mr. Santorini," explained White. "I helped your uncle prepare his will, and I am familiar with its contents. Sister Ann and Mr. Bishop have a legitimate reason to be here as you will see."

"Legitimate my ass," barked Rocco. "I'll get a lawyer of my own."

"How you choose to respond is your own business. However, I must warn you that my job is to inform all of you of the contents of this will. Your uncle was very explicit in his instructions. You are here as your mother's representative to listen and nothing more," cautioned White.

When White had finished the reading of the will, Bishop, Sister Ann, and Santorini were speechless. The value of Coach Zappala's estate was far beyond what they could have imagined.

It took several minutes for the facts to register. Zappala had left one million dollars to Holy Trinity High School to be used specifically for the benefit of the students. "Oh my God," whispered Sister Ann. "What a wonderful man!" Bishop seemed to recall that just over a week ago, the coach was nothing more than an "s.o.b." who had a winning record. Whoever said that money talks knew what they were talking about. With the economy in a downturn and enrollment slipping, thoughts of the myriad ways that she could use that money must have danced in her head. "Are you sure, Andy?"

"Mr. Zappala was very clear about his wish that the money be distributed in this way. And as you recall, he wanted whatever monies remained after all of his possessions were liquidated and all of his debts paid to be donated to a charity chosen by the executor. My guess is that will come to another four million."

Rocco jumped to his feet. "I'm getting' a lawyer! This is total bullshit! Wait until my mother hears about this!"

"Please be seated, Mr. Santorini," White replied calmly. "Of course, you may do as you like, but I'm afraid that hiring a lawyer would prove a waste of your money. You see, if Mr. Zappala had completely cut his family out of his will, there might be some basis to contest it. However, as I just explained, he was very specific in his desire to leave your mother exactly fifty thousand dollars and not a penny more. It would be almost impossible to argue that she should receive more than that simply because he had more than that."

"But that isn't enough to save the bakery and he knew it," exploded Rocco.

"I'm sorry. That may be true, but it does not constitute a valid challenge to this will."

Rocco turned to Sister Ann. His face was flushed, and his eyes were dark and menacing. "Why did he give you a million bucks? Al didn't even go to church! What did you do to get him to give you that money? You don't look like his type, you know what I'm sayin'?"

"How dare you!" Now it was Sister Ann's face that flushed. "I'm sorry that your uncle is dead. I'm sorry that your family may lose their business, but I am not sorry that he gave that money to Holy Trinity. Your uncle loved sports, and he knew how expensive these programs are to run. He didn't give the money to me. He gave it to the school for the benefit of future students and athletes." Her eyes that had been focused on Rocco like a laser beam now turned back to White.

"Is there reason for me to stay here any longer?" She must have wanted to return to the convent to tell Sister Pat the good news. They would probably celebrate the school's good fortune by dining at Barrington's, one of the finest restaurants in town.

"No, Sister. None at all. You will be contacted after the will has gone through probate. Thanks for coming."

She stood to leave and both White and Bishop stood and shook hands with her. Santorini remained seated. White walked her to the door and quietly offered an apology for the unpleasant scene that had just taken place.

When he returned to his desk, Rocco began to fire again. "What's this guy still doin' here? He isn't gettin' any dough, is he?"

"No, if you recall my reading of the will, Mr. Bishop is not named as a recipient of any money. However, he has been named as the executor of the will."

***

When Bishop first heard White reading the will, he was so stunned by the numbers and by the exchange between Rocco and Sister Ann that he had almost forgotten that he had been mentioned in the will. Executor? Why would he be named executor? What would he be required to do? How much time would it require? He was behind in his work as it was. He had missed a day of school last week and more essays were piling up waiting to be graded.

"Excuse me, Andy. Is there any way that I can decline to be the executor?"

"Yes, but I would hope that you accept. The job of executor is a thankless one, but someone has to do it and obviously, Mr. Zappala felt you were the man for the job." Rocco sat silently, still seething over the millions that had been given to strangers instead of family.

"Me? I hardly knew him. I mean we were colleagues and neighbors, but I didn't pal around with him or anything." Bishop was embarrassed. He realized that he sounded like a student trying to talk his way out of a detention.

"I have to admit that I asked him the same question about naming you as executor."

"And? What did he say?"

"I remember him saying, 'Bishop is the one I want. He's sharp for an old guy. Good with details.'"

He ignored the comment about his age. He was seventy and that was older than any other lay teacher in the school's history. "Lots of people are good with details. Andy, teaching takes up almost all of my time." Bishop thought of the mountains of paper work that might be involved. He would have to liquidate all of Zappala's assets, sort through his belongings, sell his house, his car, everything.

Rocco interrupted. "Listen, if you don't wanna do it, I will. After all, he was my uncle. You're nothin' to him."

White immediately ended that suggestion. "I'm afraid that's impossible, Mr. Santorini. Mr. Bishop is the person named in the will, and he hasn't indicated that he plans to recuse himself."

Rocco most likely didn't know what "recuse" meant, but he got the picture. "This stinks big time." With that, he got up to leave. "When do we get our fifty K?"

"As I explained to Sister, the will must go through probate. All the assets must be liquidated. This process could take up to six months or more. Mr. Bishop will keep you posted as far as the distribution is concerned."

"Thanks for nothin', White," said Rocco as he stormed out of the room and slammed the door behind him. Bishop reflected on the words, "six months or more." It sounded like a prison sentence.

White and Bishop spent some time prioritizing a list of things to do. Bishop had thought that finding the body had been the most difficult part of this experience. Now that the funeral was over, he hoped that his life would to get back to normal. Apparently, Coach Zappala had had other ideas. Bishop thought of the character in Herman Melville's "Bartelby, the

Scrivener" who when given a task simply replied, "I prefer not to." Unfortunately, Bishop couldn't bring himself to say so.

Chapter 5

The Friday night football game between Holy Trinity and Riverside had been rescheduled for Saturday. There had been some talk earlier in the week that the game would be cancelled due to the tragic death of the coach. That didn't last long. Practices were held even on Monday, the day of his death. Two of the assistant coaches, Russ Chandler and Doug Sanders, organized a team meeting that afternoon. The players decided that they wanted to play the game. They wanted to dedicate the game to their coach. Sister Ann had the final say.

Bishop was initially surprised at their decision. He wondered how much the assistant coaches had influenced the players and how much Sister Pat had influenced Sister Ann. When he mentioned his concern about the appropriateness of playing the game to Sister Ann, she got a little huffy.

"What's wrong with playing the game? That's how the kids want to honor their coach."

Bishop wanted to comment on her sudden interest in what the kids wanted, but prudently kept quiet.

Sister added, "Both Russ and Doug called a number of times on Monday to express their sympathies and to offer their help in any way. Russ told me that Zappala had promised him the head coaching position when he decided to retire. Doug told me the same story."

"What did you say?"

"I told them that I would have to think about it."

Bishop had heard that line so many times over the years. It usually meant that she had already made up her mind, and she didn't want to give you the bad news just yet. Bishop surmised that she had already made up her mind about Zappala's replacement, just as she knew what she was getting when she had hired the coach. She was willing to tolerate his flaws for the sake of his proven expertise on the field. With either Russ or Doug, the new coach would be no different in that respect.

"Sister, you do realize that either Russ or Doug lied to you about what Zappala said, don't you?"

"I guess it's possible that one of them lied. It's also possible that both of them lied and that neither had been promised the job by Zappala. It doesn't surprise me. I know how desperately they both want this chance."

"Sister, weren't both of them finalists for the position when you hired Zappala?"

"Yes, they were."

As Bishop left her office, the words of Sister Pat from a similar conversation that he had overheard were still fresh in his memory. *What right did that bastard Zappala have to tell either of those two guys who the next head coach would be? That's up to you, not him!* For a Sister of the Holy Rosary, Sister Pat's language in private wasn't what one would expect.

On his way to his next class, Bishop came up with another possibility regarding the conflicting statements of the two assistants. Perhaps both of them were telling the truth. Zappala might have said whatever he needed to say to keep his assistant coaches happy. He needed them to do the drudge work during practices, in the training room, before and after games, and on scouting trips. Bishop thought of Iago's response when he had been passed over by Othello for a promotion. "I follow him to serve my turn upon him."

***

One benefit of playing the game was that it gave Bishop an occasion to forget about the events that had transpired in H. Andrew White's office the previous day.

The game began late because of a brief tribute to Coach Zappala that Sister Ann had written herself. She mentioned nothing of his sizable donation to the school. That announcement would wait for a more appropriate moment. Bishop sat with Ron Jennings, Steve Marshall, and some of the other guys in the midst of the largest crowd of the season. There hadn't been any further talk of last week's benching of Chris Delaney by the coach. That seemed such an insignificant issue in light of this week's events. Still, Bishop wondered what Chris could have done to merit that treatment. Chris was widely admired by the staff and the student body. A gifted athlete and an excellent student, he was a polite young gentleman who didn't let success change him. He was pulling a 90+ average in Bishop's Advanced Placement English class. His essay on *Moby Dick* had been among the best in the class.

"Hi, guys. Mind if I sit here?"

Bishop was so lost in his thoughts about Chris Delaney that he hadn't noticed Stephanie Harris approach. He was a bit startled that she wanted to sit with the guys rather the group of female teachers who had gathered in the next section of the bleachers. It was a rather mild October evening and she was wearing a turtleneck and jeans.

Ron quickly moved a little to his left to make some room between himself and Bishop. "Sure, Steph. Please sit down. I was hoping that I would see you tonight." That was as good an understatement as any that Hemingway had ever written. Bishop wasn't the first faculty member to take notice of Ron's interest in Stephanie. Sarah Humphries was sure to start making comments about what might be going on between those two.

Bishop would be pleased if a romance blossomed between Ron and Stephanie. Ron was his closest friend on the staff. He had started at Holy Trinity shortly before Grace passed away. He had helped him get through the darkest days that had followed. Although neither was much of a cook, they had shared many meals together. Bishop learned that Ron had suffered his own loss several years earlier. He had been engaged to one of the teachers at the school where he had worked before joining the staff at Trinity. Paula Siracusa had even moved in with Ron. He had never been happier. Shortly before the wedding, Paula unexpectedly called off the wedding. She had reconnected with a physician she had dated previously. Paula moved to Seattle and married the doctor a few months later. Ron never heard from her again. Robert Frost described a similar situation in his poem, "The Impulse." The ties between a young married couple were broken suddenly and swiftly. If Stephanie were to fill that void in Ron's life, no one would be happier for him than Bishop.

The group spent most of the game in the kind of small talk that made everyone relax. They stood for obligatory cheering when Trinity scored or made a nice play. Delaney scored three touchdowns and the game dedicated to Coach Zappala went into the record books with a W.

Earlier in the day, Ron told Bishop that he planned on asking Steph at halftime if she might like to go someplace for coffee after the game, but he didn't get the chance. First, a couple of freshman boys came over to say hello to their French teacher. They stood there awkwardly for a moment and when their gawking became obvious, they quickly left, laughing and joking with each other. Then, several parents came over to chat about everything from the weather, to the week's events, to the game. Just as Ron prepared himself to ask Stephanie if she would like to go with him to get a coffee, she turned to Bishop.

"Mike, would you like to meet me at the Bean Tree in about twenty minutes? I need your advice."

Bishop desperately wanted just to get home, put on some classical music, and read before bed. However, that was out of the question if she needed his advice. He wondered what the problem might be but knew he would find out soon enough.

"The Bean Tree it is. See you there."

Bishop read the disappointment on Ron's face. He felt guilty that Ron's plan had been thwarted. He told himself that Ron would have other opportunities to ask her out. Perhaps this had saved him from the embarrassment of having Stephanie decline his offer in front of the other teachers. Imagine what Sarah would have done with that tidbit!

**

When Bishop arrived at the Bean Tree, Stephanie was already seated in a booth with a cup of coffee and a half moon cookie on the table. "I hope you don't mind that I already ordered."

"Not at all," he replied as he got the attention of the waitress. She was a heavy-set girl about eighteen years old. The uniform shirt and hat that all employees wore did nothing to enhance her appearance.

"What can I get for you?" she asked with a half-hearted smile.

Taking a quick glance at her nametag, Bishop said, "Amy, I'll have a cup of hot tea. And those half moons look good. I'll take one of those also."

They spent the next few minutes talking about the game and about how much paperwork they each had facing them that weekend. After Amy had brought him his tea and cookie, they spent the next few minutes more focused on eating than on talking.

When the cookies were gone, Amy came by with refills on their drinks. Stephanie looked into her coffee cup as if hoping to find the right words. At first she hesitated, then she said, "For what it's worth, I want you to know how much I appreciate your friendship. You've helped me so much since I have been here at Trinity. Letting me observe your classes, answering my endless questions, offering your insights and wisdom. I don't know how I could ever thank you." She paused again and added, "I really owe you so much!"

"Nonsense," replied Bishop. "Thank you for saying that, but I really haven't done that much. Now, what's this business about advice that you need?"

She put down her coffee cup and leaned a bit closer to him. "Well, it's really nothing, I guess, but I thought I'd run it by you."

"Go ahead." Bishop had no idea what to expect, but after so many years in the teaching profession, there wasn't much that any teacher or student could say to him that could surprise him any more.

"Over the last couple of weeks, I've noticed Sister Pat walking back and forth outside of my classroom and sometimes just standing near the door. The kids have noticed too. It's getting on my nerves."

"I have seen her out there myself, now that you mention it." It would have been hard to miss her. She was just a few inches over five feet tall, and she was well north of two hundred pounds. Bishop knew the way Sister Pat operated. She was conducting some unofficial classroom observations. If Stephanie, as a first-year teacher, was having any problems, she wanted to know about it. If her intention had been to help Steph, Bishop might have given Sister Pat the benefit of the doubt regarding her tactics. However, he was fairly certain that there was nothing positive in her motivation. She was looking, perhaps hoping, to find problems. If she noticed that Stephanie had difficulty with classroom management or if she didn't start class with a prayer, she would eagerly report that to the principal. Nothing made an insecure person feel better than to find flaws in others.

"Do you think that I should just close my door when I see her hovering around in the halls?"

"No, I wouldn't do that. You would be admitting that her presence bothered you."

"Then, what would you recommend?"

Bishop took a sip of his tea as he thought of a response. "Next time you notice her out there, go right out and invite her in."

"Really?"

"That's what I recommend. You would be showing her that you aren't intimidated by her and that you're confident in what you are doing in the classroom."

"Do you think that she actually would come in?"

"I seriously doubt it. She's not interested in sitting through a French lesson that she wouldn't understand. She'll find someone else to harass."

"You'd think that she could find something more constructive to do with her time."

That was a sentiment universally shared by the faculty. "Amen to that," said Bishop emphatically. He was pleased to have earned this woman's trust. She was quite a girl. He hoped that Ron Jennings would find another opportunity to ask her out soon. He thought that they would make a nice couple. Then he realized that he was beginning to sound like Sarah Humphries. One Sarah the Blabber was enough.

Chapter 6

Two weeks after the death of Coach Zappala, Trinity seemed to be getting back to normal. There was laughter in the halls, and the decibel level in the cafeteria during lunches was back to its typical, jet engine range. The football season was almost over. The boys had won both games under their interim coach, and they were headed for a playoff game. Who had asked whom to the Halloween dance was a major topic of discussion, not only among the students, but among most of the faculty as well.

Bishop had met with Attorney White a couple of times with questions regarding his role as executor. He still wondered why he had been selected for this thankless and time-consuming job, but he was determined to do the best that he could. He was also determined not to let any of this affect his teaching or his ability to devote the necessary time to the grading of his students' essays. They deserved no less.

Planning to grade a few papers during his prep period, Bishop walked into the faculty break room. Just as he did, Sarah Humphries and Mary Nickerson broke off their conversation. "Hope I'm not interrupting anything, ladies," he said as he took a seat at an empty table.

"No, no," whispered Sarah. "You're fine. We were just being careful. You know, some people around here are just big snoops and can never keep anything quiet."

Bishop was tempted to explain the definition of the term, "irony," but decided against it.

As the two women resumed their conversation, he pulled out a stack of essays. He wasn't sure that he was going to be able to concentrate as it was impossible not to overhear what they were saying.

"Well, as soon as Terry had given the message to Sister Ann, she gave me a buzz," Sarah explained to Mary. "Guess who wanted to talk to the principal?"

"How would I know?" replied Mary, obviously waiting for the answer.

"Lieutenant Hodge!" Terry made this dramatic announcement as if that explained everything.

Mary's response was a clueless, "So?"

"So? What do you mean 'so'? Don't you get it? Hodge wouldn't call unless something was up."

"There could be lots of reasons to call," explained Mary. "Maybe there was a party after the game, and some kids got busted for underage drinking."

Bishop was again tempted to insert himself into their conversation, perhaps by reminding them that Hodge's phone call to Sister Ann was obviously none of their business. Doing so, he realized, would accomplish nothing except alienating himself from these two colleagues. Bishop hadn't been at Trinity for over forty years without knowing that it was sometimes best to let things go.

Just then the chatter between Sarah and Mary went into silent mode again as another teacher entered the room.

"Does anyone know what's going on here today?" asked Jack Slater, one of the school's custodians. He was a short and thin man in his mid-fifties who had taken the job at Trinity after retiring from the city public works department. His rough hands told the story of a lifetime of hard, physical labor. He had a good pension, but after a few months at home, he found himself bored in retirement.

Sarah took the bait, and returned his question with one of her own. "What do you mean?"

Jack pulled up a chair and sat in it backwards so that he could fold his arms over the back. "They're having a big powwow in Sister Ann's office." He went on to explain that the door was closed and that a curtain had been pulled over the window in the door.

"Who's in there with her besides Sister Pat?" wondered Mary. It was a given that Sister Pat would be one of the participants in any high level meeting. No one had ever been able to figure out exactly why that was the case. She was living proof of the adage that those who can't teach end up in administration. Although Bishop had known several good administrators over the years, they were the exception to the rule. Pat had an opinion on everything and rarely bothered to think before she shared that opinion with the world.

Jack had managed a peek inside the principal's office from outside the building as he ostensibly picked up a few pieces of trash that the wind had conveniently blown in that direction. "Well, Hodge is in there for one." That wasn't a big surprise since they had learned from Terry that he had called that morning. In addition, a police car was parked illegally near the front entrance to the building.

"Who else?" asked Sarah as the possibilities of the nature of the meeting must have swirled in her head.

"I only got a chance for a quick look but Jennings was in there." No surprise there as he was part of the administrative team. "I'm pretty sure that the other guy I saw is Andy White." That added a little fuel to the fire. White was Coach Zappala's attorney, but he was also the school's attorney.

"Maybe it has something to do with Zappala's will. Maybe the school isn't going to get that all that money after all," said Mary without any basis for such speculation. A few days after the funeral, Sister Ann had sent an email that made reference to Zappala's "most generous" donation to the school.

Jack had saved the most interesting participant in the meeting for last. "And Sister Pascala was in there, too. And she didn't look too happy, I'm sure of that." To look at Sister Pascala, one would assume you were in the presence of a very holy person. She was a petite woman with a very plain face. She was one of the few nuns left who had kept the name she had taken when she entered the convent. She also continued to wear the old habit with its long, black, bulky skirts almost touching the floor, and an oversized rosary dangling from her waist. Looks are often deceiving, however, as they were in the case of Sister Pascala, who taught science. The kids knew her as an angry and bitter old woman whose age they often speculated to be in the 90s although, in fact, she was only a few years older than Bishop. Nothing her students did was ever good enough. She constantly berated and belittled them. Occasionally, she even resorted to slapping a student for which she always managed to escape a reprimand.

The prep period just about over, everyone headed out of the break room. Bishop hadn't been able to get through even one essay. As he walked up to his classroom on the second floor, he was concerned about the nature of that meeting. Was it possible that a student or a parent finally had filed charges against Sister Pascala?

***

It wasn't until the faculty had received an email from Sister Ann informing them that there would be a mandatory meeting after school in the library that the rumor mill kicked into high gear.

Stephanie, whose classroom was across the hall from Bishop's, appeared at his door as the last of his students had filed out. "Mike, what do you make of that email?"

Without repeating the details of what he had heard when he was in the break room, he told her that there had been a meeting behind closed doors in the principal's office earlier in the day, but that he didn't have any idea what it might have been about.

Steph's face looked pale as she said, "Well, I think I might know."

"Know what?"

"I think I know what that meeting was about."

"Really? How would you know?" Bishop assumed that the rumors about Sister Pascala were already spreading.

"The kids in my last class just told me."

"Told you what?" he asked with some annoyance. He thought that Steph was smart enough to ignore such unfounded gossip.

"The kids said that Coach Zappala didn't have a heart attack." Then, in a whispered tone, she added, "They said he was murdered."

Bishop didn't know whether to laugh at this outrageous idea or not. He was the one who had found the body. There was no evidence of foul play. Yet, in the back of his mind, fears surfaced that this might be true. It wouldn't be the first time that the students knew more about what was going on than the teachers.

***

At the end of the last class of the day, as the students rushed to their lockers, the teachers made their way to the library. Some walked in alone; others came in in groups of two or three, talking in hushed voices, deciding where to sit. Lieutenant Hodge was there, standing near the podium with a look of deep concern on his face. Sister Ann was already at the podium shuffling through some papers. Sister Pat was seated at a table near the podium, writing down names as teachers walked in. It was unlikely that anyone else would sit at that table until all other options had been exhausted. As the last of the group arrived a few minutes late, Sister Pat made her annoyance obvious as she scowled, eyed the clock, and placed an exaggerated check mark next to their names. She then signaled for Sister Ann to begin.

"If you would all place yourselves in the presence of the Lord, I would like to begin with a prayer." With that, the buzz in the room ceased, and everyone bowed their heads. The prayer, one of her old favorites, asked for God's guidance through difficult times. She then introduced the Lieutenant, and sat next to Sister Pat who shoved the attendance list towards her so that she would know who had had the temerity to skip this meeting.

Hodge stepped behind the podium and took a deep breath that seemed to tax the limits of his uniform shirt. "Thank you for coming here this afternoon." It struck Bishop that a similar sentiment had been absent from Sister Ann's opening remarks. "I'm afraid I have some rather disturbing news to share with you." At that, there was a palpable tension in the room as teachers exchanged worried glances. He went on to explain that he had received the results of a toxicology report from Albany identifying the cause of the death of their colleague, Coach Albert Zappala. Everyone had assumed that he had had a massive heart attack so no one was prepared for what came next.

Hodge took a firm grip on the podium as he said, "According to these test results, although there was a moderate level of alcohol in his system, Mr. Zappala died of acute poisoning caused by sodium cyanide." There was moment of stunned silence. A few of the female staff members reached for tissues as they became teary. Hodge went on to explain that given this new evidence, an investigation of Zappala's death had officially begun. After asking for the full cooperation of the administration and staff, he opened the meeting up for questions.

Ron Jennings, the assistant principal, who had been in on the earlier closed-door meeting, asked the first question, obviously knowing the answer but wanting everyone else to hear it directly from Hodge. "Do you mean that he committed suicide?"

"No, not at all. At this point, there is absolutely no reason to believe that he took his own life." Hodge went on to explain that no note was found. No one had reported a sudden change in mood or behavior. Although the autopsy had found the beginning stages of heart disease, he was in relatively good health, eliminating that as a possible reason to consider suicide. He concluded, "Under the circumstances, we have to look at this as a homicide."

A few people audibly gasped; others were bewildered. Bishop raised his hand. Hodge pointed at him as if he were a teacher answering the questions of his class, "Yes, Mr. Bishop?"

"Lieutenant, what happens now?"

"Excellent question, Mr. Bishop." That turned out to be the perfect segue for what he wanted to say next. "Earlier today, I discovered that a small bottle of sodium cyanide is missing from the school's science lab storeroom. I need to talk with anyone who might know anything about that."

Many of the teachers began whispering with those sitting near them. The rumor mill was already beginning to churn.

Bishop realized with a quick glance around the room that Sister Pascala was not present. According to Jack, she had seemed very upset after that morning meeting. Diane Ramos, a Spanish teacher who was one of those who had come in at the last minute, blurted out to no one in particular, "Why would we have cyanide or anything dangerous like that in the school in the first place?"

Sister Ann was prepared for that one. "It had been purchased many years ago by one of the teachers interested in the effects of that substance on metal. It hadn't been used for years, and was kept in a locked cabinet. I am sure you realize that every science lab contains any number of dangerous chemicals and compounds." She approached the podium in an attempt to end the meeting. Diane replied, "Then what makes you think that the poison used to kill him came from our lab?"

Hodge interjected, "We can't be sure that it did," he admitted. "But it does seem like a good place to start, especially since the school's bottle is missing."

Bishop raised his hand again. "Lieutenant, surely you don't believe that one of us had anything to do with this tragic event, do you?"

Sister Pat, still seated, barked out a response. "Anyone with a classroom key is a suspect!" Her eyes darted around the room as if she expected the perpetrator to confess to her on the spot. She failed to realize, of course, that she had one of those keys in the ring that she had placed on the clipboard in front of her.

Frank Wilson, who taught social studies and rarely contributed at faculty meetings, bolted out, "Then you'd have to include students as suspects since I know for a fact that teachers routinely lend their keys to kids who need to get into a locked classroom to get books that they had forgotten or whatever. I've done it lots of times myself." His face had turned red as he continued. "Why would anyone of us want to kill the coach?"

Hodge raise his hands defensively. "I'm not saying that one of you did. But it's pretty clear that somebody did, and I aim to find out who that person is." Then he added, "I'd appreciate your cooperation, that's all."

Sister Ann again attempted to end the meeting at that point, but someone was waving her hand in the air as if she were hailing a taxi. Without any hesitation, Bishop assumed correctly that that hand belonged to Mary Nickerson. The woman had gained a reputation as the human rain delay of faculty meetings. Her last-minute need to ask one more question had become the stuff of legend among the faculty. Usually, the question she asked had already been answered or was several light years off topic, generating a faintly audible collective groan among her peers. This time, however, Mary outdid herself by asking, "What about the cameras? Wouldn't the films show who went into that storeroom?"

"Theoretically, yes, ma'am, they would," replied Hodge. "The problem is that the tapes are set on a 72-hour cycle which means that older video is taped over by newer video. By the time we realized that Zappala had been poisoned and that the school's container of cyanide was missing, the window of opportunity had long passed."

Assuming that the missing cyanide was in fact the source of the poison that killed Zappala, Bishop felt a chill as he realized that the identity of the individual who had taken that bottle from the lab had been captured on tape for only 72 hours. How fortunate for the killer! Was it possible that the killer knew that proof of the theft would be so easily erased?

In her third attempt, Sister Ann finally dismissed the group. Sister Pat approached the principal, seemingly more concerned with the list of those who had missed the meeting than with what had transpired in the meeting itself. As the teachers headed for the doors, some had pulled out their cell phones to check messages or make calls. Others walked out alone, still shaken by the news.

"Steph, I guess your kids were right, after all," observed Bishop. "Did they tell you how they knew?" She briefly explained that one of the boys in that class got a text from his mother. The mother works in the same office as the wife of one of the police officers who had called to tell his wife what the investigation had revealed.

"So much for confidentiality, I guess."

"Believe me, Steph, in a small town, nothing stays a secret for long."

Just as he said that, Ron Jennings caught up with them. He didn't miss an opportunity to be close to Stephanie. "Secrets?" he said, picking up on what he had heard. "You know what they say. For three people to keep a secret, two of them have to be dead." Neither Bishop nor Stephanie responded. Jennings must have quickly realized that his remark about the dead was in poor taste considering what had recently transpired. "Sorry," he said with much embarrassment. "I guess I wasn't thinking."

Bishop was lost in thought as he walked past Stephanie and Ron without saying another word. He was thinking about the glass of beer that he had accidentally knocked over the morning that he had discovered the body. Had he unintentionally hampered a murder investigation?

Chapter 7

Bishop spent most of that evening working on his papers and plans for next week's classes. As he worked, he listened to classical music in the background. He found that it not only blocked out any distractions, it also helped him think more clearly. He had selected the piano sonatas of Scarlatti. When he was grading, he often lost track of time. The vibration of his cell phone interrupted his focus. He glanced at the screen but did not recognize the number of the incoming call that was displayed.

"Hello?"

"Good evening, Mr. Bishop. This is Lieutenant Hodge. I hope I'm not disturbing you."

Even though he had hoped to finish his work before he became too sleepy to concentrate, he replied, "Not at all, Lieutenant. What can I do for you?"

Hodge didn't hesitate to put his cards on the table. "You must realize that as the person who discovered Zappala's body, you are, shall we say, a 'person of interest' in this investigation."

Bishop was torn between shock and indignation. "Why, that's absurd, Lieutenant!"

"What makes you say that?"

"Well, for starters, as one of the teachers pointed out at today's faculty meeting, anyone with a classroom key would have had access to that lab."

"True, but you just happened to be the one to find the body," countered Hodge.

"That's true, but the only reason I went to his house that morning is that Sister Ann called me and asked me to go up there. He was late for a meeting, and she thought he might have overslept." He decided to leave out the concern about Zappala's drinking habits.

"Listen, I know all about that," said Hodge. "The point is that you had access to the cyanide, you live near the victim, your fingerprints were found at the scene, and you tampered with possible evidence in the case."

"I think you should stop right there, Lieutenant. As soon as you arrived at Zappala's house that morning, I told you that I had accidentally bumped into that table and that I had cleaned up the mess as best I could. You didn't have a problem with that then. Obviously, my fingerprints would be there!" Bishop practically spit out the words as his anger and frustration grew.

"I didn't know he had been murdered then, either," Hodge was quick to reply.

"Are you accusing me of any wrongdoing? If so, I will naturally seek the advice of a lawyer."

"No, no, Mr. Bishop," Hodge said in a much more conciliatory manner. "I realize that the missing piece to this puzzle is motive. As you said yourself, many people had access to the cyanide. I also know that the victim was in the habit of keeping his front door unlocked, so anybody could have walked right in on him."

"Wouldn't it have to be someone who knew him?" asked Bishop even though as he asked that question, he realized that he was placing himself once again in that 'person of interest' category.

"That's exactly what I think, too," declared Hodge with some satisfaction. He added, "That's really why I called."

"Excuse me. I don't understand."

"Bishop, you're a sharp guy. My daughter tells me that you were her favorite teacher over at Trinity."

"Thanks. And your point is?" asked Bishop, having no idea where Hodge was headed.

"Means, motive, opportunity. Lots of people had access to the means. Some had the opportunity. It's motive, Bishop. Who had a reason to want Zappala dead?"

"With all due respect, Lieutenant, isn't that what you are supposed to investigate?"

"Yes. And I could use your help."

"My help? How can I help?" asked a dumbfounded Bishop who had apparently gone from "person of interest" to assistant detective.

"Listen, you've been around there for ages. People respect you. They trust you. Maybe you'll pick up something that somebody lets slip."

"You mean that you want me to spy on my colleagues, my friends? I can't do that, Lieutenant."

"What I mean is that you might be more effective in certain aspects of this investigation than I would be. After all, someone did kill your colleague and friend, Mr. Zappala. I'm asking you to help me find the person who did it."

In his heart, Bishop knew that it was the right thing to do. Although he did not want to accept the possibility, what if the murder was committed by someone connected to Holy Trinity? He had an obligation to help in any way that he could. A shiver ran through his body as he realized that the murder of the coach might not have been an isolated event. What if the perpetrator decided to strike again, and he had done nothing to help prevent that from happening?

"You mentioned that you found my fingerprints there. Might I ask, Lieutenant, if you were able to identify any of the other prints?"

"My people were able to pull a number of prints at the scene. As you know, all of the faculty and staff at Trinity are fingerprinted as a requirement of working there. We could identify only yours and those of the victim." He also mentioned that the lab people had found traces of cyanide in the sample of carpet fibers where the beer had spilled. Additionally, he told Bishop that the autopsy revealed a high level of cyanide in his system, indicating the death would have occurred within minutes of ingestion.

"Are you saying that you have other prints that you can't match against your database?"

"You got it. The killer might have actually left his calling card there for us, but we have no way of identifying who that might be short of asking everyone even remotely connected to Zappala to voluntarily agree to be fingerprinted." It went without saying that the killer would be unlikely to volunteer. "It's also possible that the killer either used gloves or wiped any evidence so the faculty and staff, even the students, are not necessarily in the clear."

Bishop was beginning to see how difficult the task of identifying the murderer was going to be. The authorities could use whatever help they could get. "I'm sure that everyone in Groveland wants your investigation to be successful." He added with a newly acquired conviction, "I'll do what I can to help."

"Thanks, Mike, if I might call you by that name, I appreciate it, but you are wrong about one thing."

"What's that?" Bishop was genuinely confused.

"There is one person in Groveland who doesn't want this investigation to be successful, and that's the person we're looking for."

Bishop was quick to remind Hodge that he was assuming that the murderer was a local, and that he was not convinced that that was the case. Hodge agreed with Bishop, but he didn't sound convinced.

Hodge gave him his home phone number and his cell phone number as well. He explained that it would be preferable to make contact by phone. In that way, no suspicions would be raised about his involvement in the investigation.

***

He had not accomplished as much as he would have liked, but the prospect of grading any more papers that night had faded. He recorded all of the results in his grade book and considered his options for the rest of the evening. He could begin looking over some of the considerable number of documents that Andy White had given him regarding the estate. He was too tired to attempt that either. He could see what was on television. Other than the news and some sporting events, he didn't really care for television all that much. When his students asked him if he caught the latest episode of "American Idol" or "Survivor," he usually replied that he had missed that one. No wonder SAT scores were down.

As he got ready for bed, Bishop couldn't help but replay his conversation with Lieutenant Hodge. He could not get one question out of his mind. Who had a motive to kill Zappala?

Chapter 8

By the time Bishop took his green tea into the sunroom that next Saturday morning, the sun was already making its way into the autumn sky. School certainly had a way of making time pass quickly as there always seemed to be more work to do than there were hours in the day. Weekends were a chance to relax a bit and to catch up on his grading. As if he didn't have enough on his plate, Andy White had delivered boxes of papers that he had taken from Zappala's house. Bishop would have to go through all of that material, and White had cautioned him that there were more boxes to come. His work as a teacher was his priority. He would complete his work as executor, but not at the expense of his students.

Ever since that phone conversation with Lieutenant Hodge, Bishop found himself returning to that nagging question of motive. From his extensive readings in literature, which is as Shakespeare put it, "a mirror" of nature, a motive for murder usually involved love, hate, revenge, greed, anger, or jealousy. Greed. Don't they say that money is the root of all evil? How did Zappala get that kind of money? It certainly was possible that he could have acquired it through careful saving and frugal living. Yet, there were his expensive cars and those regular trips to Atlantic City. His Holy Trinity salary certainly covered basic expenses. Although no one at school knew of his wealth, his family knew that he had more than enough to help them save the bakery. Bishop couldn't believe that he was a Mafia hit man or that he was dealing drugs. His drug of choice had been alcohol. He realized that as his executor, he was going to get to know Albert C. Zappala much better after his death than he had ever known him in life. It was a good example of situational irony, but not one that he planned to share with his students.

Was it possible that Zappala had a jilted lover? From everything that Bishop had heard, Zappala treated women as second-class citizens. They were there to be used, not loved and respected. Who might have been hurt or angered enough to kill? Chris Delaney might have been incensed by his benching, but he was an unlikely suspect. Delaney's parents were also furious with the coach for jeopardizing their son's chances for an athletic scholarship. One or both of them might have sought revenge for their economic loss, although Chris's chances of receiving a free ride for college were still good. Rocco might have wanted the money to save the family bakery, but he was in Connecticut when the murder took place. Bishop didn't know Russ Chandler and Doug Sanders very well at all, since neither of them actually taught at Trinity. It was evident that they both badly wanted Zappala's job, but would either of them be willing to kill to get it?

Bishop's tea had gone cold while he entertained these fragments of possibilities. He hoped that the trail that would lead Hodge to the killer had not gone cold as well.

***

Bishop decided that he really needed to put in a few solid hours on his papers. He opened several windows to let in the refreshingly crisp air, settled in at his desk, and pulled out a number of folders. There was an unfinished set of *Moby Dick* essays that took priority over all the rest. Normally, students were clamoring for results before the ink was dry, but no one had asked him about those essays. They probably figured that he had been too busy to grade them or perhaps, their thoughts were understandably elsewhere.

He took a moment to look through the papers trying to recall each one that he had graded sporadically over the last week. He preferred to read an entire class set of papers within a day or two so that he could establish and maintain a consistent and fair grading rubric. He reread Colleen Snyder's paper on Ahab as a tragic hero. It was beautifully written, well organized, detailed, and convincing. Colleen was a gifted writer to be able to accomplish all that she did within the class period allowed for writing. He had been pleased to give her an "A" and was looking forward to her reaction when he returned papers to the class. Chris Delaney's paper was the next one to capture his attention. Chris had written about the internal conflict faced by Starbuck, the first mate in the novel. Starbuck understood that Ahab's monomania would lead to the destruction of the ship and its crew. He had challenged Ahab's authority and then backed down in awe, and perhaps fear, of the great Ahab. Chris argued in his paper that Starbuck would have been justified in shooting Ahab in order to save himself and the rest of the crew. Bishop recalled that Chris had also made this point rather vigorously in class discussion. Ahab was asleep in his cabin as Starbuck contemplated shooting him through the wall rather than confronting him directly. Ultimately, Starbuck decided that he could not commit this murder, and in doing so, he sealed his own fate. Ahab would ultimately be responsible for the loss of the crew (minus Ishmael, of course). Suddenly, the veteran English teacher felt flushed as that disturbing thought came up again. Could Chris have been so upset with his coach for benching him, and for jeopardizing his chances with the scouts in attendance at that game, that he would have killed him? It seemed ridiculous; Chris wasn't a cold-blooded murderer. For some reason, he could not get such thoughts out of his mind. One phone call from Lieutenant Hodge, and Bishop had become a reluctant sleuth.

***

Bishop found it hard to concentrate on the Sunday paper the next morning. Again, his tea went cold as he was absorbed in the articles concerning the murder of the coach. For a small town such as Groveland, this story was understandably big, big, news. The police had no comment on the progress of their investigation into the murder. They said they had been given a number of anonymous tips and that each one would be examined. There were rumors that the coach had left ten million dollars to the school. The dollar amount was way off, but the idea of a bequest was accurate. Had Sister Ann known that Zappala had included Holy Trinity in his will? Was it ludicrous to consider a nun as a murder suspect? Her school did stand to gain a sizable amount of money just as they faced some difficult financial decisions. If not Sister Ann, might greed have overcome her ever-faithful companion, Sister Pat? He envisioned Sister Pat Meehan, known among the students as "Sister Meany," being led out of the school in handcuffs as the students cheered. Bishop tried to rein in his overactive imagination. Another article mentioned that he had been named executor of the estate. This was one of those instances when he was glad that he had always been very judicious in giving out his cell phone number. Then he remembered that his number was listed in the faculty directory which meant that, in reality, his number was readily available to the entire staff. After all, Lieutenant Hodge didn't seem to have had any difficulty getting it. Determined to have some quiet for at least this Sunday morning, he reached for his phone and switched it off.

Chapter 9

Just as he was about to leave for school the next morning, his cell began vibrating. He had decided not to answer, but when he saw that the caller was Stephanie, he picked up before it went to voice mail.

"Hello?"

"Hi, Mike. I'm really sorry to bother you, but I need your help."

"What's the problem?" asked Bishop with a tone of genuine concern.

"My car won't start." Her frustration was obvious. "If it were the battery, I could probably ask a neighbor to give it a jump, but that battery is only a couple of months old. I think it might be the starter."

"How can I help?"

"Well, I have a towing service, but by the time they get here, I'll be late for class. I was hoping you could swing by here and give me a ride to school."

"Sure, no problem," he said. He wanted to tell her to call Ron Jennings instead, but it wasn't the right moment to play matchmaker. "But that still leaves you with a car you can't start."

"I've already asked my landlady, Henrietta, if she wouldn't mind giving the key to the tow truck driver when he arrives."

"Good enough. Where exactly do you live?"

"I'm on the Westside. It's 103 Glendale, off of Lowell Street."

"Okay. I should be there in about fifteen minutes."

"Great. Just toot your horn when you get here. Thanks so much!"

Bishop had no problem finding the house, but after sounding his horn a couple of times, Stephanie was nowhere to be seen. He kept the engine running and hopped out of his car. He rang the bell at 103 Glendale. Located on a quiet road, the house was a well maintained two-story with pale yellow siding and green shutters. A long driveway led to a single-car garage near the rear of the small city lot. When a well-dressed elderly woman with white hair and half glasses hanging from a thin chain around her neck, answered the door, he stammered, "I'm terribly sorry. I must have the wrong house. I was looking for Stephanie Harris."

"Sorry. What did you say?" As she cupped her hand to her ear, Bishop remembered that Steph had told him about her landlady being somewhat deaf. He increased the volume as he repeated his request, and suddenly, the old woman smiled. "You must be Mr. Bishop. Stephanie told me that you were giving her a ride this morning."

"Yes, that's right. And you must be Henrietta Avery." He extended his hand to her. "Nice to meet you. Do you know where Stephanie is?" Henrietta explained that the entrance to Stephanie's apartment was actually on the side of the house. As he walked to that entrance, Steph opened the door before he had a chance to ring the bell. "Sorry. I thought I would be ready before you got here."

"That's okay, but we better get a move on before we're both late!" Thoughts of getting stopped for a speeding ticket on the way to school surfaced again, and having Stephanie in the car would only provide that much more fodder for everyone.

As Bishop drove, they engaged in some idle chitchat. Still bothered by Chris Delaney's essay and his overactive imagination, he decided to share his thoughts with Stephanie so that she would tell him how foolish his theory was. He felt that he could tell her this in confidence, and he really did want another opinion. He was jumping to conclusions that were totally unwarranted, wasn't he? Steph immediately felt that Chris could not have committed such a crime.

"How could you think such a thing about Chris? He seems like such a nice young man. You're going to accuse him of murder on the basis of a paper he wrote for class?"

"No, no, of course not. I don't know why I even mentioned it. Certainly, his thoughts on a novel we discussed in class are just that – thoughts on a novel. I guess I was just reading too much into it. I tend to see too many connections between literature and life."

She suggested that being overtired and stressed could explain his flawed thought process. "You know, I was observing your class that day. I remember Chris suggesting that Starbuck should have killed Ahab to save the ship and the crew. However, I also recall that several other students also made the same argument. Are they suspects, too?"

"No, of course not. You're right, I'm sure." Still, Bishop noted to himself that none of the other students were counting on a football scholarship to a Division I school, and none had been benched by Coach Zappala. And then he remembered the anger and disappointment of Hamlet when he realizes that "one may smile and smile and be a villain." He decided to keep that observation to himself.

As he pulled into the faculty parking lot, he knew that they had just enough time to get in the door before the first bell rang. They hurriedly gathered their bags and rushed into the building to be greeted by Sister Pat.

"Well, well, well. I'm so glad you could make it," she remarked, putting emphasis on each word, her tone dripping with sarcasm. "You have exactly one minute to get to your homerooms. Those kids shouldn't be hanging out in the halls." It occurred to him that if she were that concerned about the students, she might have managed to get herself up the stairs and open the doors herself. He knew that it was best to say nothing. He hoped that Stephanie would also refrain from making a comment at such an insensitive greeting. Even the kids knew that "Sister Meany" was much better at creating a scene than she was at actually trying to solve a problem.

Between classes, Steph stuck her head in the door of his classroom. "Mike, I need another favor," she said sheepishly.

"What is it?"

"I called the repair shop, and they said that they didn't have another starter on hand and that my car won't be ready until tomorrow. Would it be possible for you to give me a ride home tonight?" Before he could answer, she added, "And another ride to school tomorrow morning?"

"Just as long as we get here way before that bell. I don't want to give Sister Pat another reason to make a comment." Stephanie shook her head in understanding exactly what he meant.

"That was a rude way to be greeted, wasn't it? How did a person like that ever become an administrator?"

"Steph, I have to say that I have asked myself that question many times, and I have yet to come up with a good answer," he said as the first students of his next class began to arrive.

***

His day at school was uneventful, but to say that it was like any other day would not have been accurate. Dealing with over one hundred students, Bishop found that no two days were ever alike. When he checked his mailbox at the end of the day, a small pink slip was on the top of the stack. That meant that he had a phone message. That also meant that Terry, the office secretary, knew who had called. If she happened to mention the caller's name to Sarah, half of the faculty already knew that he had received a call from Maria Santorini asking him to return the call as soon as possible. He decided to do just that.

"Bishop. My son, Rocco, tells me that you have control of the money left by my bruddah-that-bastard-may-he-rot-in-hell Al." She was wheezing a bit by the time she finished that sentence.

Ignoring her unsettling characterization of Zappala, he replied, "I am the executor of your brother's estate, Mrs. Santorini. What can I do for you?"

"What can you do for me? You can give me da money my bruddah had, that's what you can do for me."

"Mrs. Santorini, I'm afraid that's impossible. I'm sure that Rocco explained to you that you were left fifty thousand dollars and no more," offered Bishop in as pleasant a tone as he could muster. "If you want my opinion, your son must have had some reason to specify that amount."

"Well, I'ma not want you 'pinion," she screamed. "That's shit is what it is. Is not enough to save my bakery. I waste my money to send Rocco ova dehr."

"I'm very sorry but there is nothing I can do."

"Yes, there is," insisted the old woman.

"What is that?"

"I'ma want dat money now, unnerstan'? I want you send it right away."

"Mrs. Santorini, I'm sure that Rocco explained to you that I can't do that. The will has to go through probate. All of your brother's assets have to be liquidated. All of his debts must be paid. Only then will I be able to distribute money to the beneficiaries. I'm sorry, but that is the law."

Mrs. Santorini told him what he could do with the law and hung up.

***

When Bishop and Stephanie pulled into her driveway on Glendale Road, it was after four, and there was a chill in the air on this mid-fall evening. On the way over, he told Stephanie that he wouldn't be able to give her a ride the next morning. He remembered that he had agreed to an early meeting with Zappala's attorney to discuss some estate business. "Why don't you ask Ron Jennings for a ride? He doesn't live too far from here, and I'm sure he'd be glad to do it."

"I'll do that. Thanks for the suggestion," she replied. Bishop noticed Henrietta Avery standing to the side of her front window with the curtain slightly pulled back. Apparently, Henrietta had a lot of time on her hands and paid close attention to the comings and goings of her tenant. Stephanie asked Bishop if he wanted to come up for a cup of hot tea. He declined, citing the need to get home and finish his preparations for tomorrow's classes. She admitted that she really did need the time to do the same. As he drove off, he congratulated himself on his quick thinking. He would have to remember to call Andy White as soon as he got home to arrange that early morning meeting for tomorrow. "Ron Jennings, you owe me big time," he chuckled to himself with satisfaction.

Chapter 10

The next morning Ron and Stephanie arrived at Holy Trinity well ahead of most of the other faculty. Steph had shared with Ron the encounter that she and Bishop had had with Sister Pat the previous morning. They were both relieved that Sister Pat was not at the door ready to pounce with some obnoxious remark.

When Bishop walked in forty-five minutes later, he was certain that Sister Pat would be in her office working on her second breakfast and scanning the feeds from the numerous security cameras place around the campus, looking for some infraction. He wondered if that duty was actually written into her job description. For that matter, he wondered if her job description even existed.

"Wait a minute!" he said out loud to no one in particular. When several students stopped in their tracks, he quickly motioned for them to move along. Sister Pat constantly watched those video feeds. Was it possible that she had seen the killer before the tapes had been erased? Why hadn't he thought of that before? Was his age catching up with him? Was he simply unaccustomed to thinking like a detective? He made a mental note to have Lieutenant Hodge question Sister Pat regarding the tapes.

Of course, if she or Sister Ann had been the one who removed the cyanide from the storeroom, she wouldn't be much help. She might even intentionally cast suspicion on someone else. He could almost hear her telling Hodge that she remembered seeing Mr. Bishop in that area and wondering what he was doing. If Sister Pat was a quick thinker, he could easily become a "person of interest" again. When he considered the probability that she was a quick thinker, he began to breathe easier.

When he arrived at the copy room, a small room that housed the only copier the teachers were allowed to use as well as the faculty mailboxes, it was, as usual, a scene of controlled chaos. Some teachers were queued up for the copier, and there was some trading of positions based on whose need had greatest priority. Early on in the semester, Bishop always advised new teachers to make whatever copies they needed a day in advance in order to avoid the mad scramble for the copier at the last moment. Just then, there was a collective groan as Mary Nickerson had a paper jam. Bishop quickly removed from his mailbox another pink slip that must have been placed there either late the afternoon before or early that morning. He hoped that Mrs. Santorini had not called again.

As he walked to his classroom, he glanced at the note and was relieved to see that it was a parent who had called.

***

He decided to make the return call during his free period. On his way to the phone reserved for teacher use, Terry left her desk and called to him, "Hey, Mr. Bishop! Got a minute?"

Knowing Terry, Bishop suspected that she had a bit of "news" that she was bursting to share.

"What's up?"

Terry grabbed his arm and motioned him over to a small alcove in the hallway, a place free from detection by security cameras. Terry looked older than her forty-five years. She had been forced to give up her plans for college and a career as a nurse when she became pregnant shortly after graduating from high school. Her husband turned out to be an abusive alcoholic. When she finally decided to leave him, she took her two children with her. Terry saw her job as a refuge from a difficult life as a single parent. As the secretary for the principal, she often knew more of what was going on in the school at any given moment than almost anyone else. "Did you hear about the big meeting that Russ Chandler had with the head honchos this morning?"

"No. I didn't get in until second period, and I've had straight classes. Did Sister Ann give Russ the head coaching position?" Bishop couldn't imagine what was so interesting about that. Russ was clearly one of the favorites for that job.

Terry leaned closer so that she could whisper. "Russ did get the job, but that's not the point."

"Then what is?" he asked, mimicking her whisper. He hoped that she would just spit it out so that he could salvage what was left of his free period.

She went on to explain that Russ told Sister that he had overheard Al and Doug arguing in the coach's office after the game during which Zappala had benched Chris Jennings. She continued, "Things got pretty heated, I guess, and the coach told Doug to pack up his stuff after the game."

"You mean he fired him?" asked a puzzled Bishop.

"Bingo! That's exactly what I mean." Just in case he hadn't made the connection, she added, "And that was the same night that the coach was murdered."

"Terry, how do you know what Russ told Sister? Was her office door open?" He knew full well that eavesdropping was one of her more developed skills.

"Heck, no," she laughed. "All the good stuff happens when that door is closed. But I have my ways," she added mysteriously as she walked back to her desk. Bishop knew that Terry would readily share gossip, but she wasn't about to share any of her snooping techniques with him. As he made his way to the phone room, he wondered if Russ had been telling the truth about that argument. Perhaps he had made it all up in order to convince Sister Ann to select him over Doug as head coach. He made another mental note to share what he had just heard with Lieutenant Hodge. It might be nothing, but he couldn't dismiss it entirely. He remembered the words of Sherlock Holmes in a story by Sir Arthur Conan Doyle. "It has long been an axiom of mine that the little things are infinitely the most important." The list of suspects seemed to grow by the day.

***

Andy White had seen right through Bishop's ruse for an early morning meeting. "Trying to avoid your first period class?" Andy teased as he invited him into his office.

"Well, not exactly," he answered as his face lit up in an embarrassed grin, "but thanks for agreeing to see me."

Bishop did have some questions about procedures that White patiently answered. He planned on presenting Zappala's will to Probate Court. If there were no challenges or irregularities, Bishop would be named executor by the court. It could be several months before the distribution of assets took place. Before the property could be listed for sale, Bishop would have to go through the contents of the house, determining what should be sold, what should be donated to Goodwill, and what should be discarded. White suggested a few names of liquidators and realtors for Bishop to contact.

"What about all those boxes?" asked Bishop, hoping to be told that the contents could simply be shredded.

"I'm afraid that you're going to have to give them at least a cursory look to make sure that nothing of value is destroyed." White tried to soften the burden by suggesting that if he found anything of value, it would increase Zappala's bequest to the charity that, as executor, Bishop would have the opportunity to select.

Bishop already had been given Zappala's checkbook, and Andy thought he should start paying bills as they came in. With some hesitation, Bishop said, "There is one thing bothering me so far."

"Oh, what's that?"

"It's about that checkbook."

"His checkbook? What do you mean?"

"It's the balance. He had over $53,000 in checking." White just whistled. "I mean, who leaves that kind of money in checking?"

"I hear you, Mike. That's more money than a lot of people make in a year."

"Especially if you teach at Holy Trinity," Bishop added, having personal knowledge in that regard. "Another thing I noticed is that he only added to his checking in large sums at the beginning of the quarter." White speculated that Zappala was making withdrawals from a brokerage account as quarterly dividends were paid. A nest egg in excess of five million dollars properly invested would generate a tidy sum.

"Anything else?"

"As a matter of fact, yes." Bishop took advantage of this opening to mention a couple of other transactions that he had noticed. "Every couple of months he wrote a check to 'Cash' for two or three thousand dollars. I assume that represents his gambling money."

"You're probably right. I guess he was entitled to do what he wanted with his own money," added White, not sure where Bishop was headed with that observation.

"That assumes that it was, in fact, his money," he said, finally verbalizing his concern.

"Mike, I honestly don't know how the man got his money. He came in here and wanted a will made, and I helped him do it. It's not my business to ask those questions. If I did, I'd be out of clients pretty soon."

"Okay, I understand." Bishop decided not to tell White that he had also noticed an unusual withdrawal within the last year. It was for $25,000 paid to Holy Trinity High School. Why would Zappala make such a large donation to the school? Was it a donation or something else?

White interrupted his inner monologue. "Listen, I do know that Bob Barnstead was Zappala's financial advisor and also prepared his taxes. Maybe he can help you."

"Bobby Barnstead, the basketball player that went to Trinity?"

"I'm pretty sure he's a local product. Did you teach him?"

"Yes, I did." Bishop wasn't sure that what he did for Bobby would qualify as teaching. As he recalled, Bobby wasn't much of a student. He coasted most of the time. Did just enough to get by. There was a reason the kids called him, "Booby." He wasn't the type of student that he felt got anything out of class discussions of literature. He'd probably never read a book from start to finish. When he wasn't tripping over himself, however, that young man could put the ball in the hoop. He had to remind himself that kids do grow up. Priorities change. It was time for Bishop to meet the new Bob Barrett.

***

That night after he finished all the work that was absolutely essential for the next day, he decided to call Ron Jennings.

"Did I catch you at a bad time, Ron?"

"Not at all. Actually, I was thinking of giving you a call myself."

"Oh? Why? What's up?"

"I just wanted to thank you for suggesting that I could give Stephanie a ride. It worked out great," he added, barely able to contain his enthusiasm. "I had been thinking about asking her out."

"No kidding!" Bishop responded as if he had been told something that he didn't already know.

Ron also told him that he had asked Steph if he could take her to the Halloween dance since they both had been asked to be chaperones, and that Steph had agreed. After the phone call ended, Bishop was pleased with himself for getting two of his favorite people together. He wondered if Sarah and some of the other female faculty members would be just as pleased.

Next, he decided to call Lieutenant Hodge. He recounted his concerns about Chris Delaney. How far might a disgruntled athlete go to preserve his scholarship chances? He made sure that the Lieutenant understood that this was pure speculation on his part.

Hodge remained silent as he absorbed what Bishop was telling him.

Bishop also told Hodge about the heated argument that supposedly had taken place between Zappala and his assistant coach, Doug Sanders. He quickly added, "Of course that may not have happened at all. I'm getting that story third-hand."

"Listen, Mike, I understand what you're saying. In my experience, ninety-nine percent of what I hear in the course of an investigation turns out to be inaccurate or of no help whatsoever. But it's that one percent that I'm after. And the thing is you never know what seemingly insignificant detail turns out to be that one percent." Bishop wondered if Lieutenant Hodge had also been reading Sir Arthur Conan Doyle.

He then told Hodge about Rocco Santorini's behavior at Andy White's office when the will was read, and about the phone conversation that he had with Mrs. Santorini the day before. "How do we know that Rocco hadn't been in town earlier? With the possible loss of the bakery, he certainly seems to have had a motive."

"True. But how would he have been able to take the cyanide from the school's lab without anyone noticing?" asked Hodge with a sharpness in his voice indicating that Bishop should have asked himself the very same question.

Bishop realized that Hodge had a good point. He was allowing his eagerness to find a suspect unconnected to the school to cloud his judgment. Hodge did agree to make some calls to the authorities in Connecticut to see what he could find out about the Santorini family. "One more idea," Bishop said. "Do you think it's possible that Sister Pat, without realizing it at the time, had seen the killer on the security tapes before they had been taped over?" Hodge agreed to ask her about it. With that, he ended the call. It did not, however, put an end to Bishop's ruminations.

Before it got too late, Bishop called Bob Barrett to set up an appointment. He was looking forward to meeting his former student in the hope that he could provide a few answers regarding Zappala's finances. Bob was very receptive on the phone and agreed to meet with Bishop after school the next day.

Normally, it was hard enough for him to keep up with his papers. When Grace died, all of the routine tasks of daily life became his responsibility as well. He managed everything quite well except for cooking. There wasn't a restaurant within twenty miles of town that Bishop hadn't frequented. He often found it difficult to read more than was required for his classes although reading had always been one of the great pleasures of his life. That was one of the primary reasons that he had become a teacher. It provided him an opportunity to share his love of literature with others. He had been given another significant responsibility as executor, and he worried about how he would be able to do it all and do it well. A meeting with Bobby would be welcomed in one respect, but it was also taking time away normally reserved for other tasks. He tried to remember what his days were like just a few short weeks ago before he had walked into the murder scene.

As he pulled his bedroom curtains closed, he watched the moon dance in and out of the passing clouds. He didn't need a degree in meteorology to know that a storm was coming.

***

When Bishop first saw Bobby Barrett, he had to consciously hide any expression of shock. Some students didn't change very much over the years; Bobby, unfortunately, was not one of them. The lanky athlete with a mop of hair had gained a considerable amount of weight and lost a considerable amount of hair. His playing days were clearly well in the past. His smile was still warm and his handshake firm. "It's certainly good to see you after all these years," Bishop said. Looking around the well-appointed office, he added, "You seem to have done quite well for yourself."

"Thanks, Mr. Bishop. You haven't changed much. Are you still teaching at Trinity?"

Bishop was used to being asked that question. Not too many would have believed that he was, in fact, still there some forty years after he started. After a few minutes spent reminiscing about the old days, Bishop got down to business.

"Bobby, I need to ask you a favor."

"Sure, what it is?"

"As you may know, I've been named executor of Coach Zappala's estate."

"Yeah, good luck with that. It ain't gonna be easy. That guy had a few bucks."

"That's just what I'm talking about, Bobby. In your dealings with him as his accountant, were you aware of how he managed to acquire such a large fortune?"

"Well, he didn't rob a bank, if that's what you mean."

"How did he do it, then?"

"The way most people do, I guess."

"Hard work?" Bishop ventured.

"More like dumb luck."

"Excuse me?"

Barrett explained that as far as he could tell, a large portion of his money had come through investing in the stock market. It seems that in addition to the sports pages, coach also read the financial pages. Years ago, he had invested in a relatively unknown company. Most people who did that never saw their money again. Coach was different.

Bishop asked the obvious question. "What was the company?"

"Did you ever hear of Apple?" Barrett laughed as he asked the question.

"You're kidding!"

"Nope. He got in near the beginning for who knows what reason, and more importantly, he knew when to take profits off the table. Go figure, huh?"

Barrett provided a list of Zappala's accounts and the latest balances that were available. There was no point in converting everything to cash right away. Bobby said that he would be ready to help in the liquidation of the assets once he got the word that the will had gone through probate. They chatted a bit about the rumors circulating in town about Zappala's death. Apparently, Bishop wasn't the only individual with an active imagination triggered by such an unlikely event occurring in their fair city.

Bishop thanked Bobby for his help. He had found the answer to one question. The source of his wealth had been obtained by legal means. As he walked to his car, Bishop started to wonder if it were possible that Bobby Barrett was stealing money from his wealthy client, and when discovered, was forced to silence him before he went to the authorities. Another example of his overactive imagination? He couldn't be sure about anyone's innocence other than his own.

Chapter 11

The next day, it was raining heavily which usually added to the decibel level generated by the kids. Instead of his prep period, Bishop had cafeteria duty which was one of his least favorite parts of the job. He got to walk around the cafeteria watching about two hundred teenagers throw down their lunches, laugh and scream, push and shove, flirt and tease. As long as they cleaned up their tables, didn't have a food fight, and didn't accidentally break any windows, Bishop was content to count the minutes until it was over.

Just a few minutes before he could escape to have his own lunch, a pimply-faced junior, Aaron Metcalf, approached him. His slender frame didn't seem very well suited for football. Perhaps that explained why he was on the sidelines most of the time.

"Uh, Mr. Bishop, you got a sec?" Aaron was a bundle of nerves most of the time, but he seemed particularly uncomfortable now. Instead of making eye contact with Bishop, he kept glancing around the room as if he were afraid of someone.

"Sure, Aaron. What can I do for you?"

Aaron moved away from the tables and Bishop moved along with him.

"There's something I heard that I thought you should know about."

Perhaps Aaron had overheard something about a drinking party, and since he wasn't invited, he was going to rat on the other kids. Maybe he had heard about an instance of cheating, and his conscience was compelling him to come forward. Although Aaron was on the football team, he wasn't really accepted by a lot of the other students. For one thing, Bishop recalled that he had made a bonehead play that had almost cost the team a win earlier in the season. The coach had gone up one side of him and down the other in front of the entire team. It wasn't the right way to handle the mistake, but that was the coach.

"What is it, Aaron? What did you hear?"

"Remember the game against Central when Chris got benched?"

"Yes, of course. What about it?"

Aaron, having checked the room again to be sure that he wasn't being watched, began to whisper, "I heard him say that he wouldn't let him get away with it and that he would kill the bastard."

Bishop was surprised, but did his best to hide his reaction from Aaron. He pulled Aaron even farther away from the nearest tables. "Are you telling me you heard Chris Delaney say that?"

"No! Not Chris! It was Mr. Delaney. I heard him in the parking lot. He was talking to his wife as he got into their car. I was sitting in the car next to theirs. I guess he didn't see me."

"Have you told anyone else?"

"No, I guess I should have said something sooner."

"Listen, Aaron. You did the right thing by telling me, but I would advise you against telling anyone else. You know very well that people say things that they don't mean, especially when they're upset. There is absolutely no reason to think that Mr. Delaney actually did kill the coach. The one person you should tell your story to is Lieutenant Hodge." Before Aaron had a chance to object, Bishop added, "Don't worry. I'll arrange it so that no one here will have any idea of what's going on."

"Like a witness protection program?"

"Well, I don't think that you are going to need protection. What you've heard might not have any bearing on the investigation at all. But let's let the Lieutenant hear what you have to say. He'll take it from there."

The lunch period was ending and everyone was getting ready to move. Aaron seemed to be frozen in place. He was obviously wondering whether he should have kept what he had heard to himself.

Bishop looked directly into Aaron's troubled eyes, "Aaron. You did the right thing. Don't worry about it. It's probably nothing, okay?"

Aaron agreed to meet him in his homeroom after school as long as Bishop cleared it with Coach Chandler that it would be okay for him to be late for practice. Aaron seemed even more afraid of the consequences of missing practice without permission than he was of his impending interview with the police.

***

In the cafeteria, students from the same class tended to sit together. A freshman would not be allowed to sit with the seniors unless the freshman was a particularly cute girl or a geeky boy who didn't understand the difference between laughing with others and being laughed at.

In some ways, seating arrangements in the faculty room were similar. Male teachers generally sat together, talking sports, and female teachers sat together, talking about the students, their own kids, or shopping. All that changed, however, if Sister Ann or Sister Patricia — or both as usually was the case — were in the room. In that event, most teachers were more interested in eating their lunch and getting out of there as quickly as possible. The preferred seating was as far as possible from Sister Pat who considered all meals serious business. Her girth suggested that some serious health issues were in her future, but nothing stopped her from inhaling whatever was on her plate. Whatever comments she made were usually made at someone else's expense. Even Sister Ann was not immune to her friend's caustic remarks.

Therefore, it was a great relief for Bishop to find that the only occupant of the faculty room as he entered that day was Sister Pascala.

"How are you, Sister?" asked Bishop as he took a seat across from her and opened his lunch bag containing his usual peanut butter and jelly sandwich.

"I should be asking the same of you. I haven't had much of a chance to talk with you these last few weeks. It must have been awful to walk into a murder scene."

"Well, I didn't know it was a murder scene at the time," he explained, thinking to himself what he might have done differently had he actually known that then. "But it was still quite a shock." Sister Pascala, Trinity's version of a curmudgeon, was pushing her macaroni and cheese from one side of the plate to the other. The only other item on her tray was a small container of milk. She looked as if she had lost a few pounds recently which was more noticeable in someone of her petite stature. She reached up several times to adjust the way her rimless glasses rested on her nose. It seemed to Bishop that she, like Aaron moments earlier, was debating whether or not to tell him something.

"Sister, are you feeling all right? You've hardly touched your lunch."

"Oh, Michael!" she said as she sighed deeply. "I feel like such a fool!" Bishop was startled by her obvious distress. Admitting mistakes was not exactly ingrained in her genetic code.

"Why? What happened?"

"I keep thinking that if I hadn't kept that cyanide in my lab, Albert Zappala might still be alive today."

It was hard not to feel compassion for this crusty, old veteran whose aura of invincibility had been shattered by her sense of guilt. Bishop tried to find the words to put her conscience at ease. He told her that she was being unreasonable in blaming herself. She had kept the cyanide in a locked cabinet, and the lab storeroom also was locked. Even if the cyanide had not been there, if someone was intent on harming Zappala, that person would have found another way to do so. Nothing that he said seemed to have the desired effect.

Since no one else had yet come in for lunch, she continued to explain the source of her agony. "You don't understand. Yes, anyone with a classroom key could open that storeroom, but I was the one who practically put the poison in that person's hands." As she said this, her lips quavered as did her voice.

"What do you mean?"

"Have you ever been in that storeroom?"

Bishop had to admit that in his forty plus years at the school he had never had occasion to do so. "That's just the point, don't you see? I'm the one who goes in there most often, and half the time I couldn't find the key to that cabinet, so I decided to place the key on a little hook right next to the cabinet. I practically put the poison in the hands of the murderer!" As she said that, she pounded the table with both of her fists, making the tray jounce.

"Sister, that's nonsense, and you know it. No one could have anticipated that outcome. You're being much too hard on yourself."

"And I worry that whoever it is might use that poison again." Her eyes became moist with suppressed tears.

"I don't think that you need to worry about that. I'm fairly certain that we don't have a serial killer on the loose. Zappala was clearly the target. The man had a lot of money and a lot of enemies. As the one who found the body and as the executor of the estate, I've been pulled into this situation more deeply than I would have imagined. I can tell you, in confidence, that I am doing whatever I can to help Lieutenant Hodge find the person responsible. And that certainly isn't you."

"Oh, Michael, thank you, thank you!" Allowing the old nun to vent her concerns was a gift that she deeply appreciated. "You're a good man. I hope that you find the truth."

"I'll certainly do what I can, but don't expect miracles. After all, I'm only a Bishop." With that line, Sister Pascala smiled, squeezed his hand gently, picked up her tray with its unfinished contents, and left the lunchroom.

***

As soon as his last class of the day ended, Bishop rushed to the main hallway, dodging students looking at their phones, and hefty backpacks being swung over shoulders as students rushed out for their rides. He was appalled at the amount of time these young people spent looking at those screens. A few years earlier, he had given in and purchased a smart phone for himself, but he still preferred actually talking with someone in person as opposed to texting.

He had to find Russ Chandler, and he guessed that he might be hanging around as the final bell rang, waiting for his players to make their way to practice. The word from some of the players was that the newly appointed head coach was so intent on trying to prove that he was as good as Zappala if not better, that he was pushing the kids too hard. Some had even talked of quitting the program for next season. Practices were longer, and the hitting was punishing. Anyone who was late for practice ran laps to the point of collapse. Apparently, he didn't realize that such tactics would doom his chances for success. No one claimed that he had been a Rhodes scholar.

Russ was standing in the middle of the hallway with a clipboard in his hands. He was wearing sweat pants, and a tee shirt that emphasized the results of his hard work in the gym. He was chewing gum so forcefully that the pencil he had tucked behind his right ear moved to the rhythm of his chewing. "Hey, Russ. Got a minute?"

"Yeah, what's up?" Bishop noted that Russ could talk and chew gum at the same time, but kept that observation to himself.

"I need you to excuse Aaron from the first half hour or so of practice tonight."

"Look, we're preparing for the final game of the season. What do you need him for?"

Bishop couldn't tell him the truth and hadn't thought out an explanation. He hadn't anticipated resistance. He had to think fast and be convincing.

"I have my suspicions that Aaron plagiarized part of his paper on Mark Twain. If he can't convince me that it was entirely unintentional, he may be lost to your team for a lot more than a half hour." He surprised himself with the ease with which he had lied.

"Okay, but keep it as short as possible, hear?" Russ's confrontational tone seemed to melt away. Bishop thought that the reference to plagiarism might have sparked a painful memory from Russ's own educational journey. He made a mental note to be sure to find Russ the next day to explain that he had been mistaken about the charges of plagiarism against Aaron.

"By the way, congratulations on being named head coach."

"Yeah, thanks."

"I hear that you have a new assistant. What happened to Doug?"

"He was pissed that he didn't get the head job, so he quit."

"That's too bad. He seemed like a good guy," offered Bishop. He had hoped to nudge Russ into further comment, but his silence told him otherwise. He couldn't help wondering how far Russ might go if he were 'pissed' badly enough.

"I'll send Aaron to practice as soon as I can." As he began to walk away, he added, "And good luck with the game this weekend." Russ didn't bother to respond, but his pencil moved up and down.

***

When Bishop returned to his homeroom, Aaron was in a front row seat doing some math homework. After closing the door, Bishop used his cell phone to call Lieutenant Hodge. He briefly explained that a student had approached him earlier in the day with some information regarding the Delaneys and Coach Zappala. He then gave the phone to Aaron. "Tell the Lieutenant what you told me in the cafeteria."

The conversation between Aaron and Hodge took less than three minutes. Aaron told the Lieutenant exactly what he had told Bishop earlier that day. Hodge mostly listened, but must have asked for a few quick clarifications that Aaron provided. When he was finished, he gave the phone back to Bishop. "He wants a word with you."

"Okay. Thanks. You can head down to practice now. I cleared it with your coach." Aaron breathed a sigh of relief. Bishop wondered whether it was relief that the conversation was over, relief that he had told the authorities what he felt obligated to tell, or relief that he would be able to get to practice without getting laps for being late.

After Aaron had closed the door, Bishop asked Hodge, "Well, what did you think?"

Hodge replied that Aaron's account of Mr. Delaney's encounter with the coach was accurate. In fact, his own investigation had already led him to talk with Mr. Delaney. It seems that a number of other people had heard similar remarks. Hodge was convinced it was nothing more than talk. Delaney had been very cooperative and apologetic. He just wanted his son to be treated fairly. "That scholarship means a lot to them. Otherwise, they can't afford to send Chris to college."

"I see," said Bishop, not convinced by Mr. Delaney's words of contrition. He had had more kids than he could count pull that act on him over the years. He then switched topics. "Did you have a chance to question Sister Pat about the tapes?"

"As a matter of fact, I did. What a piece of work she is!"

"What do you mean?"

"Well, this is just between us, but she became very defensive, almost belligerent. She claimed that she was much too busy to pay anything more than cursory attention to the security cameras, and that she never saw anything unusual in the lab area. She actually accused me of accusing her of withholding information."

"I should have warned you that overreacting was in her DNA." He thought of Gertrude's response when the player queen professes her innocence: "Methinks the lady doth protest too much."

Before he ended the call, Hodge added, "And by the way, you know you were right about Rocco Santorini."

"In what way?"

"I called a Detective Scalera in Connecticut, and asked him to see what he could find out about Rocco. As luck would have it, a number of officers frequent that bakery. Rocco practically lives there, but the officers say that they remember Rocco was noticeably absent for about a week around the time of Zappala's murder."

Did that mean that Rocco might have been in Groveland before he showed up for the funeral? From his brief encounters with him, Rocco struck Bishop as a man with a volatile temper. Might he have killed his uncle in an attempt to save the family business? Even if he had been in town at the time of the murder, how would he have gotten the cyanide? Could he have had an accomplice? After thanking the Lieutenant, he ended the call and packed up the books and folders that he needed to take home that night.

Chapter 12

With the sun setting earlier and earlier, Bishop decided to use the fireplace in his living room for the first time that season. It took only a few minutes to feel the warmth of the crackling fire. Staring into the flames, he thought of how much Grace enjoyed sitting by the fire with a good book. It was moments like this that reminded him of how much he missed her.

He had been able to catch up on his grading, so he decided to take advantage of this time to examine the contents of one of the boxes that Andy White had given him. This box had originally held a ream of multipurpose printer paper that Zappala had probably salvaged from the copy room at school. Bishop often did the same thing, although in his case, instead of storage, the box served as a makeshift podium. He simply placed the box on a desk in the front row and placed his book on the box. That served a dual purpose: one, it brought him much closer to the students, and two, it enabled him to refer to his book at a distance he could manage comfortably with his bifocals.

The box in front of him had a bit of a musty odor having been stored in a closet. Zappala had not placed any identifying marks to indicate the nature of the contents. As he flipped open the top, he found the contents in a jumble. Reaching in, he pulled a fistful of papers out and began skimming through them. Zappala had attended a football clinic at Penn State University and had kept an itinerary for the event and a certificate of attendance. There were a bunch of handouts with such titles as "Seven Strategies for Success" and "Concussion Protocols." He must have been bored by some of the presentations as his notes contained a lot of doodling. He had written out and highlighted a quote by Vince Lombardi, "You never win a game unless you beat the guy in front of you. The score on the board doesn't mean a thing. That's for the fans. You've got to win the war with the man in front of you. You've got to get your man."

Lombardi was undoubtedly one of the greatest coaches in the history of the NFL. Bishop was certain that Lombardi had used those words to motivate his players to play their best. Could the same be said for Zappala? How many times had he won the war? It didn't matter. The words lingered in Bishop's thoughts, "You've got to get your man." Someone finally did. If he could figure out why it was done, he would know who had done it.

After putting all of the papers back in the box, he put the lid back on, and set it aside. He placed another log on the fire, causing a burst of embers to escape up the chimney, taking with them his frustration.

Just then his cell phone rang. It was Ron Jennings.

"Did I catch you at a bad time?" asked Ron, obviously hoping that he had not.

"No. Not at all. What's up?"

Ron was speaking a little faster than he normally did, reflecting his excitement over the news he wanted to share. First, he wanted to thank Michael again for setting him up to give Stephanie that ride to school. It seems that that was just the jumpstart that he had needed. Bishop realized that he hadn't had much of an opportunity to speak to Ron privately. Even when they happened to see each other in the halls and stopped to chat for a few minutes, there was inevitably a student or teacher or an open classroom door within earshot keeping any exchange to the most mundane pleasantries. Ron had met Stephanie after school for a coffee at the Bean Tree. They really seemed to be getting along well.

"Ron, I'm really happy for you. Steph seems like a very nice young lady."

After giving Ron a chance to extol all of her wonderful qualities, Bishop decided to steer the conversation in the direction of the Zappala investigation as he had come to label the thoughts that consumed more and more of his time. "Ron, do you remember the question Mary Nickerson asked Lieutenant Hodge at that faculty meeting?"

"Who can forget the questions that that woman comes up with," he said with a laugh, "although asking about the tapes from the cameras was a good question." He paused, then added, "for a change."

"I've been wondering about the security cameras for the outside entrances," said Bishop as he sought a way to confirm a theory that he had developed. "Do you know if those cameras work on the same 72-hour loop?"

"Those cameras were installed earlier, I'm afraid. They run on a 24-hour loop. Why do you ask?"

"Well, it's possible someone outside of the school population walked into the building, used the signs to find the science labs, found the storeroom unlocked, and walked out with a murder weapon." Ron listened as his friend played out this scenario.

"Unless the person drew attention to himself in some way," Bishop theorized, "most of us would simply assume that the individual was a parent or had some business at the school." It was true that if someone looked lost, most of the students and staff would certainly ask if they could be of assistance, but what if they acted as if they belonged?

"Maybe now the board will decide to provide the funding for a buzzer system at the main entrance," Ron said sarcastically. It was a sensitive topic with some of the faculty who had been asking for some sort of security system at Holy Trinity given recent national tragedies. Bishop had been one of the most vocal advocates for such a safety precaution. He recalled the way Sister Pat had put the idea down. "This is Groveland," putting exaggerated emphasis on each word. "Nothing like that is going to happen here," she stated with the certainty that only revealed how clueless she really was.

"You know, Ron, there is some question as to when Rocco Santorini first arrived in town. He could have very easily walked right into our building with the pretext of looking for his uncle if he were questioned."

"Michael, are you kidding?"

"All I'm saying is that we shouldn't dismiss the possibility that an outsider is responsible." The phone call that had begun with Ron in such good spirits ended on that sobering note.

***

Bishop had just put some water on for tea, when the phone rang again. "Sorry to bother you, again," Ron started. "I was thinking about what you just said about Rocco. He then went on to suggest that it might be possible to determine if Rocco had been in town the night of the murder. Since there were only a handful of places offering lodging in Groveland itself, he thought that a few inquiries might yield a big payoff.

Bishop hadn't considered that approach but thought that it was worth a shot. He informed Jennings that Lieutenant Hodge did have the authorities in Connecticut checking on his whereabouts around the time of his uncle's death. With that, he ended his conversation with Ron for the second time and got back to the business of making some tea. As the water boiled, he wondered if Rocco would have been so careless as to use his real name in registering at a motel. Would he have stayed in town, or would he have sought out the relative anonymity of one of the busier chain motels such as the Hampton Inn about 20 miles outside of town? Perhaps he could be tracked by the car he was driving. Bishop had noted a white Ford Taurus with Connecticut license plates parked in front of Andy White's office on the day the will was read. He hadn't, however, picked up the plate number. He began to understand in a new way what Sherlock Holmes meant by the necessity of observing details. Attention to detail was always what led him to solving the most baffling case. He had been explaining that to his freshmen just the other day in their discussion of *The Hound of the Baskervilles*. Holmes certainly didn't believe in a supernatural hound or in the legend of the curse on the Baskerville family. Concentrating on the details worked. As he placed an Earl Grey teabag to steep in his favorite mug, one with the words, "Keep Calm and Carry On," in red letters across a tan background, he picked up his phone as well as a telephone directory.

He struck out with his first call to the Budget Motel; however, he hit a homerun with his second call to the Weary Traveler Inn. To his surprise, the owners, Hank and Marcia Proulx, were the parents of Janice Proulx, Trinity Class of 1986. After some small talk about Janice who was now married with two kids, living in San Diego, and working in real estate, Marcia verified that Mr. Santorini had stayed at her place. "It was such a shame about his uncle," she said sympathetically, "and having to return just a few days after he left must have been quite a shock for him." Luckily, she did not question why Bishop would be interested in knowing where Rocco had stayed.

Bishop could barely contain his interest. "What do you mean 'his return'?"

"Well, he had been here for a couple of nights just before, well … you know, just before Mr. Zappala died, and then he came back for the funeral, of course."

"Are you sure about the dates?" queried Bishop. He was incredulous that he had just been handed solid evidence for placing Rocco Santorini at the top of the list of suspects.

"Oh, yes. In fact, he had also been here for a couple of nights about six months ago. At least he had the chance to spend some quality time with his uncle before his tragic death."

Quality time, indeed, Bishop thought to himself. He thanked Mrs. Proulx for her time, and asked her to give his best regards to Janice.

His next phone call was to share this new information with Lieutenant Hodge who told him that he would pass it along to the authorities in Connecticut. He also cautioned him against jumping to conclusions. "Even if he was in town the night of the murder, it doesn't prove that he did it." Bishop had to agree, although in his mind, it did make it more plausible.

Chapter 13

Just before Bishop's alarm was about to sound at 5:30 a.m., he reached over and turned it off. As usual, he was already awake. His internal clock never seemed to fail him. He had gotten into the habit of waking up before the alarm so that Grace could catch a little more sleep. Since she had passed away, he had thought of selling their king size bed and replacing it with something smaller. Yet, part of him wanted to keep everything the way it was when she was alive.

As he shaved and showered, he thought about his plans for each class that he would have that day. Grace had often told him that if he wasn't thinking so much, he could shave and shower in half the time. She was right about that, but old habits were hard to break. With one class of 9th graders he was discussing a short story, "They Grind Exceeding Small," by Ben Ames Williams. The other 9th grade class was discussing excerpts of Homer's *The Odyssey*. His juniors were studying *The Scarlet Letter* by Hawthorne while seniors in his Advanced Placement English were starting an examination of *Hamlet*. He was pleased that all of his classes that day would be focused on literature. At this stage of his teaching career, he had promised himself that he would only teach works of literature that he truly enjoyed himself. Doing that, he felt, gave him a better chance of conveying his passion for literature.

Some of his colleagues thought that he was insane to try to teach four or sometimes five different works of literature at the same time. They thought that it would be too much work to have so many different preps. On the contrary, Bishop always felt that teaching something different in each class prevented him from getting bored with the material. He disliked the idea of teaching the same material two or three or even four times a day, and since today's classes were all focused on a discussion, no new essays would be added to the stack he already had. At least for today, he reminded himself.

***

Because he liked to arrive at school early, there were only a handful of teachers in the copy room picking up their mail before heading to their homerooms. They were buzzing about something. As soon as he walked into the small room, Diane Ramos turned to him and asked, "What do you make of *this*?" with a mixture of anger, confusion, and curiosity in her voice. She waved the half sheet of paper back and forth rapidly as if she could make the words fall off of the page if she tried hard enough.

The notice apparently had been placed in every teacher's mailbox. "EFFECTIVE TODAY TEACHERS WILL HAVE ACCESS TO THEIR NAILBOXES ONLY BEFORE HOMEROOM PERIOD AND AFTER SCHOOL. THANK YOU. THE ADMINISTRATION."

Bishop laughed as he read it out loud. This was clearly the work of the ever-plotting Sister Pat. The "nailboxes" typo was as good as her signature in identifying the source. She was the one who was constantly harping to others that typographical or grammatical errors were unacceptable. Based on her own writing, Bishop concluded that her desire for error-free messages applied to everyone except herself.

"Well, Diane, since I don't have a 'nailbox,' I'm not going to worry about it," as he handed back her copy of the memo, intentionally left his copy of that memo in his mailbox, and walked out of the room. As he did so, he heard Kim Mitchell, one of the gym teachers, offering her opinion, "This is nuts!" Bishop couldn't argue with her assessment.

Once in the hall, he passed by Jack Slater, the maintenance man. "Morning, Jack, how are you doing today?"

"Oh, I'm doing just dandy. Did you see the memo yet," he asked hoping to stir up some reaction. When Bishop refused the bait and just smiled, Jack said mysteriously, "Oh, it's gonna be an interesting day," and kept on walking.

***

After his first period class, Stephanie popped into his classroom. She was dressed in her always professional manner: sweater with a silk scarf draped around her neck, skirt that came just above the knee, and comfortable-looking low-heeled shoes. "Did you hear what they did?"

Although he assumed that this had something to do with the memo, he still asked, "Who's they?"

"Why, the administration, of course!"

"What did they do?" He was tempted to add "this time" to his last question. The administration had a habit of making arbitrary decisions that usually turned out badly. There was that time when they decided that all teachers would be required to turn in their lesson plans on Friday afternoon. That didn't go over too well with teachers who used the weekend to plan their classes for the following week. There was another occasion when they decided that all teachers would be required to attend games, concerts, and drama productions. That didn't go over too well with teachers who either had small children, a part-time job to supplement their income, or a considerable commute to school each day.

The source of these impractical ideas was almost always the belligerent Sister Patricia Meehan. She was something of an enigma. Although she spent her entire career in education, her words and actions revealed how little she cared. She often remarked that school is great "as long as the kids aren't here." Bishop was sure that whatever idea she had cooked up would soon backfire once again, and Sister Ann would be there to minimize the damage.

Since some students were already filing in for the next class, Stephanie whispered to Bishop, "They're attaching a metal grate to the cabinet with the mailboxes. According to Terry, they're going to put a padlock on the grate." She needn't have whispered since, by the grins on their faces, it was clear that most of the students already knew what was going on.

"That's brilliant," whispered Bishop in return, "as if communication around here wasn't bad enough already." Then, he added, more seriously, "I wouldn't worry too much about it. My bet is that by the end of the week, the padlock will be gone." He didn't explain whether he thought that the administration would reverse course, or if one of the teachers would simply use some bolt cutters to remove the padlock.

Conversation in the faculty lunchroom was particularly animated that day. Frank Wilson, one of the younger teachers on the staff, had made the mistake of asking Sister Pat why teachers were being denied access to their mailboxes. Pat didn't hesitate to lay Frank out in front of some teachers and students. She launched into a fiery tirade over the fact that teachers were using the excuse of checking their mailboxes to congregate in the copy room. In her view, they were simply wasting time and that wasn't what they were paid to do. Any communication during the day would be done through email, telephone, or voice mail. The scene between Sister Pat and Frank was replayed for other teachers as they came in with their lunch trays. As long as Sister Ann and Sister Pat were not in the room, the teachers were unanimous in expressing their outrage.

Mark Fletcher, a tall man with a neatly trimmed beard who taught math to the 10th graders, spoke for everyone when he said in a dejected tone, "It's an insult to be treated like a child. As a matter of fact, you wouldn't even treat a child that way!"

"Do they seriously think that we are neglecting our responsibilities by spending maybe five minutes in the copy room chatting with a colleague?" asked Sarah Humphries.

"Who knows what's next?" asked Roger Willis, who taught theology. "Maybe they'll put a limit on how often we can use the bathroom or how long we can be in there."

"Don't give them any ideas!" Sarah blurted out, as they all laughed.

***

Bishop decided to finish his lunch quickly and head right down to Sister Ann's office. If he were lucky, she would be free for a quick conversation. If he were really lucky, Sister Pat would not be involved. Her office door was open, so he peeked in. She was alone, looking at something on her computer. Was she working on the budget? Was she preparing a report for the board? Bishop caught a reflection of her computer screen on the window behind her desk. He didn't feel guilty about disturbing her when he realized that she was playing solitaire. He knocked on the open door and asked as if he didn't know the answer, "Sister, do you have a minute?"

"Yes, I do," she said somewhat tentatively, perhaps anticipating what Bishop might want to discuss. She hit a key on her computer, and her screen saver popped up. "What can I do for you?"

As Bishop entered the office, he said, "It might be best if I closed the door." At that point, he was certain that she had not only figured out the topic, but also her response. He sat down in the chair facing her on the other side of the desk. Her chair was an expensive leather swivel rocker. Knowing Sister Ann as well as he did, he assumed that the straight-backed wooden chair he was seated in was chosen with the intent of making the occupant uncomfortable and less likely to linger.

"I was wondering if I could talk to you about the lock on the mailboxes."

"What's there to talk about?" she said defensively. "Teachers will have access to their mailboxes before and after school. They don't need to check them twenty times during the day."

Bishop wondered whether that was an exaggeration or if someone had actually watched surveillance camera feed and counted the number of visits. "Well even if one or two faculty members are going into the copy room an excessive amount of times, I would think that a private comment made to the offending individuals would suffice. Why punish the entire staff for the actions of a few? If a teacher punished the whole class for the misbehavior of a few, you wouldn't consider that an effective strategy, would you?" Sister picked up a pen from her desk and studied it as if she had no idea what it was. Since she gave no response, Bishop continued, "What will happen on Friday when many teachers will want to pick up their paycheck from their mailboxes and go to the bank during their lunch time?"

Sister's face flushed as he mentioned the paychecks. It had obviously not factored into her decision. He added, "It's just my opinion, but given all that has happened around here in the last couple of weeks, you might want to reconsider that lock on the mailboxes." He had said what he wanted to say, so he got up to leave. Sister grudgingly said, "Well, I'll think about it." What she probably meant was that she would have to think of a way to break the news to her cohort, Sister Pat, that the mailbox idea wasn't going to fly. "Just sit back down for a minute. I have a question for you." Bishop had no idea what might be coming. He looked at the clock in her office and realized that he would have to leave for his next class in a few minutes.

"Michael, do you know when the school might be receiving Mr. Zappala's bequest?" she asked in a tone that had turned much more congenial.

"I don't know for sure. It depends on the Santorinis to some extent. If they contest the will, it could be quite some time. Andy White doesn't think that they have much chance of success. Moving the will through probate could take a few months."

"Well, we certainly could use those funds around here," sounding as if she already decided how the money would be spent. "And what about the other four million?"

"What about it?" he asked, again feeling caught off guard.

"You are to give that money to a charity of your choosing, is that right?" knowing that it was, in fact, correct.

"Yes."

"Have you decided on a charity?"

Bishop wanted to ask her what business that was of hers, but he refrained. Instead, he said, "No. There will be time for that. Right now my greatest concern is that the authorities find the killer."

Sister straightened in her chair. Perhaps she had forgotten that someone had murdered Zappala, someone who might be associated with the school in some way. "Of course, I hope they find the perpetrator, and quickly. It's just that I was thinking that Holy Trinity deserves your consideration for the remainder of his bequest." Judging from his raised eyebrows, she quickly added "or at least of a portion of the remainder."

Even with that adjustment, Bishop had to control the impulse to laugh in her face. Zappala had left the school a million bucks, and she has the nerve to ask for more? He decided to give her a taste of her own medicine. "Well, I'll think about it!" he said as he got up to leave. As he opened the door, another thought occurred to him. He turned around and asked, "Do you remember when we were talking about his financial resources before the funeral?"

"Yes, now that you mention it, I remember that we were interrupted."

"You knew that Zappala was a very wealthy man, didn't you?"

"To some extent, yes. During the summer, he came in to my office and demanded all new helmets, pads, and uniforms for his team. He also wanted big raises for his coaching staff. When I told him that it was out of the question because the budget was tight enough as it was, he stormed out. The next day he came into my office and dropped an envelope containing a generous check on my desk."

She tried to mimic the gruff voice of the coach. "'*Here. Buy my kids what they need!*'"

There was a flash of recognition in Bishop's mind. "That check was for $25,000, wasn't it?"

"Yes, but how would you know that?" she asked with a look of amazement.

"I've looked through his checkbook and came across that transaction."

Sister quickly added, "When I realized how much money he had given me, I wrote him a thank you note and told him that I would be happy to add his name to the list of major donors to the school. He called me when he received the note and asked me to keep his donation confidential, and so I did. I hope that you will do that also."

Instead of responding, he just nodded, looked at the clock, and said that he had to get to class. He had just been discussing Hazen Kinch from the short story, "They Grind Exceeding Small" with his students. Hazen was so greedy that he unwittingly caused the death of his only child, and lived the rest of his life with that guilt. If Sister Ann knew that Zappala was a very wealthy man, and if she had shared that knowledge with Sister Pat, what might either one of them, or both of them, been willing to do to acquire a large sum of money for the school? Hadn't Sister Ann just revealed her interest in the remainder of the bequest? Could she have known that Holy Trinity had been named in his will? Obtaining the cyanide would not have been a problem. Motive? Yes. Opportunity? Yes. Would she have aroused suspicion by being seen on the security cameras? No. Could Sister Pat have talked Sister Ann into it just as she had persuaded her to place the lock on the mailboxes?

Only the sight of the students in his classroom shook him from this line of thought.

Chapter 14

Although some people complained that the school week always went by so slowly, Bishop felt that the days went by so quickly that he had to work hard to keep up. Maybe that feeling was a product of his age. He sometimes thought about how many more years he would be able to do this. Perhaps it was time to start thinking about the next chapter of his life. If Grace were still with him, he definitely would have chosen to retire in order to spend more time with her and to travel.

He had received a call the previous evening with an update from Lieutenant Hodge. He told Bishop that Detective Scalera had had a conversation with Rocco Santorini. Rocco had been quite upset that his whereabouts at the time of his uncle's murder were being questioned. He had, however, admitted what Bishop had already learned from Marcia Proulx, the owner of the Weary Traveler Inn. Rocco had been in Groveland the night of the murder. Rocco had asked Scalera if it was a crime to visit his uncle. He even admitted that he had been at Zappala's house the night that he was poisoned, but he insisted that Albert was very much alive when he left.

Bishop thought that it was smart of Rocco to admit that he had been in town on that night. He probably realized that it was just a matter of time before the police would figure that out anyway. Of course, the fact that he was in town did not mean that he had committed any crime. On the other hand, it didn't eliminate him as a suspect either.

When he arrived at school, he went straight to the copy room which was bustling with activity. Mark Fletcher greeted Bishop with a high-five. "Look, man, the grate is down! The mailboxes are back!" He had a backpack slung over one shoulder and a coffee cup in one hand.

"That is good news," replied Bishop as he picked up his mail and headed towards his classroom. He noticed that although the metal grate had been removed, it was still visible behind a filing cabinet. Perhaps that was to serve as a not-so-subtle reminder to the faculty that it could be used again.

Terry, the office secretary, left her desk and rushed to catch up with Bishop. "I guess we have you to thank for regaining access to the mailboxes," she said with a knowing look.

"What makes you think that?" asked Bishop, unsure of how his private conversation with Sister Ann could have become public knowledge.

"Well, for starters, I noticed that you were in a closed-door meeting with Sister Ann the other day, and…" Bishop cut her off by interjecting, "But that meeting could have been about anything."

As soon as he had finished making his point, Terry continued as if what he had said was irrelevant, "…and another reason is that I overheard a rather heated exchange between Sister Ann and Sister Pat right after you left Ann's office.

"Is that so?" said Bishop wanting details and knowing that Terry would happily provide them without much prodding.

"Yeah, you should have heard them! Sister Ann marched right in to Sister Pat's office, and she needn't have bothered to close the door because it wouldn't have made any difference. Ann told Pat that denying teachers access to their mailboxes during the day was a bad idea, and that the grate had to be removed ASAP. Pat bellowed, 'Why the hell should I do that?' When Ann mentioned that you had been in to discuss it with her, Pat really blew a gasket. 'Why should I care what he thinks? When is that guy going to retire? He's nothing but a pain in the ass!'" Terry wasn't the only member of the staff who did a not-too-flattering imitation of the assistant principal.

If Terry thought that Bishop would be upset to hear of himself spoken about in this manner, she was going to be disappointed. She continued, "Ann said something about not wanting to antagonize you right now because a lot of money was at stake." Terry admitted that she didn't quite understand what Sister Ann had meant, and Bishop was not about to explain to her that he knew exactly what she had meant. As he headed off to his classroom, he simply said, "The important point is that the mailboxes are open again." However, he had no intention of forgetting what "Sister Meany" had apparently said about him. That, and the reference to Zappala's money.

***

There was a tangible air of excitement in the halls that built through the day. The stresses of student life were about to be relieved at least temporarily. The last football game of the season was that night against neighboring Roosevelt High. Everyone was hoping that Chris Delaney would break the school record for touchdowns in one season, twenty-two. Win or lose, there were parties planned. Students, all of them under the legal age, would be imbibing their favorite brew. There was nothing that school officials could do about it. The kids often drank with their parents' approval. Many of them even provided the booze. It was a mentality that Bishop had never understood.

Bishop knew that Ron was excited, too. Ron was taking Stephanie out for pizza after the game, and if she asked him up to her apartment afterward, Ron confided to him that he had would accept the invitation.

Before he knew it, his classes were finished. The weekend had begun. Since he had decided that he was too tired to attend the game, he went over to Stephanie's room to wish her a nice weekend, but she had a student in with her and the door was closed. He straightened his desk up a bit, and checked back about fifteen minutes later. The door was now open, and Stephanie was just sitting at her desk, looking a bit pale.

"Are you okay, Steph?"

"Me, yeah. I'm fine."

"What was that conference about, if you don't mind my asking?"

"Oh, that. Nothing really." She started shoving folders into her book bag. "That was Bonnie King. She hasn't been doing very well in French III, and she was curious to know if the retest had helped her grade." Bishop knew all about the retest. Steph had discussed it with him earlier. She had handed back some tests to her French III class that were less than stellar. Instead of coming down hard on them, she wanted to give them another chance. After all, the last couple of weeks had been hard for everyone, and she thought that adding some new material and scheduling another test soon would give them their best chance at improving their average before the end of the first quarter. It was the type of strategy that Bishop himself had used on occasion in the past with great success. Here she was a rookie teacher, and she already had figured out some of these techniques on her own. An impressive young lady, thought Bishop, one that he hoped would stay at Trinity for years to come.

He thought it was a bit strange that Stephanie would have closed the door if that was all Bonnie had wanted to talk about, but he didn't say anything. After a moment's hesitation, Stephanie spoke again tentatively. "Well, there's more to it than the retest," she admitted, thus confirming Bishop's suspicion.

Having jammed as much as she could into her bag, she dropped it to the floor next to her desk and began to tell the story. She had promised

Bonnie that she wouldn't tell anyone, but she felt that she had to tell someone, and Bishop was one of the few people she could trust.

"It all started a few weeks ago. I had asked to see Bonnie after class because of her poor work. She broke down and told me that she hadn't been able to study because she was so worried."

"Worried about what?" he asked, still not understanding how this could be so important.

"She had missed her period."

"Oh, my!"

"That's not all," added Stephanie. She went on to explain that Bonnie had told her that she had been sleeping with her boyfriend and that she was a week late. She was too frightened to tell her parents. She had made Stephanie promise that she wouldn't tell anyone. Bishop now understood why Steph had been upset, but he didn't understand why she had decided to tell him at all.

"Don't you know who her boyfriend is?"

"No." He had made it a habit of not paying too much attention to the latest hot couple.

"It's Chris Delaney!"

Michael was surprised but not overly so. Despite the fact that the official word at a Catholic school was "abstinence," he knew that a fair percentage of upper classmen were having sex. He could only hope that they were practicing safe sex. Apparently not always. He still did not quite understand why Steph had been so shaken by this. She explained that Bonnie had returned a few days later to announce with great relief that her period had finally started. Steph had taken the opportunity to talk with Bonnie about the risks that she was taking in having sex with Chris or anyone for that matter. Bonnie had listened politely, but clearly she was unlikely to change her behavior. Everything had changed when Bonnie had come in this afternoon. Bonnie was interested in her grade on the retest, but her real purpose in coming in was to share some other private concern. Bishop listened, hoping that all of this would come into focus for him.

"Bonnie told me about a conversation between Chris and Coach Zappala."

"What conversation?" Once the coach's name was mentioned, his interest was piqued.

"It's why Chris got benched that night."

"Because he had sex with Bonnie? I don't think that the coach was the type to get too upset over something like that." He thought about some of the less-than-flattering comments that Zappala had made in the past about women.

"It wasn't about the sex. Bonnie said that during halftime, the coach pulled Chris into his office and reamed him out about his poor play that night. Chris made the mistake of trusting his coach. He told him why. He told him that his girlfriend was late with her period and that was all he could think about. He apologized for playing so poorly. Apparently, Coach lit up."

"What do you mean?"

Steph went on to recount the events of that closed-door meeting as she had it from Bonnie. Zappala berated him for being so stupid as to get a girl knocked up. He asked him if he had ever heard of protection. He told him that if the girl were pregnant, he would take care of it. When Chris asked him what he meant by that, the coach rubbed his thumb across his fingers suggesting a payoff. He asked him if it was Bonnie. Chris told him that it was. The coach apparently laughed and said, "Cheerleader right? Nice piece of ass." Bonnie explained to Stephanie that Chris got so furious that he started calling the coach all kinds of names. He threatened to tell Sister Ann what he said. Zappala then challenged Chris to do just that. He wasn't afraid of her, he said. It would be his word against Chris's. Then coach threatened to tell the Delaneys that Chris was sleeping with his girlfriend. That was when Chris said he'd kill him.

Bishop couldn't believe what he was hearing. "He said what?"

Stephanie repeated, "Bonnie told me that Chris threatened to kill the coach. That was why he benched him for the rest of the game. Later that weekend, the coach was murdered." Steph was clearly upset as she asked, "Oh, Mike, do you think Chris did it?"

He shook his head. "Both father and son threatened to kill the same man on the same night! No, I really don't think Chris is responsible. He wouldn't have told Bonnie what he had said if he had really done it." Then he said as much to himself as to Stephanie, "Zappala was a nasty, nasty man. I'm beginning to understand why a lot of people might have wanted him dead."

Chapter 15

Despite the fact that it was Saturday, Bishop woke around 5:30 a.m. as usual. After showering and having breakfast, he put in a CD of Lizst's Hungarian Rhapsodies. He did some paperwork which always made time disappear quickly. His concentration was disrupted by his cell. He didn't recognize the number, but it was local so he answered.

"Hi, this is Cindy Walker. Is this Michael Bishop?"

"Yes, it is. What can I do for you?" he asked as he racked his brain trying to remember who Cindy Walker was. The name was familiar. Was she a parent of one of his students? They didn't always share the same last name.

He quickly realized that Cindy was one of the real estate agents that had contacted him hoping to win the listing of Zappala's house. He had forgotten that he had agreed to meet her at the coach's home on Saturday at 10:00 a.m. Keeping that appointment was something that he had pushed out of his mind. The last time he had been in that house, he had found a dead man. He wasn't anxious to return.

He drove up the road to Zappala's house just as he had a couple of weeks earlier. Zappala's Lincoln was still in the driveway. He would have to talk to some car dealers about selling it. The realtor wasn't there yet. He parked his Corolla next to the Lincoln, and as he got out, he felt that he had learned more about this man in a matter of days than he had learned in the time that they were colleagues with not much in common. The police had removed the crime scene tape. The lawn definitely needed mowing one more time before the end of the season. He realized that it would be his responsibility to see that it got done. It was his responsibility to see that everything got done.

Before long, Cindy Walker pulled up in a bright yellow Mazda Miata. Bishop knew very well that the real estate business could be quite lucrative if you were a go-getter. She hopped out of the car, grabbed a notebook, and rushed up to greet him. She had her long blonde hair pulled back with her sunglasses pushed up on top of her head. Without much need for makeup, she still managed a cover girl look.

"Hi, I'm Cindy. I'm so glad to meet you." Her warm handshake and photogenic smile undoubtedly contributed to her success. "I've sold houses to lots of people whose children you've taught. I've heard a lot about you." Statements like that always were unsettling to him. Just which people did she mean? What kinds of things did they say? If they listened to their kids, they probably weren't getting an unbiased view. He let all those thoughts go as he began to focus on the task at hand. He had the key, and he opened the door, and stepped back to let her go in first.

Bishop walked behind her, attentive to every detail of the house unlike that earlier occasion when his dual concern had been to relay a message to the coach from Sister Ann and try not to miss homeroom. The house had a musty smell, and the carpets had a number of tracks made by the various investigators who had worked the scene. The section of the carpet where the beer had spilled had been removed for the lab analysis that had found traces of the cyanide.

"Mr. Bishop, you must have been a very close friend of Mr. Zappala. I am so sorry for your loss," Cindy began. She seemed to mean every word as all the vivacity in her voice and that warm smile temporarily vanished.

"Cindy, please call me Mike, and to be honest, I was really wasn't that close to him. I was quite stunned to learn that I had been named the executor."

"I'm sure he made a wise choice." It was the polite thing to say, especially if it helped her acquire the listing. "Now, what, if any, furnishings are you planning to include with the house?" The vivacity and smile had returned. Cindy was back to business.

The will was fairly explicit in that regard. Bishop was charged with going through Zappala's personal effects to determine what should be discarded, what should be given away, and what should be sold. He made it clear to Cindy that that process was nowhere near complete. Furthermore, he reminded her that the house could not actually be put on the market until the will had gone through probate.

"I totally understand, Mike," she replied as if she had been expecting his comments. "I'm not here to pressure you into a commitment. I simply want you to know that I am extremely interested in listing this property at the appropriate time, and I'll do everything I can to help you through every step of the way." Bishop found her approach very comforting, and understood what made her so successful in her work.

She suggested that he contact an estate liquidator to assist him in determining what items were appropriate to give away and what items were of value. They would offer a price for the remaining contents of the house. After briefly looking through the house, she added that she thought only the appliances would be appropriate to include with the sale of the house itself. She went through taking measurements and making notes while Bishop relived that horrifying moment when he realized that the coach was dead. When Cindy was finished inside, she asked if she could walk around outside. He was more than happy to oblige since being in that house made him very uncomfortable. As they walked around in the crisp October morning, Cindy advised him that it would be a good idea to get the house painted, both outside and inside using neutral colors.

"From my experience, I'd say that you — or rather the estate, would get more than two dollars back for every dollar spent. With a bit of work and some imagination, some young couple could turn this into a wonderful country home." She made a sweeping gesture toward the surrounding countryside. "This a great location to raise kids." He realized that she was not just giving him a pitch. He had read about the return on such investments before marketing a house. What struck him more deeply was her comment about a young couple raising a family out here. His own home was only a mile and a half down the road. He and Grace never had any children. It was one of the sad facts that he lived with each day. What a comfort children and grandchildren would have been to them in their later years, but they had managed to lead a full and happy life regardless. Once he lost Grace, that reality became more difficult for Bishop. He liked to think that instead of having a couple of kids of his own, as a teacher he had over a hundred kids to care for each year.

Cindy made a few more suggestions. Instead of replacing the carpet in the living room, she thought that it would be better to remove the carpet completely as she had noticed that there was a hardwood floor underneath. She knew someone who could refinish it, make any necessary repairs, and make it look like new. That would really add to the appeal of the house. She also cautioned him that one factor that might make the house more difficult to sell was the fact that a murder had taken place there. It was information that had to be disclosed. She promised to work up some comparables in order to determine a fair asking price. She thanked him for his time, promised to keep in touch, hopped in her sporty car and left.

He stood outside for a few moments until the sight and then the sound of her car on the cinders faded away. He forced himself to go back into the house. He wasn't sure why. Perhaps seeing more closely how Coach Zappala lived would provide some clue as to how he died. He didn't have to look hard to find something.

***

Wandering into the coach's study, he found himself surrounded by trophies, medals, certificates, and photos on the walls. In one of the photos, a beaming coach was vigorously shaking hands with Bill Belichick of the New England Patriots. Apparently, that was part of the official celebration of Madison's third state title under Zappala. Bishop thought it strange that there were absolutely no family photos anywhere. He wondered what had turned him against his sister and her family. Why would he refuse to help them save their bakery if he had the money to do it? He had only left the fifty thousand so that would have a harder time contesting the will. Perhaps Zappala was like Pip from *Great Expectations*. Pip's older sister, Mrs. Joe, had been forced to raise him, and she did so "by hand." Could Al have been mistreated as a youth? Pip, however, with the help of his benefactor, ultimately became a gentleman. What about Al? He became his own benefactor, but all of his money didn't make him a gentleman. Far from it.

Bishop sat at the coach's desk. As he pushed some newspapers around, he noticed that the coach kept a large calendar on his desk as a type of blotter. He noticed that the score of the Central game had been filled in in red pen in the appropriate space on the calendar. "W, 28-3." There was nothing marked in the spaces for that Saturday or Sunday. Although that Sunday date would certainly be etched on his tombstone, it had just looked like any other date to coach. There was something written in black pen in the space for Monday: "Delaney 7." So he had planned on attending that meeting after all. It wasn't like him to have been afraid of anything. Underneath that was another notation: "BK 25,000." He took a slip of paper from his pocket and copied it down. Whatever it meant, someone had made sure that Zappala never saw Monday.

***

Not long after he had returned to his own home, Ron Jennings called. "Hi, Mike. You busy?"

"Not really. What's going on?"

"You missed a good game last night. We trounced Roosevelt. Chris Delaney broke the school record for touchdowns in a career by scoring four more. It was hard to tell who was more excited, Chris, his father, or Russ Chandler."

"There was quite a write-up in this morning's paper. Sister Ann must be pleased that we're getting some positive coverage in the press to offset all of the rumors surrounding the Zappala's murder."

Ron agreed, noting that the principal had not been herself lately. It was his observation that Sister was quite troubled when it was revealed that the cyanide was missing from the lab.

"Do you think that explains her poor judgment in that mailbox fiasco?" asked Bishop. "Had she sought your opinion on that one?" he added, teasing his good friend.

"No way!" said Ron without any hesitation. "You know very well that I am excluded from most of the decisions at that school." Indeed, Bishop did know that, although he did not understand it. Sister Ann could have prevented many awkward and embarrassing moments by simply running an idea by Ron, a guy who had a reasonable amount of common sense, and whose advice would be invaluable. Instead, she chose to listen to Sister Pat whose understanding of complex issues was minimal and whose interpersonal skills were non-existent.

Ron had heard that Bishop had convinced Sister Ann to remove the lock on the mailboxes, and he expressed his gratitude. He also told Bishop a little bit about his date with Stephanie. They had gone out for a pizza after the game, and when he drove her home, she invited him up to her apartment. He hadn't stayed there very long, but he did ask her if he could give her a ride to the Halloween Dance, and she had accepted. Ron noticed that Stephanie's landlady, Miss Avery, was peering out from the curtained window of her front room, both when he had arrived and when he left.

Talk of the dance prompted Ron to ask, "Are you coming to the dance tonight?"

"Sure. I was planning on stopping by for a while anyway. It's always a hoot to see the kids in costume."

"Are you coming as Mark Twain again?" Ron hopefully.

"I suppose so. The kids seem to enjoy it."

"We all do." He noted that activity at the dances was often difficult to monitor, so having a seasoned veteran there would be a help. "Luckily, I don't have to wear a costume. Do you think that Steph will be in costume?" He was running through some possibilities as he asked the question.

"She might. Some of the chaperones do." He was running through some possibilities as well, but as it turned out, the reality topped anything that he had imagined.

"Well, so far so good with Steph. I'm happy for you, Ron. She seems like a wonderful person."

"Don't I know it!" Ron's happiness was obvious. "And I have you to thank for the jumpstart." Bishop inwardly hoped that Ron would continue to feel the same way as time passed.

***

After having a quick lunch of tomato soup and a grilled cheese sandwich, he called Lieutenant Hodge. "I hope that you don't mind me calling on a Saturday."

"Not at all, Mike. What's on your mind?"

"It came to my attention yesterday that Chris Delaney had a verbal altercation with his coach during that Central game, and that was the reason that Delaney was benched for the second half."

"What are you suggesting?" asked the Lieutenant, forcing Bishop to be more precise.

"Apparently, that verbal altercation included a threat to kill the coach. Now, understand that I have this information indirectly, but I think that the source is credible."

"And that young man that I talked with, Aaron, claimed that he heard Delaney's father threaten to kill Zappala."

"Yes, that's right. I know that it sounds rather bizarre, but both the father and the son appear to have threatened to kill a man who ended up dead two days later."

"I looked into that business regarding the father."

"What did you find?"

"Well, it seems that Dave Delaney had done the same thing to one of his son's coaches at a summer camp a few years ago. Happened in Jersey somewhere. That coach didn't have a sense of humor about it and filed a complaint. A restraining order was issued and that was that."

Bishop said nothing. He felt that this made Mr. Delaney's recent threat more ominous. The man was clearly obsessed with his son's athletic career. Could he have been driven to murder over Chris's benching? Wouldn't that previous incident make him even more likely to act on his anger? Or was he thinking that way because he didn't want to believe that Chris might be involved?

"One more thought, Lieutenant, and I'll let you go."

"Okay. What is it?"

Bishop had been bothered by the torment that Sister Pascala was putting herself through. "I was thinking that our assumption that the cyanide came from the lab at Trinity might be mistaken."

"Why do you think that?" asked Hodge, intrigued by the idea.

"Well, I did a little Internet search the other night, and I found that cyanide and all types of other poisons are readily available for purchase online. All you need is a credit card, and you could have whatever you wanted delivered right to your door within a few days."

"Does that mean that you don't believe the perpetrator was connected to the school?"

"Not exactly. It means that anyone from the outside could have acquired that poison, but it doesn't eliminate anyone within the school community either." Bishop ran through the list of suspects in his mind. He put Rocco at the top of his list. He had a strong motive, and he had admitted to being in town when the murder took place. Also on the list were Chris Delaney and his father, David. It was hard to believe that a student could do such a thing, but anger and fear were powerful emotions. The fact that the father had previously threatened another coach certainly didn't work in his favor. Then there was Russ Chandler who threw Doug Sanders under the bus to get the position of head coach. And Doug had been fired by Zappala, at least according to Russ. Revenge was also a powerful motivator. Finally, although he hadn't said anything to the Lieutenant, he thought of Sister Ann and Sister Pat. Could they have been so desperate for funds that they might have done it, knowing that, as members of a religious order, they were unlikely to be considered suspects?

Hodge interrupted his reverie. "By the way, I talked with Russ. He claims that he went to a movie with his girlfriend the night of the murder, and they spent the night at her place. That all seems to check out unless she's lying about his staying over. There are witnesses that saw them at the theater. On another front, I haven't been able to talk with Doug."

"Really? Why not?"

"He moved out of his apartment, and no one seems to know where he went."

"Didn't he leave a forwarding address with the post office?" As soon as he asked that question, he realized that it might sound as if he were questioning Hodge's investigative abilities, so he apologized. Hodge assured him that he had not taken offense. He knew how invested Bishop was in solving this case.

When he looked at the time, he realized that he needed to get ready for the dance. As he enjoyed the hot water of his shower, he could not help but think whether Doug simply moved away to pursue another opportunity, or whether he was running away from something. His conversation with Hodge had brought many vexing questions back into focus. As the water soothed his body, one answer popped into his head. He had been reading an essay, and in the space for name, the student had simply written, "TJ." His name was Thomas Jefferson Donnelly. Everyone including Bishop called him TJ. The shower magic had worked again. He had, at least, a good idea that the BK in Zappala's calendar notation, "BK 25,000," stood for Bonnie King. That led to another question: Could 25,000 refer to dollars? Was the coach going to give her twenty-five thousand dollars? Chris had told Zappala that Bonnie might be pregnant, and Zappala had told him that money would take care of it. Could the money be for an abortion? Could it be to buy her silence as to the identity of the father? These questions swirled around in his head as the soapy water swirled down the drain.

Chapter 16

The Halloween dance was held from 8:00 to 12:00 p.m. in the school's gymnasium. Ron and several chaperones were there an hour early to supervise all of the preparations. It was their job to check that students were not drunk when they arrived and that they were not bringing alcohol into the dance. For the most part, Trinity kids were very cooperative with school policy. What they might do after the dance was another matter.

Bishop arrived dressed as Mark Twain. He was wearing a light tan suit that he had borrowed from a friend. His costume included a wig, an unlit cigar, and a walking stick. He didn't need a fake mustache as his own full, gray mustache served the purpose nicely. As the students began arriving, he heard a few "Cool costume, Mr. Bishop" comments, but mostly, they were too busy reacting to what their friends were wearing. There were squeals of laughter when three football players walked in dressed as Trinity cheerleaders. Cell phone cameras were everywhere capturing images for uploading to the Internet.

Ron had been at the entrance greeting everyone as they came in. He smiled and winked approval of Bishop's costume, leaned in to quickly whisper, "Check out Stephanie," and refocused on another group of students just arriving. At first, Bishop didn't see her. Then he noticed a group of boys who were gathered on the far side of the gym. As he made his way there, he realized that Stephanie was the focus of their attention. "Oh, my God!" he said to himself. Stephanie was dressed as Catwoman. Her black, form-fitting body suit left little to the imagination. She had claws, a mask, and her hair was completely hidden under a black wrap. No wonder that a number of boys had gathered for a closer look. One student verbalized the reaction of many when he shouted, "Awesome!" That wasn't the word to describe Bishop's reaction. He was shocked at

Stephanie's attire. He realized that there were things that he did not know about this woman.

"Mr. Twain, how nice to meet you," Stephanie purred. "I do so enjoy your books." Framed by her mask, her eyes seemed larger than normal.

He wasn't sure what to say. There were students everywhere at this point. He hoped that Steph wasn't going to remain in the Catwoman mode all evening. He decided to send her that message by responding as himself rather than trying a Twain witticism. "How is everything going so far?"

"Purrrfect!" she replied.

Bishop smiled feebly and walked away. He was thinking about the words of Polonius, "The apparel oft proclaims the man," and wondering how they might apply in this case. The music hit him like the blast from a furnace. He had never appreciated hard rock or heavy metal. Its pulsating rhythms instantly began to give him a headache. If it hadn't been for the fact that Ron had asked him to help out, he would have made a quick escape. Now that he had seen Stephanie's costume, he wondered if Ron's reaction had been similar to his own. What could she have been thinking? She obviously wasn't wearing a bra, and every movement she made accentuated that fact. At least it was dark on the dance floor except for the swirling strobe lights that occasionally illuminated the glitter on her dark figure.

Walking over to the refreshment table turned out to be a mistake. He greeted Sister Ann and Sister Pat who were there, exchanging derogatory comments. Sister Ann held a plastic cup of punch in one hand, probably wishing that it contained something a bit stronger. She was grousing, as usual, about the way the kids were dancing. Bishop was tempted to remind her that times had changed since she was a teenager going to a sock hop. Imagining her in that situation brought a smile to his face.

Sister Pat, who had a heaping plateful of munchies, was making one critical comment after another. "Did you see Ellen Frangiamore? Where's the rest of her costume? How could her parents have let her out of the house looking like that? It's disgraceful! Ann, you should call that girl's parents right now and make them take her home."

Bishop managed to drift away from that table before the desire to confront Sister Pat for her insensitivity became unbearable. He wondered if they had seen Stephanie yet. He hoped that they had enough sense not to embarrass her in front of the students, but he had his doubts. He wanted to ask Stephanie if she had brought a change of clothes.

He was having a hard time getting that image of Sister Ann as a teenager out of his mind when he heard someone screaming above the music, "Get out of my face or I'll deck you!"

As he moved in the direction of the confrontation, he caught a glimpse of Ron Jennings sprinting ahead, pushing past students who were blocking his path. He quickly got between the two young men, pushed them apart, and calmly announced, "If anyone gets decked, it's going to be by me." All the students in the immediate area who had stopped dancing in anticipation of what might happen next were told that the show was over and to get back to dancing. Ron made note of some of the faces he recognized so that he could talk to them later for their version of what had happened.

Ron pulled one of the students involved away with him, and Bishop grabbed the other and took him in a different direction. It wasn't until he had gotten back out to the lobby that he realized he was dealing with Chris Delaney.

"Chris, what got into you back there?"

"It's that nerd, Eric Munro. He was at me and Bonnie right from when we got here, and I wasn't gonna listen to that all night. I just wanted to make him back off. I wasn't gonna deck him."

"What was he saying?"

"Nothin'. It's over now. Are you going to let me back into the dance? Bonnie's still in there."

"Whatever Eric said wasn't 'nothin'' or you wouldn't have reacted the way you did. You're not getting back in until I get the whole story. I'm sure that Eric is giving his version to Mr. Jennings right now."

"That little weasel is probably lying through his teeth." The way he practically spit out those words convinced Bishop that this incident was far from over.

"Then why don't you tell me the truth, and I can try to convince Mr. Jennings not to throw you out of here and call your parents."

"Leave my parents out of this, please. They've been through enough already lately." Chris explained that as soon as Bonnie and he arrived at the dance (they were dressed as gangsters Bonnie and Clyde), Eric started making comments such as "Where's the gun, Clyde? Oh, I forgot. You didn't use a gun. Too messy, huh?" Eric also had kept saying, "Don't drink the punch. Who knows what Chris did to it." Chris told him several times that it wasn't funny and to knock it off, but he kept doing it. When he asked Bonnie what she was going to do when they put Chris in jail, he couldn't take it any more. That's when he threatened Eric.

A quick check with Ron revealed that Eric at first tried to lie his way out of trouble. Ron wasn't buying it. He talked to a couple of kids who were close by when it happened, and they independently verified

Chris's version of events. Ron called the Munros to come and pick up their son. He would receive additional punishment later.

Ron thanked Bishop for his help.

"No problem. You know, the way you went after those guys before somebody got hurt was the best move on the dance floor all night!" They both broke out laughing.

***

Bishop snuck out of the dance when it became clear that the fireworks were over for the evening. He made eye contact with Ron and gestured with his cane towards the door. Ron gave him a thumbs-up. As he drove home, he mulled over the implications of the evening's events. Stephanie's appearance and behavior were nothing short of bizarre. It would be interesting to get Ron's take on it. Chris Delaney had surprised him. He wouldn't have expected Chris to let a kid like Eric get to him. Bishop realized that the events of the last month had taken their toll on Chris. He was not going to make high honors for the first quarter. He hadn't received an offer yet from a Division I school. Both he and his father had been questioned regarding the murder of Coach Zappala. He knew that Chris had other reasons to hate the coach including his comments about Bonnie, his offer to pay her off, and his threat to tell the Delaneys that their son was sleeping with his girlfriend. He hadn't thought that Chris was capable of murder regardless of how persuasively he had spoken and written that Starbuck should have murdered Ahab. Yet, as evidenced tonight, Chris was capable of losing control, and that was a troubling fact.

Something else was troubling Bishop. It was something that Sarah Humphries, the guidance counselor, had said to him during the dance. They were both standing near the door, watching the kids, and trying to be as far from the music as possible at the same time. Stephanie (a.k.a.

Catwoman) was actually dancing with the kids. It was as if wearing that mask had allowed her to escape being Miss Harris for a brief moment. Perhaps encouraging Ron to pursue his interest in her had been a mistake.

Sarah looked Bishop up and down. "Twain again?" she said disapprovingly. Bishop chose to ignore her petty comment. She had not even bothered with a costume. Never had. Doing so would have made her the object of possible derision. She much preferred to be the one dishing out the snide remarks. She kept her eyes on Stephanie as she danced closer to them. Speaking loud enough to be heard over the music, she said, "She's a beautiful woman, isn't she? I'm glad that she and Ron seem to be hitting it off so well."

Bishop chose not to comment on her remark. He wanted to see where she was going with this line of talk. Knowing her penchant for gossip, he didn't think he would have to wait long. Then she added, "Steph had me worried when she went out with the coach, God rest his soul, but it didn't take her long to figure out that Ron was a much better choice."

He was shocked. "She went out with Zappala? I didn't know that!"

"Well, I guess I shouldn't call it 'going out.' I know that she met him at least once right at the beginning of the year."

"Did Steph tell you about it?"

"No, she never mentioned it and neither did I. I had walked into the teachers' lounge, and I guess they didn't hear me. They both had their backs to the door. I heard her tell him that she would meet him after practice."

"Then what?" Bishop's mind was racing at the number of questions he wanted to ask.

"That was it. I turned around and left, so I don't think that they knew I had been there. She didn't seem all that happy to have made the date if you ask me. I wouldn't have looked twice at that guy, but I figured that she was a grown woman, and it was none of my business. I hardly knew her myself. She must have found out what he was like because I never saw them near each other again. And then…"

"And then what?"

"And then he was dead."

As Bishop reflected on what Sarah had told him, he wasn't ready to believe that Stephanie had gone on a date with Zappala. There might have been other reasons for them to meet after school although he couldn't think of any at the moment. He wondered if Ron knew about this.

***

As expected, Ron called the next day. "Am I interrupting?"

"I was grading a set of essays, and was just thinking about a break, so you did me a favor." He got up from his chair at the desk and plopped into a recliner.

"I wanted to thank you again for your help last night with Chris and Eric. That scene might have gotten ugly in a hurry if you hadn't been there to deal with Chris."

"No problem," Bishop replied dismissively. "I'm worried about Chris, though. He's been under a lot of pressure lately."

"No doubt. And Eric certainly was asking for it. I probably would have popped him one myself if I were in Chris's shoes," Ron admitted. "I plan on calling each of them in on Monday just to be sure that this taunting is stopped in its tracks."

"Good idea."

"I'll give Eric an in-school suspension and call his parents."

Bishop agreed that that was a good approach. Suddenly, Ron turned the conversation in a different direction. "By the way, what did you think of Stephanie last night, or should I say, Catwoman?"

Trying to be diplomatic, he simply said, "It was a bit of a surprise."

"That's putting it mildly." Ron explained that when he picked her up, she was wearing a cable knit sweater and slacks and carrying a duffle bag. She told him that she had her costume in the bag and that she would change when she got to the gym. She didn't mention what the costume was, and Ron hadn't asked. When they arrived, she went off to change, and he started supervising the last-minute preparations. When he caught a glimpse of her in that outfit, he was flabbergasted. By that time, the kids were arriving and it was fairly hectic, so he didn't have a chance to warn her that she might be taking this masquerade business a bit too far.

"She definitely made a rookie mistake, and she hasn't made many of those," Bishop said, trying to put a positive spin on her poor judgment. "Did either Sister Ann or Sister Pat say anything?"

"Luckily, no. Pat was giving her dirty looks all night, though."

Bishop commented that it was better if she confronted her directly. At least she would have the chance to defend herself, and Pat was likely to back down as is the case with most bullies. However, her other course of action was to talk disparagingly about her behind her back. Ron agreed with Bishop's assessment. Just about anyone who worked at Trinity had Pat figured out pretty quickly.

He decided not to mention to Ron what he had heard from Sarah about Steph meeting with Zappala. He had two reasons: first, considering gossipy Sarah as the source, he wanted to ask Steph about this directly; and secondly, if true, he thought that Ron should hear it from Steph herself, not him.

Before he could ask, Ron answered the obvious question. "Neither one of us mentioned it on the way back to her place. We talked about the kids, mostly." When he pulled up at her apartment, Steph said that she was tired and just wanted to get some sleep. That was fine with Ron who waved at Miss Avery who was watching from her living room window as he pulled away from the curb.

After ending that call, Bishop decided not to return to his desk and the stack of ungraded papers. His thoughts turned to the boxes of papers that had been removed from Zappala's closet. Ever since he had discovered that the coach had given $25,000 to Holy Trinity, the thought plagued him that amidst all of those papers was something else of importance. He grabbed another box and decided that he would allow himself an hour on this search. Making it harder was the fact that he didn't know what he was looking for. As he shuffled stacks of sports programs, newspaper clippings, and bundled stacks of financial statements, Bishop began to realize that Zappala had apparently never met a bank that he didn't like. He had accounts with most of the banks in Groveland as well as with a number of financial institutions in Madison where he had lived until coming to Holy Trinity a couple of years ago.

He may not have known what he was looking for, but as soon as he saw it, he knew he had found something. It was a check register from the People's Trust of Madison from about three years ago. What caught Bishop's eye was the entry that the coach had made for a withdrawal of twenty-five thousand dollars. The notation was simply, "HJ." This was an account that otherwise had very little activity. Bishop had marveled at how large a position that man had in cash. Why would he withdraw that large a sum? He might have purchased a new car. He could well imagine Coach Al Zappala walking into the showroom and plunking down the cash for a luxury car. But if he did that, word would have spread about his wealth, and since most people didn't know about it, it was unlikely that he would have used the money that way. Besides, "HJ" reminded him of the "BK" notation he had found on the calendar on the desk at his home.

    Bishop regularly told his students that having the right answers was often not as important as asking the right questions. Coach was prepared to use twenty-five thousand dollars to buy Bonnie King's silence. At least that was the theory. More recently, he had used that same amount to buy influence with Sister Ann. This withdrawal had been made while he was still a teacher and coach at Madison. Who was HJ? It was at that moment that Bishop decided that he would be taking a drive to Madison the following weekend. He had a friend who taught there, and it was time he paid him a visit.

Chapter 17

Monday arrived all too soon as it usually did. Bishop pulled his Toyota Corolla in next to a shiny new maroon Nissan Murano. At first, he thought that one of the seniors had parked in the faculty lot hoping that no one would notice. Then, he realized that someone was still in the car, checking phone messages. It was Jim Davenport who taught math at the school. Jim's wife was a successful lawyer in town which explained how he could afford that car.

When he saw Bishop, Jim put his phone in his pocket, grabbed a book bag and his brown bag lunch, and greeted him with a huge grin. With his rugged good looks and his designer clothes, he looked like he was going to a photo shoot for a fashion magazine. "Seems like we never left, doesn't it?"

Bishop had heard that line many times before and had even used it himself on more than one occasion. It was certainly hard to argue with the fact that the weekends always seemed so short. Add in class preparations, grading, and attending a school function, and the weekend during which one had hoped to accomplish so much had quickly disappeared. He had gotten used to the feeling over the years. "Yes," Bishop replied, "I know what you mean." Then he added, "Nice car."

"Thanks. Just picked it up on Saturday. It's actually Sue's car, but she's working from home today so I thought I'd give it a spin."

"Good luck with it. I hear that Muranos are really nice. You can expect that Steve will give you a hard time about it when he figures out that that baby is yours." He looked around the lot, but didn't see Marshall's beat up minivan. "He tends to get a little jealous when someone gets a new car."

"Don't worry. I can handle him, but thanks for the warning." Before they arrived at the front entrance, Jim changed the subject. "I hear there were some fireworks at the dance on Saturday."

Bishop was quick to reply. "Oh, that scuffle between Delaney and Munro? That was nothing really. No punches thrown. Just some trash talk and some posturing." He hoped that that was the incident that Jim was referring to and not the spectacle caused by the appearance of Catwoman. Before Jim had a chance to say anymore, they were greeted by the scowling Sister Pat. They both said, "Good morning, Sister."

"What's so good about it, I'd like to know. Look at some of these kids. Walking in here half asleep, carrying no books." The look of disgust on her face matched the tone of her words.

Neither teacher responded. They were familiar with her sour disposition. It wasn't likely that Sister Pat would ever get a job as a Walmart greeter.

***

In addition to lunch time, twice a month, Bishop was assigned to monitor the cafeteria before homeroom. It was an assignment that he didn't care for very much since he would rather spend that time in his own room getting ready for the day. Several years earlier, there had been a nasty fight between two senior boys. One of them ended up in the hospital, the other was expelled, and the school barely escaped a lawsuit for allowing students to wait for school to start in an unsupervised cafeteria. Thereafter, a teacher was assigned to the cafeteria at all times of the day.

For the most part, the kids were no problem. Some of the early arrivals busied themselves with the homework that they had failed to complete the previous night. Some played cards. Some tapped to the beat of the music pounding in their earbuds. Others were too sleepy to do much of anything except chat with their friends. Bishop sat at a desk placed at one end of the cafeteria.

Reading an essay and writing comments on it took much longer than normal in that environment. Despite his best efforts, there was just too much noise for him to concentrate on anything of substance. Usually, he spent the time just grading quizzes or reading the morning newspaper.

He was working his way through a set of spelling quizzes, dismayed at the number of times he encountered, "buisness," when he picked up the voice of a girl. "Yeah, I hate that bitch." Such language was unacceptable, and he was just about to make that point to the offender when he heard more. "I'll have that bitch crying by the end of the day." The sounds of approval from those of around her, kept her going. He didn't recognize her voice. He kept his head down as if he was totally absorbed in his papers. He wanted to hear more.

It was a source of amazement to him that students spoke so freely in the presence of a teacher. Were they so caught up in themselves that they didn't realize he was sitting close enough to hear what they said? Did they think that he had a hearing problem? Did they think that he wouldn't care what was said? Was it possible that they didn't care whether he heard them or not? In the few years since this morning proctoring had begun, he had heard all sorts of things from arguments that students had with their parents to incidents that had occurred in classes to what they did or didn't do on their dates. Nothing much surprised him any more.

He kept grading and listening. Who was "the bitch"? Her mother? Another student? Sister Pat? Why did she hate her? What was she planning to do to her? Within a few moments, the picture became clearer. This girl's boyfriend, Tommy, had recently dumped her, and he was now dating "the bitch." She was sure that this girl didn't even like Tommy and that she was dating him only to make her jealous. If that was the case, Bishop thought, it certainly had worked. Her anger was clearly directed at the other girl, not at Tommy.

As he continued to appear to be absorbed in his grading, Bishop picked up details of this girl's intentions. She had left a threatening and anonymous note in her locker. She had enlisted some of Tommy's friends to convince him that his new girlfriend was a slut. She had arranged for one of her friends to slam her in gym class later that day. The list went on. This girl, whose reedy voice Bishop was unlikely to forget, had developed her plan as carefully as any politician preparing for a campaign or any student outlining before writing an essay. This was her outline for revenge.

It struck Bishop that whoever had killed Zappala had done much the same type of preparation. His death had not been a random act of violence. It had been carefully plotted by someone who perhaps had been hurt by him and sought to hurt him in return. Whether the motive was revenge, jealousy, anger, greed, or something else, the result was the same. Destroy the enemy. But how? What weapon to use? How to obtain that weapon? When to use it? How to avoid suspicion? There were many steps to be considered. Someone had written an outline for murder.

Suddenly, the bell rang, signaling that it was time to report to homeroom. Bishop stuffed his papers into his briefcase and left the cafeteria before many of the students had begun to move. He made no attempt to make eye contact with the jilted girlfriend. Before going to his room, he had two quick detours to make. One was to Terry in the main office. She was a veritable encyclopedia of knowledge of who was dating whom. There were only a couple of students named Thomas in the school. He had Thomas "TJ" Donnelly in class. He happened to know that TJ was dating Mary Flanagan. Without explaining why, he asked Terry if a young man named Tommy had recently broken up with his girlfriend. Not one to disappoint, the secretary informed him that Tommy Calhoun had dumped Shelley Olson for Hannah Driscoll in a rather heated exchange in the student parking lot the day before.

His second stop was at Ron's office. After giving the assistant principal a concise summary of what he had overheard in the cafeteria, he rushed up to his homeroom, arriving just before the second bell.

***

Bishop was discussing the novel, *A Separate Peace,* by John Knowles in his first period class of juniors. Although the story itself is fairly straightforward, the students were having difficulty with some of the novel's implications.

Mary Flanagan, a bright and self-confident girl, raised her hand. "Why would Gene jounce that limb on purpose and cause Finny to fall? I mean, Finny is his best friend."

"That's an excellent question, Mary. If jouncing the limb had been an accident, which is what Finny believes or wants to believe, then there's really no problem. No sin. No guilt. So why did a good person such as Gene intentionally do something so harmful?" He looked to the rest of the class. "Who wants to explain that to us?"

At first, there were no takers, but Bishop knew that if he gave them a few minutes to think about it, someone might contribute a comment that would move the discussion forward. Just as Bishop was about to suggest that the class look at a particular passage for insight, Charles Petrillo, raised his hand. He was one of those well-rounded students who did as well in math and science as he did in the humanities, all while being a three-sport athlete. "I think it … like … took Gene himself quite a while to figure out why he did it. Doesn't he come to understand that there is within him ... like ... something dark? He realizes that, even though he is basically a good person, he is ... like ... capable of evil."

These were the moments that kept Bishop teaching long past the age when others had retired. Through their analysis of good literature, these students were gaining valuable insights about human nature in general, and about themselves in particular. He would mention his overuse of "like" some other time. "I think that you're absolutely correct, Charley! Gene is a good person, but Gene also confronts the reality that evil comes from within the human heart. Once he accepts that, it liberates him, doesn't it?"

Just as Phil Perry was going to add something to the discussion, everyone heard a burst of laughter from the class across the hall, and then Miss Harris shouting, "That's quite enough! One more remark and I'm putting the whole class on detention!"

Bishop was tempted to quickly peek into Stephanie's room just to make sure that she was okay, but he just as quickly realized that she would be far better off without the interference of a veteran teacher. He could talk to her about it later if she wanted to, but for now, he had to draw his students back to their discussion of Gene.

***

As his students filed out of class, some were still talking about the novel, and others were dreading a Calculus quiz that they were about to take. Stephanie made a quick appearance at his door. "I'm sure you must have heard the commotion. Sorry about that," she said with an apologetic laugh. She had evidently regained control of the situation, whatever it had been, and was back to her normal self. If she didn't volunteer an explanation of what had happened, Bishop was not about to ask for one. "I've got another class coming in. Gotta go!" and with that she went back to her room. There were no further outbursts for the rest of the day.

***

As Bishop was headed down to the lunchroom, he was stopped by Sister Pascala, who looked better than she did the last time they had talked. "Michael, do you have a minute?"

"Of course, Sister."

She asked him to walk with her to her room. They exchanged only superficial chitchat as they passed throngs of students and occasionally another teacher. Her classroom door was closed. Sister took a ring of keys from her pocket, quickly sorted through until she found the one she needed, unlocked the door, and let Bishop in. It had been quite some time since he had had occasion to be in this classroom. He sat at one of the student's stations as Sister settled in behind her desk. On the wall behind her was an enormous chart of the Periodic Table, and on the whiteboard, she had written, "Endothermic vs. Exothermic Reaction." For Bishop, the reaction was a queasy feeling as he flashbacked more than fifty years to his own struggles with Chemistry.

Sister Pascala snapped him out of his reverie. "You know, Michael, I've been thinking quite a bit about this cyanide business." Not knowing where she could be going with this topic, he urged her to continue.

"I have my doubts that the cyanide used to murder Zappala was actually taken from my storeroom."

When he asked her to explain, she said that it was possible that Sister Wilhelmina, the teacher who had originally acquired the cyanide, had also disposed of what remained of it after her classes had conducted their experiments. Bishop vaguely remembered Sister Wilhelmina as being on the faculty when he first arrived so many years ago. She was elderly then, in frail health, and as Jim Croce once phrased it, "meaner than a junkyard dog."

"What made you think of that possibility?"

"Believe it or not, I had a dream and Wilhelmina kept telling me that she had sent the remainder of the bottle's contents back to the supplier. She kept asking me, 'Don't you remember? Don't you remember?'"

It was obvious that this poor woman had been blaming herself for what had happened, and that this dream provided her a way of alleviating her guilt. He was not about to take whatever solace this dream provided away from her. "Well, Sister, that may be exactly what happened. I've learned that there are lots of places on the Internet that make obtaining such poisons relatively easy." As he left her room for a quick lunch, he smiled at Sister Pascala who looked relieved that she had shared her dream with someone who did not dismiss her theory out of hand.

If Pascala was right, then Rocco Santorini's name went to the top of the list of suspects since he was least likely to have obtained the cyanide from the school in the first place. And Rocco admitted to being at his uncle's house on the night of the murder. And Rocco's family needed money to save their business. "Foul deeds will rise…" as Shakespeare wrote in *Hamlet*.

***

One class quickly followed another, giving Bishop little time to give any more thought to what had prompted the outburst in Stephanie's classroom. Had it anything to do with Shelley Olson and her plans to torment Hannah Driscoll? As the last student left his room that afternoon, Ron popped his head in the doorway. "Say, Mike, got a minute?"

"Sure. I was on my way down to see you anyway. I couldn't believe what I was hearing this morning from Shelley. I assume you clipped her wings."

"She won't be trash talking in the cafeteria any time soon. I'll fill you in on that one later. I have something more pressing that I need to discuss with you."

"Okay. What's up?"

"Why don't we go back down to my office?" There was nothing friendly in his tone, and the clenched jaw emphasized the tension that he felt.

Ron usually chattered nonstop, but on this occasion, they walked down to his office silently. Once inside the office, Ron shut the door. Bishop didn't know what to expect. He tried to catalog all of the possibilities. Had a parent called to complain about a grade? Had he sent a student in to see Ron and then forgotten? Had he forgotten to show up for a class? Did Ron want him to serve another semester on the Sports Eligibility Committee? Then his thoughts took a different turn. Had someone else been poisoned? Had Zappala's killer been identified? Apprehended?

"For God's sakes, Ron, what's going on?"

"I'm sure you know that there was an incident in one of Stephanie's classes today," he began rather tentatively.

"Well, yes, I did hear a bit of a ruckus, but it only lasted for a couple of minutes."

"She's really quite embarrassed by the entire situation. She was in my office for about fifteen minutes earlier this afternoon."

"I hope that you told her that there's no need to feel embarrassed. We've all had our share of bad days. Steph came in to my room after that class to apologize although there was really no need for her to do that," he said, rather dismissively, relieved that this was "much ado about nothing." He started to get up to leave, but Ron asked him to sit down again. "There's more," said Ron with obvious discomfort.

As Bishop settled back into his chair, Ron told him what had led to the outburst that he had heard. Even before her class had begun, as some of the boys walked in and saw Stephanie writing on the board, they started meowing and laughing as they took their seats. They were obviously making reference to her ill-advised appearance as Catwoman at the dance on Saturday night. She ignored them, at first, but they continued to make noises during the class. Then one of them said something about her being "hot." The rest of the class joined in the laughter as Steph lost her patience. "Then it got worse," Ron said ominously.

"What do you mean?"

"Connie Goldblatt got everyone's attention by asking Stephanie, 'Are you sleeping with Mr. Jennings?'"

"Oh, brother!"

"Steph told me that her first impulse was to slap that girl silly, but she managed to get control of herself. I think that some of the other kids were stunned by Connie's question. Steph threatened them all with detention, and that diffused the situation for the moment."

Bishop listened attentively. Ron went on to say that Stephanie felt that she had to report Connie's comment to him as the assistant principal, but that she didn't want to discuss it with anyone else. He had Steph give him the names of the boys who had made comments and promised her that he would have a chat with each one of them. He also planned to call Connie in to get her side of the story. Assuming that she admitted that what she said was totally inappropriate and disrespectful, he planned on giving her two nights of detention, and asking her to write a letter of apology to Miss Harris. He also planned to inform her parents of what had happened.

Bishop told Ron that he agreed with his approach. He added that Stephanie needed to realize that kids are going to talk, and that sometimes kids ask stupid questions without thinking. He was confident that Stephanie would develop strategies to cope with such situations in the future. "Steph is a natural as a teacher from what I have observed. Her only mistake here is to let some sophomores get to her. She lost it, that's all. Happens to all of us at one time or another."

The tension seemed to have disappeared from Ron's face. He asked him not to mention to Stephanie that they had discussed the situation. "And thanks for the heads-up on Shelley. I had her in here for over a half an hour. She broke down after about two minutes. I don't think that she'll be threatening anybody anytime soon."

It had been a long day, and Bishop was looking forward to getting home.

**

He made it into the parking lot, and he had his car key in his hand, when he heard someone rapidly approaching. "Mike, I'm glad I caught you!" said Diane Brennan, somewhat breathlessly. Diane, who taught art classes at Trinity, was in her early forties but not in very good shape. She was wearing a floral-patterned dress that was all wrong for a person of her build and a plain white sweater that she probably couldn't have buttoned if she wanted to.

"Hi, Diane! I didn't see you at all today. How are things?"

That was exactly the opening she needed. Right in the middle of the parking lot, she started unloading on him all of her frustrations of the day. Bishop listened patiently, interrupting her barrage of stories about who did what to whom, and who said what about whom. He politely interjected a brief "Really" or "Oh, my!" when he could. Then, she relayed a story in which he actually took some interest.

Diane served as the moderator of the student council, and they were the ones who had put on the Halloween dance. She had written checks from the club's account for the DJ, refreshments, flowers and decorations, and security, and paid for some other odds and ends with her own money. She saved her receipts and expected to be reimbursed by the school. The problem was that the ticket sales came in about $300 short of expenses. Knowing that the SC account had over $3,500 in it from the previous school year, she didn't give the shortfall much thought.

However, as she explained to Bishop, earlier in the day she gone into the business manager's office. Annette Dunkirk had been the business manager for years. She was thin as a rail, always smelled of smoke even though Trinity was a smoke-free campus, and she wore her long gray hair piled in a bun. Whenever anyone asked Annette a question, she always acted as if they were accusing her of a crime. Most of the faculty avoided her if they could. She made people feel as though she didn't have time for their stupid questions. When Diane gave Annette her receipts and asked to be reimbursed at her convenience, Annette smugly said, "I'm afraid that won't be possible."

At that point, Bishop opened his car door, and put his briefcase in the backseat. He was tempted to get in the car so that he could get off his feet after a long day, but he remained attentive as he leaned against the side of the car. Diane continued without skipping a beat, "So, I ask her, 'Why is that impossible?' and she tells me that the student council account has a zero balance."

Bishop was suddenly more interested. "I thought you just told me that you had $3,500 in there?"

"I did!" she practically screamed. When she told Annette that there had to be a mistake somewhere, Annette explained that there was no mistake. At the end of last school year, Sister Ann directed her to transfer the remaining monies in all club accounts to the general fund. The school was having some cash flow problems, and it made more sense to use the monies in those accounts than it did to borrow what she needed from a bank. When Diane asked Annette if Sister intended to reimburse the student council, Annette laughed and said, "You'll have to ask her yourself." As Diane left the office, Annette added, "Good luck with that!"

"What are you going to do?" queried Bishop. He hoped that she read into his question that there was nothing that he planned to do about it.

"What can I do?" she responded in frustration. "I can't afford to confront Sister about this. I need my job, and I'm afraid that if I complain, they'll find a way to let me go. You know very well that without a union, we have no job security." Diane was right. Challenging Sister Ann on her questionable behavior was a foolhardy proposition. Over the years, the staff learned that she could be a very vindictive person, especially when encouraged by Sister Pat. They had said on more than one occasion that they didn't get mad. They got even.

Bishop told Diane that he was sorry for her troubles. If all of the club moderators got together, they might be able to get their funds restored, but the chances of getting all of them to agree to anything was remote. There didn't seem to be much of anything that he could do about it. When Diane was talked out, he finally was able to start his car. Diane's story did get him thinking. How desperate was the school's financial position that the principal would resort to such shady bookkeeping? What else might she be capable of? Did she realize the extent of Zappala's wealth? Had he possibly mentioned to her that he had named the school in his will? Was she any less likely to commit a murder simply because she was a member of a religious order?

***

By the time Bishop pulled out of the parking lot, there were only a few scattered spaces that were not empty. He turned the radio on to NPR, but he wasn't able to concentrate on the discussion of the increasing power of Political Action Committees (PACs) in American politics. Money and power in Washington. Was it much different at Holy Trinity? He decided to stop and pick up something for dinner. Ever since Grace died, he had struggled with meals. He had never been very interested in taking the time required to cook nutritious meals. It just didn't seem worth all the trouble to cook for one. Even dining out had lost its appeal. Although he loved to read, he hated sitting in a restaurant with a book for a companion.

As soon as he arrived home, he grabbed the mail from his box at the end of his driveway, and unlocked the door. The emptiness of the house always gave him a momentary pause. Skipper, their West Highland White Terrier, had died about six months after Grace. The dog had been good company for him in those early days after Grace's death. Perhaps Skipper had died of a broken heart. He wouldn't have been surprised if that had been his fate as well. But he had survived. For a man the age of seventy, he was doing quite well. Holy Trinity brought with it its share of problems, but it was clear to him that his teaching kept him in the game.

He put his ham and cheese sub in the fridge, checked through the mail that was mostly ads and solicitations for money. It was hard for him to remember the last time he had received a handwritten letter in the mail. That was rapidly becoming a lost art. Now everything was email and texts and Skype. He made himself some tea, put a CD of Scriabin's piano sonatas in the player, and settled into his favorite chair in the sunroom.

Just then his phone started vibrating and ringing. He had been turning off his phone when he was at home, but had not done so this time. It was Lieutenant Hodge.

"Hello, Lieutenant. Any news?"

"As a matter of fact, there is a bit of news," he said without giving any hint as to whether the news was good or bad. Bishop waited for Hodge to elaborate. Doug Sanders had been pulled over by the state police for speeding in the town of Avalon, about a hundred miles west of Groveland. He blew a 0.93 on his BAC so they arrested him for DUI. When they ran his plate, they realized that it was his second violation and that he was also wanted for skipping out on his landlord. Apparently, he was a couple of months behind on his rent. When they contacted the Groveland police because of the rent issue, Hodge picked up on the opportunity to ask Sanders a few questions of his own.

"Did you find out anything interesting?" Bishop recalled that Zappala had fired Sanders just a couple of days before his death, at least according to Russ Chandler.

"A few things," Hodge started. "For one, he was carrying about $2,300 in cash at the time of his arrest, and he refused to explain where that money had come from."

"That is interesting," said Bishop as he mulled over the possibilities. "If he had that kind of cash, he probably could have squared up with this landlord." He also remembered Jack, the custodian at school, telling him that Doug had lost his part-time job as a driver for UPS about six months earlier and that his coaching stipend was his only source of income. Perhaps the earlier DUI had cost him his job. The question remained: Where did Doug come up with that amount of cash?

"Did you ask him if it was true that Zappala had fired him?"

Hodge explained that not only did Sanders admit that that was true, he also said that he had driven up to Zappala's house on the night of the murder.

"You've got to be kidding!" said a flabbergasted Bishop.

"No kidding! But wait, it gets better! He said that he went up there to beg the coach to give him his job back."

"And Zappala refused…?"

"No."

"He gave him his job back?"

"No."

"I'm confused," admitted Bishop.

"Here's the catch. He claims that when he got to Zappala's house, there was another car in the driveway besides the coach's Lincoln. He wanted to talk to the coach alone, so he turned around and went home. He swears he never went into that house that night."

"Did you ask him if he recognized the other car?"

"Yes, I did. Unfortunately, he doesn't recall anything about that car. It could have been Rocco Santorini's. He's admitted that he was there," Hodge added.

"And if Rocco is telling the truth when he says that his uncle was alive when he left, then the car that Doug saw was more than likely the car driven by the murderer."

Bishop thanked the Lieutenant for the update and asked him to keep him posted on any new developments. As he prepared to have his dinner, he considered what he had learned. It was obvious that Russ was telling the truth when he told Sister Ann that Zappala had fired Doug. That still didn't entirely clear Russ who might not have wanted to wait until Zappala retired to become the head coach. Sanders admitted that he was there the night of the murder. He could also be lying about seeing another car in the driveway. He might have gone in, tried to get his job back, and failing that, slipped the cyanide into Zappala's beer before he left.

Then there was the fact that Doug had been carrying a large amount of cash, the source of which was a mystery since he hadn't had a substantial paycheck in months. Just as he was about to take the first bite of that submarine sandwich, Bishop remembered something. When he had looked at Zappala's checkbook register, he had noticed that the coach made rather regular cash withdrawals of $2,000 and sometimes $3,000. He had always assumed that that was Zappala's gambling money. But what if it wasn't? What if Zappala was giving the money to someone? Or paying someone off. But whom? And why? If he were paying Sanders off, why would Sanders kill him and stop the gravy train? Could Sanders have been there that night asking for more? Had Zappala threatened to stop payments? And then he remembered the cash withdrawal for $25,000 made about three years earlier. Who or what was "HJ"? That was something he hoped to learn on his upcoming visit to Madison.

Chapter 18

The next day Bishop and Stephanie pulled into the faculty parking lot at the same time. Since they both preferred to get to school early, most of the faculty had yet to arrive. If the usual pattern held, to the great annoyance of Sister Pat, the keeper of the gate, a good number of the teachers would arrive within a minute or two of the first bell. They would each receive a frosty glare from her as they arrived. She saved her wrath for the unfortunate soul who might have been stuck behind a school bus, thus arriving after the first bell.

Steph gathered all of her belongings and hopped out of the car with youthful energy. She greeted Bishop warmly, and made a comment about the cold morning temperatures that were becoming the norm. She was wearing a light blue sweater, charcoal gray pants, and an unzipped jean jacket. She slung the strap of a large carryall bag over her right shoulder, followed by her book bag slung over her left shoulder, and her handbag on the right. Her walk was a bit charliechaplinesque as she made her way to the entrance. She chatted about the weather as if her appearance as Catwoman and the incident with Connie Goldblatt had both been erased from her memory. Bishop knew that the ability to let such matters go was essential in the teaching profession, and he had no plans to mention either of those events to her. However, he did want to question her about something else that had been bothering him for a few days.

After checking their mail, they both headed upstairs to their rooms. Some students who were unlucky enough to ride an early bus were already in the halls. Some were seated on the floor making a desperate attempt to complete last night's assignments or cramming for a test. Others were just wandering around looking for someone to talk to. After getting settled in his room, Bishop went across the hall to talk to Stephanie. She seemed a bit surprised to see him since they had just walked into the building together.

"Got a minute?" Bishop asked.

"Sure. What's up?"

He sat in one of the students' desks opposite her desk. He explained that someone (and he wasn't going to identify who that someone was) said something about her that he didn't necessarily believe so he wanted to ask her about it. Not having any idea what he was referring to, Stephanie urged him to go on.

Bishop wished that Sarah Humphries had never spoken to him at the dance, but since she had, he needed to get a straight answer. Ultimately, it was none of his business, but what if it were true? Somewhat sheepishly he asked, "Did you ever go out with Coach Zappala?"

All of the early morning cheerfulness drained from her face. "How did you know about that?"

He reminded her that he was not going to name the source. "Let's just say that it's a small school, and people talk, but they don't always have all of their facts straight." Then he added, "You don't have to answer the question if you don't want to. I'll understand." He wasn't sure that that last statement was entirely correct. If she didn't want to talk about it, perhaps there was something to what Sarah had observed. Stephanie couldn't look at him directly. She hesitated for a moment and then began to explain.

"It was within the first week or so of school. I didn't know much about him or any of the rest of the faculty for that matter, including you. He said he wanted to talk to me about possibly helping to coach the cheerleading squad. He guessed that I had probably been a cheerleader myself and suggested that it would be a good way to get to know some of the students. I agreed to meet him at the Blue Moon after his practice one afternoon." She stopped there, lost in thought.

The Blue Moon was one of the seedier restaurant/bars in town. It was a place he might expect Zappala to frequent, but not Stephanie. He prompted her to continue. "Well, what happened when you met him? You obviously didn't accept his offer."

She was staring out of the classroom windows as if there were something there that demanded her full attention. Bishop felt that what she was about to say was going to be difficult for her. He wasn't sure that he really wanted to hear it, but it was too late now. She took a deep breath, turned her focus back to him, and began to tell her story in a soft voice.

"I got to the Blue Moon around 6:00 p.m., but he wasn't there. That place is a real dive. I felt so uncomfortable being there alone. I ordered a coffee and pulled some papers from my bag to grade. He showed up about half an hour later. He apologized, saying that practice ran late 'because those morons can't remember plays' to use his words. He ordered a coffee and after the waitress left, he told me that he thought I was...." She hesitated before the next words as if they brought back a painful memory. Her voice began to quaver as she fought back tears. "He wasn't interested in me for cheerleading. He was interested in me! He said that I was '... a good-looking broad.'"

Bishop urged her to say no more. He did not wish to cause her any further upset. They both sat quietly for a few moments until she had gathered her composure. He asked her if she was going to be all right, and she assured him that she would be fine. Bishop said, "I'm so sorry," he whispered. "It's really none of my business."

"I didn't want you to know...*ever*. I was so ashamed."

"You have nothing to be ashamed of. You didn't know what he was like. Apparently, that's how he operated."

"Please don't tell Ron."

"No, of course not. There's really nothing to tell. You didn't do anything wrong."

As he went back to his room, he was ashamed to admit to himself that he was glad that Zappala was dead. What a bastard!

***

The remainder of the day was thankfully uneventful until last period. His group of twenty-three freshmen was discussing the importance of the author's choice of point of view in telling a story. Bishop explained that an author's decision to tell a story from a particular point of view changes the story that is told.

To help them understand what he meant, he posed these questions to the class: "What if Mark Twain had not chosen Huck as the narrator of *The Adventures of Huckleberry Finn*? What if Jim had been the narrator? How would the story have been different?"

Heather Sanders raised her hand, displaying a collection of about ten bracelets of varying widths dangling from her wrist. "Jim wouldn't be able to tell us about Huck's experience in that feud between the Grangerfords and the Shepherdsons … not unless Huck told him about it first."

"That's a good example of a limitation imposed by the choice of narrator, Heather, and that works both ways, doesn't it?" She scrunched her face suggesting that she didn't quite follow. "Well, if Jim were the narrator, he would be able to give the readers information that Huck couldn't. Can someone give me an example of that? What about it, Jamie?"

Jamie Rogers often had good ideas but was usually hesitant to contribute in class. Bishop wanted to encourage her to be more involved, not only for her own sake, but also for the benefit of the class as a whole. She thought for a moment and then replied, "I guess Jim would be able to tell us how it feels to be a runaway slave. Huck couldn't possibly understand that."

"You're exactly right!" She seemed pleased with herself for coming up with that example, and Bishop was glad that he had given her that chance to shine. "An individual narrator can only tell the story from his own perspective. It's the same in the real world. If there were a fender bender in the parking lot, each driver would tell what happened. They may not tell the same story even though they are discussing the same event. Even eye witnesses might disagree about what happened."

Greg raised his hand. "Then how do you know who is telling the truth?"

"Good question. Each of them may be telling the truth as they understand it. They also may be trying to put a 'spin' on the story to make the other person look guilty. That's exactly why it's so critical to look at the author's choice of a narrator. That narrator is putting a 'spin' on the plot, and ultimately, the theme of the work."

Bishop noticed that two students in the back of the room were grinning about something. Perhaps they saw the irony in Bishop using Mark Twain's work as an example so soon after having made his appearance at the dance as one of America's most beloved writers. "Do you have something to add to the discussion, fellas?" He assumed that they didn't, but that they would get the message to get back on task. He was surprised when Pat Hanrahan spoke.

"It's like at the dance on Friday."

"Excuse me?" Bishop should have seen this coming, but he didn't.

"You know. The fight? I guess it depends on who you ask if it's true that Chris pulled a knife on Eric." Suddenly, the classroom became extremely quiet. They were waiting to see how their teacher would react.

Bishop's face flushed, and he was tempted to launch into attack mode but regained his composure quickly. He defused the tension by simply saying, "If a narrator isn't credible, no one is going to pay attention. End of story." Luckily, it was also the end of class.

***

As he packed up his bag for the evening, he was still seething over the comment made by Pat Hanrahan. How did such rumors start? How could students be so unfair? Of course, he had been teaching long enough to know the answers to both questions. It happens all the time. It simply is human nature to want to embellish stories. It is also typical that people often do not consider the harm that their words might do.

He had barely managed to unlock his front door when his phone started vibrating. He dropped his bag on the floor and fished out his phone. It was Ron Jennings.

"Sorry to bother you again, Mike."

"No problem. What's on your mind?" Bishop had not talked with Ron during the day. He assumed that Ron wanted to share with him the results of his conversation with the impudent Connie Goldblatt and her parents. Did Connie try to deny that she made that comment about Ron and Stephanie sleeping together? That would be ludicrous as the entire class had surely heard her remark. Were her parents refusing to admit that their daughter's comments were inappropriate and disrespectful?

"It's about what Connie said in class about me and Stephanie."

"Go on," urged Bishop. This was exactly what he had thought had prompted the call.

"Sister Pat got wind of it somehow and ..."

"Sister Pat?" Bishop said in disbelief. His guess as to the nature of the call had only been partially correct. "What does she have to do with it?" Knowing her as well as he did, he could almost anticipate what Ron would say next.

Sister Pat had barged into Ron's office, slammed the door shut, stood across from his desk, and launched into a verbal attack. She expressed her outrage and shock in learning of his immoral behavior. Gesturing wildly, she told him that if he didn't stop seeing Stephanie, she would see to it that the two of them were fired. She concluded her diatribe by spitting out the words, "This is a Catholic school. We are held to a higher standard!"

That comment made Bishop cringe. Catholic school? Higher standard? Was there no limit to that woman's hypocrisy? Didn't she realize how often she and the principal had failed to live by those higher standards? Words from the Bible came to mind, "Let he who is without sin cast the first stone."

"Ron, I hope that you didn't let her get away with bullying you that way."

"No, I didn't," he answered proudly. "I may get fired when Pat reports back to Sister Ann, but I wasn't going to take that sitting down. As a matter of fact, I stood up, and that made Pat take a step backward. I said, 'First of all, you are assuming that Stephanie and I are having an affair. Where did you get that information? Did you bother to confirm that with either one of us? No! Instead, you accept rumor and innuendo as fact. And secondly, even if that were true, what business is that of yours? Steph is a single adult. I'm a single adult. What we are or are not doing is frankly none of your business.'"

"Good for you, Ron! I agree with you one hundred percent!"

Ron explained that Sister Pat just stood there, obviously regretting her decision to start the conversation, and unable to think of a good response. Before she left the office, he had also reminded her that it was common knowledge that more than a few teachers had engaged in some "extracurricular" activities over the years. He reminded her that a former faculty member, Jerry Dunlap, had had an affair with the mother of one of our students, and the administration did not have one word to say about it because that woman just happened to provide some very generous financial support to the school.

"Sounds as if you handled the situation perfectly," Bishop said. It was time that Sister Pat was put in her place. "Did you tell Steph about this?"

"No, not yet."

Bishop advised Ron to tell Stephanie everything so that she wouldn't be blindsided if Sister Pat tried to pull that holier-than-thou act on her.

**

When he finished that call, Bishop saw that he had one unheard message from Andy White, the attorney. He tapped the button to hear the message. "Hello, Mike. Andy here. I just wanted to let you know that I received a phone call from a Vito Petrocelli. He's been hired by the Santorini family to contest the will. Call me back when you get a chance. Thanks. Bye."

As he mulled over the implications of this news, he kept asking himself, "Why did that man ever name me his executor?"

**

Just as he was about to go to his bedroom to change into some casual clothes, there was a knock at the door. Normally, he would have heard a car pull into his driveway. As he approached his front door, he caught a glimpse of the car in the driveway, and he knew who it was. "Lieutenant Hodge! What are you doing here?"

Hodge had left the engine of his cruiser running, and he was still in uniform, so this wasn't a social call. "One of my boys was patrolling through here this morning, and he noticed that the windows at Zappala's place were soaped pretty bad. I'd like to borrow your key so I can take a look inside, just in case."

Bishop's face registered his concern. As executor, he felt responsible for that place. "Sure. Let me grab the key. It's in the study." When he returned, he asked Hodge if he could tag along. He didn't have a good feeling about what they might find.

It took only a few moments to drive up the hill. Bishop, who had never been in a police car, sat quietly, partially fascinated by all of the electronics, and partially reliving those moments not that long ago when he had driven up to the coach's home at the request of Sister Ann.

Nothing much had ever happened on this road before Zappala had been murdered. After his death, Bishop had noticed an increase in the number of cars slowly passing up and down the hill. They were drawn to the scene of the tragedy, needing to gawk at the house, imagining what had happened there. None of them would have dared to actually stop at the house. It was as if the yard had still been cordoned off during the actual investigation phase.

As Hodge pulled into the driveway, Bishop exclaimed, "Oh, my!" Every window on the front of the house had been soaped. He wondered who might have pulled such a prank. The houses on Pleasant Hill Road were so spread out that he hardly ever had a trick-or-treater at his place even though Grace had always insisted on buying bags of candy just in case. The few that did come were driven to each house by a parent.

"I'm lucky that these knuckleheads didn't pick my house," he said with a faint smile as they both exited the vehicle. "I was at the dance that night and didn't leave the outside light on so as not to disappoint the little tikes."

"Let's take a look inside," as the Lieutenant gestured for Bishop to unlock the door. He placed the key in the keyhole, turned it to the right, heard the lock release, pushed the door open, and held it as Hodge entered first.

"I just have a feelin' that …" Hodge stopped in mid-sentence as he glimpsed the look of absolute shock on Bishop's face. They both surveyed the place from where they stood. It looked as though a small twister had passed through. Furniture was strewn about. Cabinets had been opened and their contents scattered. Every box that had been neatly packed and taped had been cut open. Articles of clothing and pieces of paper had been flung in every direction. As they began to make their way through the rest of the house, Hodge cautioned, "Watch where you step. And don't touch anything."

Bishop felt fortunate that the intruder, or intruders, had not decided to burn the house to the ground. "Does anyone else have a key to this place?" Hodge wondered.

"I'm pretty sure that Andy White does. At least, I think he does. I got my key from him. Why do you ask?"

"There's no sign of a forced entry. That lock on the front door hasn't been tampered with. None of the windows that I can see are broken or unlocked."

"Then how did they get in?"

"That's a damn good question," Hodge said as he exhaled deeply. "That and why," he added.

When they reached the study, they saw that every certificate had been ripped from the walls. The frames were bent and twisted. There was broken glass everywhere. Papers had been tossed around the room like confetti. Trophies had been smashed. Some had been thrown against the wall where they left gauges. Pieces of trophies lay on the floor like broken toys. The desk had been thoroughly ransacked.

"This isn't the work of a disgruntled trick-or-treater," Hodge said soberly.

"I've never seen anything like this. Whoever did this was either looking for something or venting their anger," observed Bishop.

"I'll call this in and get some lab boys up here. Whoever did this might also be the person who poisoned the coach."

"The criminal returns to the scene of the crime?"

"If we're lucky," added Hodge.

***

After the Lieutenant dropped him off at his home, Bishop put on some classical music, the Polonaises of Chopin, made himself a cup of Earl Grey tea, sat in his favorite chair in the sunroom, and tried to make sense of what he had just witnessed. Why would anyone so thoroughly trash the place? It was almost as incomprehensible as Zappala's murder itself. He might have understood this destruction if it had been part of the murder scene that morning in early October. Revenge? That didn't make sense. Zappala was already dead. Looking for something? What could anyone possibly hope to find? Now that the extent of Zappala's wealth was common knowledge, perhaps whoever did this was hoping to find some cash left behind. But no one would have murdered him if the real intent were theft. There would certainly have been opportunities to ransack the house while he was out. He was at school every weekday. He had a schedule of practices and games. A robbery could have been committed then unless, of course, the perpetrator also went to school everyday, and attended practices and games as well. Chris Delaney fit that description.

Then Bishop remembered Hodge telling him that when Russ Chandler had been picked up he had about $2,300 in cash on him. Was it possible that Chandler had decided to return to Zappala's house after he had been frustrated in his earlier attempt to talk the coach into giving him his job back? But the trashing of that house had taken place on Saturday night at the earliest. Chandler was already in custody in Avalon. What about Rocco, someone who was high on Bishop's list of likely suspects? He made a mental note to check with Mrs. Proulx to find out if Rocco had stayed at the Weary Traveler Inn recently. But why would Rocco rip the place to shreds? He couldn't have expected that his uncle kept his fortune under his mattress. If not money, what could he have been looking for? When Bishop remembered the phone message from Andy White indicating that the Santorinis were going to contest the will, the thought crossed his mind that Rocco might have been hoping to find another, more recent and more favorable, will. Only one point seemed clear to Bishop — whoever had ransacked that house was not the person who had murdered the coach.

Considering the late hour, he decided to wait until tomorrow to return Andy White's call. The music and the tea had done little to soothe Bishop. He hadn't managed to grade a single paper. As he prepared for bed, he knew that he was in for a night of restless sleep.

Chapter 19

The end of the first marking period was rapidly approaching, and the added tension was palpable among students and teachers. Bishop made an attempt to schedule tests and essay due dates in such a way that his students did not face three or four major tests on the same day. A few teachers rather relished watching the kids stress out. Perhaps that was the way they were treated when they were students. Then again, most teachers had their own sources of stress when faced with the daunting task of grading all of the end-of-the-quarter assessments and submitting grades on time. A few teachers solved the problem by giving mostly multiple choice tests, preferably ones that they found online so that they not only didn't have to spend time grading papers, they didn't spend much time developing their own assessments either. Heaven help any teacher who failed to meet that deadline. They faced the fury of Sister Pat unleashed. Of course, she didn't have any papers to grade or deadlines to meet. The absence of any defined duties other than watching what everyone else was or was not doing and reporting all to her best buddy, Sister Ann, made this time of the year all the more enjoyable for her.

If Bishop was going to devote all of Saturday to his search for information in Madison, he knew that he would have to work feverishly to complete his grading as well as solidify his plans for each class for the upcoming week. He believed in the theory that the amount of work one faces expands to fill the time one has to devote to it. He would never allow the quality of his work in the classroom to suffer. Not only was it a matter of personal and professional pride; it was also a matter of survival. The students would know immediately if he was not giving his job top priority. He knew that he would find the strength to do whatever needed to be done.

It would be done well and done on time. The thought of a five-day break at Thanksgiving brought him a measure of comfort.

***

Bishop and Andy White played telephone tag all day Wednesday, but they finally did have a chance to talk on Thursday. White had received a call from Vito Petrocelli, the attorney hired by the Santorini family. They planned to contest the will on the grounds of undue influence. Since Zappala had left only approximately one percent of the value of his estate to his family, they would contend that Sister Ann, the Principal of Holy Trinity, had befriended her employee, Albert Zappala. Having knowledge of his vast wealth, she sought to manipulate him into naming her school as a beneficiary of a large portion of his estate.

When Bishop commented that Zappala hardly appeared to be the type of person to be so easily manipulated, White agreed. He said that if the case went to court, he would line up a number of witnesses who would give testimony to that fact. Sister Ann would be questioned. White added that it was somewhat troubling that Zappala had essentially cut his family out of the will without any explanation. Nevertheless, he felt that their attempt to contest the will would ultimately fail just as ninety-nine percent of all attempts fail. He suggested that Bishop not let it trouble him too much. Bishop thanked him for his time, and given everything else that was on his plate at the moment, he was determined to take that advice.

***

Bishop was listening to NPR as he drove to school on Friday morning. After the hard work of the last few days, all of his grading was complete. Most of his students had done quite well. For those who had not, Bishop planned to make calls home early the following week. He had discovered over the years that parents were usually very receptive to his expression of concern. He would offer some suggestions for improvement. Keeping the parents fully informed ultimately made his job easier. As he pulled into the parking lot, he was looking forward to a quiet day at school.

His morning classes went smoothly. Once the students were in front of him, he could easily block out all of his other concerns and focus solely on the business of teaching. Although some of his students might have felt differently, he was usually surprised at how quickly the forty-five minute class period passed. When he walked into the teachers' lunchroom, he greeted the few people who were already there. He sat down next to Ron Jennings. Their talk was interspersed with the serious business of eating lunch. Ron told Bishop about a conversation he had had that morning with a junior boy to whom he had assigned detention for repeated tardiness to class.

"Josh looks at me in disbelief and says, 'Detention? That's not fair! I know at least five other kids who have been late to the same class that didn't get detention.' I tried to explain the difference between being tardy on occasion and being tardy habitually. Then Josh said, 'You just don't like me, I guess.'"

"What did you say to that?" Bishop asked, although he had a fairly good idea of the answer.

Ron polished off the last of the macs and cheese on his tray before answering. "I said, 'That's not true, Josh. In fact, you are my second favorite student.' Then he asked me, 'Who's your favorite student?' and I answered, 'Everybody else.'"

Bishop had heard that one before, but they both shared a good laugh over it. Ron had used that line many times over the years. This bit of normalcy was just what Bishop needed. The conversation then turned in a different direction.

Ron gulped down the remaining contents of his carton of milk, crushed the carton, and launched it into a trash can on the other side of the table. "Are you planning anything special for Thanksgiving break?"

"As a matter of fact, I am. Stephanie invited me to have dinner with her parents in Fairmont," his pleasure in announcing this quite evident.

"Really, that's great! I'm happy for you both."

Just then Sarah Humphries entered the room. She took a moment to survey the occupants. Once she saw Ron, she headed directly for the vacant seat next to him. Now that Ron and Stephanie were dating, Sarah seemed to have renewed her own interest in Ron.

"It seems as though I hardly ever see you, Ron. How are you doing?"

"Fine, thanks. And you?"

She launched into an account of her life's little trials and tribulations. Bishop thought it rude that Sarah had barely acknowledged his presence, but he had learned to expect that from her. If she needed something, she'd be all sweetness and light. She was telling Ron that she didn't know how she was going to remove the air conditioner from her bedroom window. It was, it seemed to Bishop, a not-so-subtle invitation for Ron to offer to help her with that chore. He was saved from having to respond by Sister Ann who had rushed into the room.

"Mike, I need you in my office right away. Ron, you better come, too." She then left as quickly as she had entered. They both immediately got up, dumped their trash into the bucket, placed their trays on the stack near the door, and headed down the hallway.

"Any idea what's up?" Bishop asked.

"No. I was going to ask you the same thing."

When they arrived at Sister Ann's office, the door was closed. Ron knocked, and Sister Pat opened the door. "Well, it took you two long enough!" she said in a tone of disgust. Neither of the gentlemen responded to her taunt. One look at the distress on Sister Ann's face said it all. Something was up. Lieutenant Hodge was seated at a conference table. Had the killer been identified? Was the killer in this room? Bishop felt his pulse quicken. When they were all seated, Hodge broke the silence.

"As you all know, Coach Zappala's house was vandalized this past weekend. I know who broke in and how it was done. I've come to make an arrest."

For a moment, no one spoke. Ron finally asked the question.

"Who did it?"

Hodge studied his hands as if the answer were written there. He took no pleasure in being the bearer of this news.

"Chris Delaney."

***

For a moment, everyone was speechless. Sister Pat began to shake her head affirmatively as if she had known this all along.

"Chris Delaney?" Bishop repeated in disbelief. "What makes you think Chris did it?"

Hodge cleared his throat and leaned forward. "Well, after we went up there the other day to check the place over, something kept bothering me. The door was locked when we approached. Since there was no sign of a forced entry, I figured that someone had opened it another way."

Ron wasn't following. "How else can you open a locked door? You just said that there was no sign of damage to the lock."

"That's exactly right, but there are other ways of working the lock, especially a cheap one like Zappala had on there. I took a credit card and slipped it in the lock, and it popped open like a jack-in-the-box. It was easy. Anybody could have done it."

"Then why do you think it was Chris?" Bishop asked, not wanting to believe that Chris could have caused so much damage.

"Because when the lab boys went through the place, they found this under a pile of magazines," and as he spoke, he reached into his shirt pocket, pulled out something, and placed it on the conference table. They all stared at the evidence. It was Chris Delaney's Holy Trinity ID card, complete with his photo and signature. All the students received laminated photo ID cards that were used for admission to dances and games among other things. Bishop picked up the card. It was the card for the current school year. He wished that he could think of some explanation that would trump the card that Hodge had played, but he couldn't. He had to admit to himself that Chris seemed guilty of something, but even if he had broken into the house, that didn't mean that he killed the coach. Sister Ann broke the silence.

"Lieutenant, should we ask Chris to join us?"

"Yes, Sister, I think that would be an excellent idea."

Ron interrupted. "Don't you think that he should have a lawyer present or at least his parents?"

"Don't worry. I'll inform the boy of his rights. He won't have to answer any questions if he doesn't want to, but if he cooperates, it might make it better for him later."

"Wait a minute, Lieutenant," Bishop cautioned. "You are talking as if you already have him convicted. There may be some reasonable explanation." Although he spoke with conviction, he inwardly doubted that such an explanation existed. Ron went to find Chris. As he left the office, Bishop said, "While you're out there, would you please find someone to cover my next class? Have the students read quietly until I get there. This should only take a few more minutes," he said hopefully. As the door opened, Bishop caught a glimpse of the custodian, Jack Slater, picking up a scrap of paper in the hallway. If Jack had heard what had been said in that office, a good portion of the school would soon know as well.

Ron left to get Bishop's class covered and to check Chris's schedule. He needed to make calling Chris out of class as routine as possible. However, with Hodge's patrol car in the visitor's parking lot, it would not take some students long to figure out that Chris was involved in something serious.

The young man looked shaken as he was led into the closed-door meeting. Bishop looked directly into his eyes. It was Shakespeare who had described the eyes as "the window to the soul." He wanted to determine if the shaken look was also the look of someone who knew he had been caught in a wrongdoing. Sister Ann indicated a chair for Chris to be seated. Hodge explained to Chris why he had been called in and asked if he was willing to answer some questions although he was under no obligation to do so. Chris agreed too quickly Bishop thought.

Hodge had placed the ID card back in his shirt pocket, and now he produced it again with more dramatic flair than he had the first time. He felt that he had solved the mystery. Everyone studied Chris's reaction. He picked it up nonchalantly, looked at it briefly, and put it back on the table.

"That's mine, all right." Bishop was in disbelief. Did Chris really understand the seriousness of the situation? Was he confessing to the break-in and the destruction of personal property? Was he confessing to murder?

"That's mine, all right," Chris repeated. "The only problem is that I haven't received my ID card yet this year. When everybody else received their cards, mine was missing. I had another picture taken, but the retakes haven't come back yet."

"He's right about the retakes, Lieutenant," Sister Ann quickly added. "The company has had some computer glitches. Those IDs aren't expected until next week."

"Chris, did you have your picture taken at the beginning of the year?" asked Ron.

"Yes, I did."

"Then how could it be missing?"

"I don't know. All I know is that everyone in my homeroom got one except me. At first, we thought it must have gotten mixed in with cards for another homeroom, but it never showed up so I just waited for a retake."

"What homeroom are you in?" Sister Pat asked.

"303."

Bishop felt his face flush.

Sister Pat slammed her pen down on the conference table. She asked with obvious pleasure, "And whose homeroom is that?"

"My homeroom teacher is Miss Harris."

***

Chris was dismissed from the meeting and urged by Sister Ann not to discuss this matter with his classmates. She knew that he would undoubtedly tell his parents, and she knew that it would not be a question of if, but only when, Mr. Delaney would call. Ron left again to check Stephanie's schedule. She was teaching a class of French II. He asked Terry, the main office secretary, to call her room, tell her that there was an important phone call for her, and that Ron would be up to cover her class.

That was the only way to get her out of the classroom without arousing the suspicions of the students too much.

When Ron explained that she was needed downstairs, Stephanie tried to contain her anxiety.

"Is it my parents? Is it Henrietta? Did something happen?" she whispered.

"No, no. Nothing like that. Really. There's a meeting in Sister Ann's office, and she needs your input. That's all," he said smiling in a reassuring way. Inwardly, he was hoping that his words of reassurance would prove correct.

"A meeting? What could be so important that she has to interrupt my class?"

"Steph, the sooner you get down there, the sooner you'll be back."

Those who remained in the office sat quietly around the conference table while they waited for Stephanie's arrival. Bishop wondered if Stephanie could have taken Chris Delaney's ID card and used it to frame him for the break-in. It made no sense, he told himself. There had to be another explanation.

Sister Ann answered the gentle knock at her door. When Steph saw Lieutenant Hodge and Bishop at the table, a look of extreme apprehension came over her. She knew immediately that this had nothing to do with her parents or Henrietta. She was about to be interrogated, but for what?

"What's going on?" she asked in a shaky voice.

"Please sit down, Stephanie," Sister Ann said curtly.

Hodge began. "Are you Chris Delaney's homeroom teacher?"

"Of course, I am. You wouldn't need to take me out of my class to ask me that. What's wrong?" Her voice sounded more confident now.

Hodge showed her the ID card.

"Do you recognize this?"

"Of course. It's Chris Delaney's ID card." She turned to Sister Ann. "Is this the retake?"

"No, it isn't. The retakes haven't come back yet. That's the problem," she explained.

"I don't understand."

Hodge jumped in again. "We found this card at Zappala's house. It was probably used by the intruder to open the lock on the front door. Delaney says that he never received his original ID card in homeroom. Is that right?"

"Yes, it is. I picked up the cards from my mailbox that morning, and when I distributed them, his wasn't there. It never did turn up."

"You're wrong there, ma'am. It did turn up, as I said, in Zappala's house. Do you think that Chris Delaney vandalized that property?"

"No, of course not. He never had that card."

"Ah, but you did, didn't you?"

"Me? What is he talking about?" Steph had turned her focus from Hodge to Bishop.

Although it was hard for him to respond, he managed to say, "I think he's trying to suggest that you intentionally kept Chris's ID card."

Sister Pat suddenly erupted with her finger wagging at Stephanie. "You could have used that card to break into the house and left it there to make Chris look guilty." She spoke so confidently that Bishop felt obligated to discredit her theory.

"And exactly why would she want to do that, Sister?"

"Well, you can't expect me to know everything!" she snapped, still trying to maintain ownership of her dubious deduction.

***

Bishop left the meeting hurriedly as he wanted to resume his schedule of classes for the remainder of the day. He didn't see Stephanie in the halls, and in between classes, she remained in her room. Wild rumors were spreading around school. Chris Delaney had been questioned regarding the murder of the coach. Miss Harris had been questioned about her conversations with Bonnie King, Chris's girlfriend. Mr. Bishop had threatened to resign if Chris was charged without sufficient evidence. He wondered how all of these falsehoods got started. Most of his students never seemed to be that creative in their written work for class. Sister Pat might have blabbed to Terry who would tell Sarah who never kept a juicy rumor to herself. He doubted that Steph would have said anything to anyone about what had transpired in that meeting. Ron might have said something in confidence to one of the faculty members or even to one of Chris's friends and his words could have been misunderstood or misstated when they were passed on to another and yet another person. Bishop hoped that, when nothing more came of the meeting, the rumors would fade and someone else would become fodder for the gossip mill.

***

With Pavarotti singing "Nessun Dorma" in the background, Bishop barely heard the vibrating of his phone the next morning. He was hoping to get an early start on his drive to Madison. He wasn't going to answer until he saw Stephanie's name on the screen.

"Am I interrupting anything? I hope I didn't call too early. I know that you're an early bird." She spoke in a friendly tone.

"No, of course not. I'm glad you called. I'm sorry that I didn't get to talk to you about that meeting at school yesterday."

Stephanie explained that although she was initially upset by Sister Pat's accusation, given the rest of the day to reflect, she had concluded that Sister Pat was just being Sister Pat.

"It does seem a bit strange that Hodge has an unsolved murder on his desk, and he's seemingly more concerned about who vandalized the house."

"Maybe he thinks that the two events are connected," offered Bishop.

"Right! The murderer returns to the scene of the crime," she said with fake sarcasm. "That only happens in badly written novels."

He agreed with her. He felt that the murder and the break-in had been committed by two different people, although he left open the possibility that the two events were connected in some way.

"I know Hodge won't find my fingerprints on that card, and he won't find Chris Delaney's prints either because I never gave him the card. It just wasn't in the stack."

Bishop suggested that the Lieutenant had probably already come up empty in checking for prints.

Stephanie spoke emphatically, "I'm willing to take a lie detector test if that is what he wants. I didn't have the card, and I didn't break into that house."

"I'm sure that won't be necessary," he replied, conveying his complete confidence in her innocence and suggesting that it was very unlikely that he would even make such a request. "I need to spend more time going through the coach's papers. Someone killed him for a reason. I still think I'm missing something."

"I'm still betting that it was Rocco Santorini, although they may never be able to prove it," Stephanie theorized. "Some of the most horrible crimes are committed within families."

He realized the truth of that last statement. It happened all the time in literature. Hamlet killed his stepfather, Claudius, because Claudius had killed Hamlet's real father. Othello killed his wife, Desdemona. The list went on.

Stephanie then explained that there was another reason for her call. She wanted to invite him to celebrate Thanksgiving with her and her parents in Fairmont. Bishop knew that she had already invited Ron, but said, "I appreciate the invitation, but don't you think you should invite Ron? I know that he's very fond of you."

"I already did invite him, and he's accepted, but I'd like you to come as well. I don't want you spending the day alone. You've been so good to me. Even standing up to Sister Pat on my behalf in that meeting yesterday. I've told my parents so much about you. They'd really like to meet you, so what do you say?"

He was looking forward to the break from school, but holidays had been difficult for him since he lost Grace. He had planned to volunteer serving meals at the community center that day and then just watch some football on television.

"Okay, you've convinced me. I'd be happy to join you. Thank you very much."

Bishop knew that unless the murder had been solved by then, he would be taking that burden with him wherever he went.

Chapter 20

It was still dark that Saturday morning when Bishop went to take his shower. The hot water was relaxing, and it always seemed to help him sort things out. He had called an old friend, John Harrington, the week before. He and John had gone to Boston University together. John had retired from teaching English at Madison about five years ago. He had seen him briefly at Zappala's funeral, but there hadn't been much time to talk. John had invited him to come up for lunch some day. Bishop hoped that John knew Al Zappala better than he had. He hoped to return to Groveland that night having uncovered some detail that would help him fit the pieces together. The longer the killer remained unknown, the more likely that person's identity would never be known. As he rinsed off, he thought of Tennyson's Ulysses who inspired generations "to strive, to seek, to find, and not to yield." He didn't know what he would find, but he was convinced that he was headed in the right direction.

Shortly after the coach had moved up to Pleasant Hill Road, he had sold his house in Madison for $122,500. Bishop had stumbled on those papers in one of his searches through the boxes. There was a folder that contained documents from the two closings. He took the cash from the sale of his home at 6560 Imperial Road, added the rest from his savings, and paid all cash for his place in Groveland. A visit to his old neighborhood seemed in order. Maybe he could get some of the neighbors to talk about the coach.

Driving within the speed limits, he still managed to reach Madison by 9:00 a.m. With his GPS, he had no problem finding Imperial Road. He passed by 6560 and parked a bit farther down the street. It was a middle class neighborhood with nicely kept single-family homes. There was a man in his thirties raking leaves at the place that Zappala once owned. He was wearing a flannel shirt that was open down the front, a pair of faded jeans, and sneakers. Two chubby little tikes were gleefully jumping into the piles of leaves that their father had just created. Bishop couldn't help but smile to himself at the Norman Rockwell scene. The property had landed in good hands. After hesitating a bit, Bishop walked onto the lawn and introduced himself to the man. Joel Lindstrom gave his hand a firm shake and introduced him to his two-year-old twins, Jessie and Jenna.

"I understand that this house once belonged to a colleague of mine," observed Bishop, not wanting to sound too inquisitive.

"Who's that?"

"Al Zappala"

"Oh, yes. You've got the right house. My wife, Libby, and I bought this place from him a couple of years ago. It was shortly after we closed on the house that we found out we were expecting these two," as he gestured to the twins who were too entertained by tossing leaves in the air to pay any attention to Bishop.

They had only met Zappala at the closing. Joel said that everyone thought that he had been a heck of a coach. Madison had three state titles in football to prove it. Yes, his murder was a real shame. He did admit that the coach must not have had much time for upkeep and maintenance as the place needed a lot of work. That must have explained why Zappala had accepted his lowball offer without even bothering to counter. Bishop shook Joel's hand again, said that it was nice meeting him, and waved at the twins as he walked back to his car. He hadn't learned much.

***

He followed Imperial Road into town. He passed Madison High on his right. It was a three-story brick building that had obviously been upgraded with energy-efficient windows that reflected the morning sun. He noticed a few cars in the parking lot and a team out on one of the practice fields. When he saw a sign for Betty's Café, he decided to stop for a cup of tea and a pastry. It was mid-morning and business was slow. He struck up a conversation with a waitress named Lily. She was about forty-five, bleached blonde, and heavy on the makeup.

"I suppose a lot of teachers come in here. I'm a teacher myself."

If she thought he looked too old to still be teaching, she kept that to herself. No sense insulting someone and then expecting a good tip. Instead, she asked, "Married?"

"Widower. We were married for thirty-seven years," he said as he stirred some sugar into his tea.

"Sorry about your wife, but thirty-seven years is a lot more than most couples these days. Me, I'm divorced. Three times. Seems every one I thought was Mr. Right was Mr. Wrong." When she smiled, she revealed a mouthful of large, stained, crooked teeth.

They chatted pleasantly for a while. He had a second cup of tea. They talked about the restaurant business. There was no Betty; Lily bought the place from her years ago and never bothered to change the name. She claimed to know most of the teachers at Madison. They knew her breakfast special was the best deal in town. She had dated a few teachers over the years, as if to suggest that if Bishop were thinking of asking her out, the chances that the answer would be a "yes" were pretty good. He took the opportunity to ask a different question than the one she thought might be coming.

"Did Coach Zappala ever come in here?"

"That creep? Yeah, I knew him. Can't say as I feel too bad somebody nailed him."

He tried to draw her out on the topic by suggesting that he had only a cursory knowledge of Zappala. Lily was more than willing to talk about the dead. She had dated him for a while several years before he moved away. All he ever talked about was sports, but she didn't mind going out with him because he bought her expensive gifts. He was an odd guy according to Lily because he never wanted to go over to her place, and he never invited her over to his. Every month or so, he'd asked her if she wanted to take off for the weekend. They'd drive up north for a couple of hours, find a cheap hotel, and they didn't leave the room until it was time to drive back.

"If you get my drift," was the way Lily put it. Bishop certainly did. Still, he didn't understand what had happened between them to leave her so bitter. He worked his way around the question for a while hoping that Lily would answer the question without having to ask her directly. She didn't disappoint.

"One time I went out into the parking lot after I closed up at 1:00 a.m., and I noticed Al's car. I thought he was waiting for me or something. When I got up to the car, I saw he had some broad with spiked hair in the front seat. That's when I broke it off with that bastard."

Bishop had to admit to himself that he wasn't very surprised by anything that Lily had said. Clearly, she hated the man. Was it possible that she had come to Groveland years later to get even? Why would she have waited so long? How would she have obtained the poison? And if she had done it, would be she be talking about her hatred for Zappala with a perfect stranger?

Still looking for that elusive detail, he got in his car and headed for John Harrington's house. It was pleasantly warm for early November, and he had left the windows open. He hadn't driven more than a mile, when he noticed a bee darting around inside the car. He instinctively swatted at it, and as he did, he felt a sharp pinch on his right hand. "Damn!" he shouted to himself. Bishop, who was severely allergic to bees, had been stung. Quickly, he pulled over to inspect the area of the sting. He found the stinger lodged in the fleshy part of his palm and carefully pulled it out. He then reached into the glove compartment for the epinephrine that he always kept with him. He administered the shot right through his pants into his leg. Within seconds, his hand started to itch and swell and within a few more seconds, he started to break out in hives on his arms and upper body. Knowing that he needed to get to an emergency room, he got out of his car, and started walking toward a group of teenagers who had just come out of a Dunkin' Donuts. The venom was quickly taking over his body. He had time to say, "Bee sting. Please call 911" before he crumpled to the ground.

Bishop woke up startled by the dose of adrenaline that he was given through an IV in his arm. He was in a hospital emergency room surrounded by a doctor and several nurses. His clothes had been removed, and he was hooked up to a machine monitoring his heart rate and blood pressure. His heart was racing, and he felt cold despite the blankets covering him. One of the nurses held his hand and looked into his eyes as he awoke. He wasn't sure if the adrenaline the doctors had given him was causing hallucinations.

"Cheryl?"

***

"Cheryl ... Khoury?"

"Yes! But it's Cheryl Bates now. I wasn't sure that you would recognize me," she said in amazement. "It's been over twenty years," she laughed. "How are you feeling, Mr. Bishop? Looks as if you arrived here just in time. You were in the early stages of anaphylactic shock."

He felt woozy. The injections of adrenaline had reversed the effects of the sting, but they had their own side effects.

"A bit shaky, but I'll be all right in a few minutes." Then he added, "This has happened to me before. That's why I carry the pen. I gave myself a shot in the leg. That bought me enough time to get to a hospital. There was a group of kids outside the Dunkin' Donuts. They really saved my life. I remember asking them for help before I passed out."

"That must be such a helpless feeling. We're getting some antihistamines and fluids into your system, so you should be getting back to normal very soon. I've got to check on another patient, but I'll be back. Just to try to rest." She gave his hand a squeeze and left the room.

A short time later, a dark-haired nurse with heavy eye makeup came in, checked the monitor, and removed the IV. She told him that he could get dressed, but that he should call if he felt dizzy. She pulled the curtain around his station as she left. "My name is Joanne. I'll be right out here if you need me," she reminded him.

Bishop was feeling quite a bit better, cheered by the prospect of putting this incident behind him. He was worried about his car which he left hurriedly near the Dunkin' Donuts. He was fairly certain that he had locked the car before he approached those kids for help. He wished he knew who they were so that he could thank them.

Cheryl called from the other side of the curtain, "Mr. Bishop, how are you doing?"

"All dressed. You can come in."

As she pulled the curtain back, she looked at him and smiled, "I still can't believe that you remembered me!"

"Well, I guess I have a knack for remembering names and faces. It helps that you haven't changed at all!"

"Neither have you! I would recognize you anywhere. Are you sure you are feeling okay? Would like something to drink? How about some crackers?"

"No, thank you. I'm fine for now."

Her curiosity got the best of her as she asked, "What are you doing these days?"

Bishop got that question quite often. "I'm still teaching at Trinity," he replied.

"Wow! That's remarkable!"

Bishop got that response quite often as well. She asked him about a few of the teachers she remembered from her days at Trinity. Bishop was struck by the fact that not one of the teachers she mentioned was "still there." A few had passed away; others had retired. He decided to steer the conversation in a different direction. "So tell me about yourself. I know that you're married and that you're a nurse," he said with a grin.

"After Trinity, I went to Nazareth and got my degree in nursing. My husband, Allen, was already in med school at the University of Rochester at the time. He's a cardiologist. We lived in Baltimore for a while when he was doing his residency. We've been in Madison for about eight years. We have two adorable little girls, Laurel and Ivy, who are six and four. That's my story," she said with obvious pride in what she had achieved in her life.

After a few more moments of catching up, Bishop asked, "Do you know when I will be able to leave? I'm really feeling much better."

Cheryl explained that the attending physician would have to officially release him. They would probably restrict him from driving for twenty-four hours until the effects of the injections and other medications wore off. If he needed a place to stay, she would be glad to let him use her guest room.

"No, thanks. That is so kind of you, but I don't think that that will be necessary. If I could call my friend, John Harrington, he may be able to come and pick me up. He's probably wondering where I am. I was supposed to be at his place around noon." As he glanced at the wall clock, he realized that it was already after 3:00 p.m. He also realized that he didn't have his phone, his wallet, or his keys.

"Do you know where my personal belongings might be?"

She went across the room to an area of small, locked storage compartments, opened one, emptied it, and returned with all of his possessions. She then left so that he could make his call. When he looked at his phone, he found several messages from Harrington who was understandably worried when Bishop failed to arrive at noon, and increasingly worried when Bishop failed to respond to his messages. John was quite relieved when Bishop called. He said that it would not be a problem for him to pick him up at the hospital or to stay the night. John said that he would bring his wife, Missy, along so that she could drive Bishop's car back to their house.

Cheryl came back about ten minutes later with some paperwork for him to sign. She carefully went through all of the discharge instructions and asked him if he had any questions. He thanked her for all that she had done for him and told her how very glad he was to have had a chance to catch up with her. She was very happy to have met him again after so many years although she wished that the circumstances had been different.

"Agreed," he laughed as he gave her a hug. Almost as an afterthought, she said, "I never did say how sorry I was to read in the papers about Coach Zappala. What a terrible tragedy!"

In his own mind Zappala's death was an unsolved mystery rather than a tragedy. It occurred to him that Cheryl and her husband were unlikely to have known Zappala because her children were too young for high school and neither one was originally from Madison. Still, he thought he would ask.

He was surprised to find out that she had met Zappala at the hospital on several occasions. She went on to explain that he had come in to visit a cheerleader who had been raped. The doctors had decided to keep her under observation for a few days. "He was so kind and attentive to her while she was here," Cheryl added.

Kind and attentive? That didn't describe the Coach Zappala that Bishop had come to know.

"When did this happen?"

"About three years ago, I guess."

"I don't know if you can answer this, but was that girl raped by a football player?"

"She refused to say who it was. The police were forced to drop the case." Bishop was thinking rapidly. If that girl had been raped by one of the coach's players, then it was possible that the twenty-five thousand dollar withdrawal with the "HJ" notation had bought her silence.

"Cheryl, this might be very helpful in the ongoing investigation of Zappala's murder. Do you remember that girl's name?" He realized that he had no right to ask such a question, but was overwhelmed by the desire for any possible bit of information.

"I do remember her name. Such a sweet girl. Her name was Honesty Jones. It's the type of name you don't forget."

Suddenly, Bishop felt chilled. HJ. Yes, it was a name he wouldn't forget.

Chapter 21

Bishop spent Saturday evening catching up with his old friend, John Harrington. He and his wife, Missy, had two granddaughters staying with them, Sarah and Bridget, who delighted in having a houseguest. They made lemonade for "Uncle Mike." They were determined to make him all better. Bishop again felt that loneliness. He regretted that he would never experience the kind of happiness that grandchildren brought to John.

The retired life suited John well. He and his wife had taken several trips to Europe. His hair had turned almost completely white which accented his tanned skin. John talked about his golf game and his daughters and their children; Bishop talked about his teaching and about meeting a former student at the hospital.

John had worked with Zappala for a number of years, but didn't really know much about him. He and a few other current and retired teachers had attended the funeral as representatives of Madison High rather than out of a sense of personal loss. Like Bishop, he hadn't liked the man, and he had avoided him as much as possible. John had heard rumors of Zappala's womanizing, but nothing that ever involved a student. He had also heard rumors of his being a millionaire.

"Are the police any closer to solving that murder?" John noted that after a few days, the story had dropped out of the Madison papers.

"Let's just say that there are several 'persons of interest.'" He didn't elaborate, and John didn't push the issue.

Their dinner of roast beef, baked potatoes, zucchini from the garden, and homemade bread was a special treat for Bishop who often frequented local restaurants. He had learned that restaurant food was never quite the same as home-cooked no matter how good the restaurant. After devouring a big piece of apple pie a la mode for dessert, Bishop asked John if he knew of a woman by the name of Honesty Jones. He kept up with many of his former students through social media, and she was one of them. John got online, sent her a brief message, and received an instant response. John turned the computer over to Bishop who explained who he was and asked if he might talk with her for a half an hour in person. He thought that she might be able to help him resolve some questions about Coach Zappala's financial records. He took the chance of implying that he knew about the payment that she had received to end the rape case. He assured her that he was not a lawyer, nor was he a detective. As he waited for her to type out a response, he was convinced that she would refuse. She did not want him to come over, but she agreed to try to answer his questions over the phone. He ended the chat and dialed the number that she had given him.

His assumption about the withdrawal of the twenty-five thousand dollars had been correct. Honesty admitted that she had taken the money to drop the charges against the man who raped her. Bishop was very careful in his approach. He did not expect her to reveal the name of the man; he simply wanted verification that Zappala was protecting one of the players on his football team.

"I'm afraid you're wrong, Mr. Bishop."

"About what?"

"The man who raped me wasn't on the team."

His heart sank as he realized that he had arrived at a dead end. Surprisingly, Honesty continued. "I guess I can tell you now since he's dead."

"Tell me what?"

"The man who raped me was Coach Zappala."

***

"Hello? Are you still there?" Bishop had been too shocked to speak.

"Yes, of course. Forgive me."

"That's why he gave me the money. He assured me that nobody would ever know. He begged me to keep quiet. Told me it would be the end of his career if anyone found out. I took the money and refused to cooperate with the police. Everyone assumed that because I was a cheerleader, the guy had to have been a football player. I let them believe what they wanted. My parents are divorced, and my mom was unemployed. We needed that money." She went on to explain that the coach always had his eye on the cheerleaders. She then went on to tell her story.

"One night, Zappala found out that some of his players were at a party and alcohol was involved. I was there, too. The coach grabbed his players, got them in his car, and took them home. Then, he came back and offered me a ride. I was drunk, and I later realized that he had been drinking too. Instead of driving me straight home, he drove out on a country road. I was in the backseat. He parked the car, and climbed in the backseat with me. That's when he assaulted me. Afterwards, he drove me home, and told me that if I told my parents or anyone else, he would deny it and have me thrown in jail for making a false accusation. When he found out that I had gone to the hospital, he offered me the money and I took it." As she finished her story, she was crying softly. "I guess I was just stupid."

"No, you weren't. I'm so sorry that I made you go through this again."

She also told Bishop that weeks later she was still so angry at what the coach had done to her that she told the principal about what had happened that night and about the money that he had given her to keep quiet.

"Who was the principal then?"

"Mr. Bostwick."

"How did he respond?"

"He told me that there was nothing that he could do. That it would be my word against his. He advised me to keep the money and keep quiet." Bishop couldn't imagine that anyone in a position of authority would respond to such allegations that way. He was determined to confront Bostwick if he were still in the area.

"Mr. Bishop?"

"Yes?"

"I'm glad that he's dead!" She was the second person in Madison to have said that to him that day.

"I understand, Honesty. He can't hurt you or anyone else ever again."

Bishop thanked her for all of her help. She had lived up to her name.

***

Only moments after he concluded that conversation, Bishop was on the phone again. He had enlisted John's help in locating the principal of Madison High at the time of the rape, Edward Bostwick. He had since retired and was living in nearby Parkwood. Bishop called, apologizing for the intrusion on a Saturday night, identified himself, and pressed for a chance to speak personally with him about a matter of some importance. Bostwick agreed.

Since Missy had driven Michael's car back to their house, he convinced John that he was feeling much better and perfectly capable of driving the short distance to speak with Bostwick. He put the address in his GPS, and promised to return within an hour.

When he rang the bell of a large home in an upscale neighborhood, he was greeted by a tall man with a neatly trimmed beard wearing an expensive suit. Bostwick and his wife had plans for the evening, but the urgent tone of Bishop's call had convinced him to delay his departure. With some reluctance, Bostwick invited Bishop into his home. They sat in a living room half the size of Bishop's entire house. There were two sofas facing each other with a glass-topped coffee table between them. On the table were a number of oversized art books, one devoted to Picasso at the top of the stack. Bostwick sat on one sofa and gestured for Bishop to be seated on the other. On the wall behind Boswick was a gold-framed etching and nothing else. Noting the books and the etching, Bishop remarked that someone in the house must be an art connoisseur. Bostwick pointed to the etching behind him and proudly revealed that the work was titled "The Ark Carried to Jerusalem" and that it was signed and numbered by the artist, Marc Chagall. Bishop pretended to be suitably impressed, but found this man's pomposity annoying.

Bishop quickly turned the conversation to the purpose of his visit. He explained that he had been a colleague of the deceased Coach Zappala and that he had been named the executor of the estate. Bostwick didn't seem surprised to learn that Zappala had been a very wealthy man. When the name of Honesty Jones came up, Bostwick's demeanor changed considerably. He suddenly became tense and uncomfortable.

"Mr. Bishop, as I told you on the phone, my wife and I have plans for this evening. Exactly what is that you want from me?"

"How much do you know of what happened between Albert Zappala and Honesty Jones?"

"Why don't you leave this business alone? It's all in the past. Jones refused to press charges, and Zappala is dead. What is the point of dredging all of this up?" He clearly was becoming increasingly agitated as he glanced at his watch.

Bishop explained that a pattern of behavior was beginning to emerge relating to the character and activity of the coach. Understanding that pattern might lead to identifying his killer.

"Isn't that a job for the authorities?" asked Bostwick with a sense of finality.

"Ultimately, yes. But as the executor of the estate, as a teacher at Holy Trinity, and as a resident of Groveland, I have a vested interest in helping them to find the truth if at all possible." Bishop had not quite thought of it that way, but once he had articulated it to Bostwick, he realized that it did accurately explain why he had not been able to simply let go of the mystery surrounding this man and his murder.

Bostwick hesitated for a moment before he began. It was as if he were deciding how much to share. He admitted that Jones had come to him with her complaint against Zappala. She had wanted him to fire Zappala on the spot. It was possible that Jones was telling the truth. She also told him about the twenty-five thousand dollars. He knew that Zappala had been in some trouble years earlier, and the principal at that time, now deceased, had chalked it up as a youthful indiscretion. Bostwick didn't know more than that about it.

"Zappala had a bit of a reputation, but he kept his name out of the papers. I felt terribly sorry for Jones, but I warned her that it would be very difficult to prove the allegations against him and that, if it came to a trial, his lawyer would undoubtedly ask a number of very embarrassing personal questions about her sexual activity. She decided not to pursue the matter. She wasn't exactly a saint herself," indicating with a roll of his eyes that there was a lot more to her past.

"Regardless, if you had a suspicion that a member of your staff had raped and bribed a student, how could you stand by and do nothing?"

"Who said I did nothing?" he responded defensively.

"Well, you convinced Jones not to testify…"

"Yes," interrupted Bostwick, "but I also forced Zappala to resign." Bishop couldn't believe what he had just heard. Forced to resign? That would explain why he moved out of town and took the job at Trinity for a lot less money. Bostwick went on to recount his confrontation with Zappala over Jones's allegations. "I remember his anger as he pounded his fist on my desk, 'I paid that bitch to keep her mouth shut.' At that point," Bostwick continued, "I fired him on the spot." Zappala, however, threatened Bostwick.

"He told me that Jones wouldn't testify, and if I fired him, the union would come after me like a pack of barracudas."

"So?" prodded Bishop.

"Well, I didn't want him around anymore, but he could be a very intimidating man. I told him that I would keep quiet if he promised to resign at the end of the school year." Bostwick seemed exhausted by recounting the story.

Bishop had one more question. "Why in heaven's name did you let him come to Holy Trinity? How could you just let him loose on another school?"

"That was part of the deal. He insisted that I write him a clean letter."

Bishop thought it odd that the principal characterized their conversation as a "deal."

"Certainly, as an educator, you must understand the situation I was in," he pleaded. "I couldn't say anything about what he had done in my recommendation. He could have sued me for defamation of character."

"But it would have been true!"

"True and provable are two different things, Mr. Bishop. I wrote about his success as a coach. That was true."

Bishop got up to leave. "And what would you have said to the *next* girl he raped?" As he left, he walked past the etching and noticed the numbers "32/100" on the lower left and the letters "M.Ch" on the lower right. It certainly looked like an original. Despite his love of art, Edward Bostwick was a morally bankrupt and despicable man.

***

On his way back to the Harrington's, Bishop sifted through what he had learned in the last twenty-four hours. Zappala treated women with no respect. When he wanted something, he went out and got it. He had been involved in a "youthful indiscretion" as Bostwick phrased it. He wondered what that had been all about. He used his money as a means of manipulation and intimidation. Bishop had spoken to two of his victims, Lily and Honesty. One had been hurt far more seriously than the other, but there were probably others, many others. For what he did to Honesty Jones, Zappala should have been sent to prison; instead, he was given a free pass into another school. And then someone decided to be his judge, jury, and executioner.

The next morning, Bishop was served a wonderful breakfast of eggs, bacon, home fries, with rye toast and a cup of green tea by his two little hostesses, Sarah and Bridget. They were sad when it was time for him to leave. He promised that he would come back some day. He thanked

John and Missy for everything that they had done and promised to keep in touch.

Chapter 22

On his drive back to Groveland, Bishop had popped a CD of Liszt's Hungarian Rhapsodies in the player. Music helped him think. Had his trip to Madison been a waste of time? Was he any closer to figuring out who had killed Zappala and why?

Tomorrow marked the start of the second quarter of the school year. It seemed that each year passed more quickly than the previous one. He was prepared for his classes from a teaching standpoint, and he relished the thought of his time in the classroom. That was his sanctuary, the place where all of his worries could be forgotten, at least for the moment.

It was about noon when he turned up Pleasant Hill Road. Since he had had such a big breakfast only a few hours earlier, he wasn't ready for lunch. He decided to drive past his house and go up to Zappala's place. Hodge's people had completed their work, and he had the key once again. Since the house had been thoroughly trashed, he needed to hire someone to do the cleanup and repairs. He planned on asking Cindy Walker, the realtor that he had met, to recommend a service. He knew that it was probably a waste of time to look around, but he couldn't escape the feeling that there was something that he was missing.

He pulled in the driveway and parked behind the Lincoln that sat there just as Zappala had left it. As he walked by the car, he wondered if anyone had checked the contents of the car. Looking in through the windows, there was nothing out of the ordinary. Some clothes and a pair of sneakers were visible in the backseat. Some fast food wrappers had been tossed on the floor of the front passenger's side. Could there be something important in the glove compartment? What about the trunk? He made a mental note to ask Lieutenant Hodge if they had searched the car.

When he unlocked the front door, he found that everything looked just as it did when he had walked in with Hodge the other day. What on earth would have possessed anyone to do this? What were they looking for? Had they found it? Once he was in the kitchen, he noticed a couple of opened doors. One was a pantry closet whose contents had been scattered about. The other led to the basement. He had never gone down to the basement although he was certain that the police would have done so. He decided that it was worth a look.

He flipped the light switch which didn't do too much to illuminate the stairs. He descended the old wooden steps carefully, each one creaking as he reached it. It felt as if the entire staircase was about to collapse under his weight, but if it held for Zappala who had him by a hundred pounds, he reasoned that it should hold for him. The thin railing on only one side didn't instill much confidence, but he held it firmly for lack of something better. Once he reached the bottom, he saw that the floor was covered with various mismatched pieces of old linoleum that had buckled and cracked. It was obvious from the extent of the cobwebs that whoever had trashed the upstairs had not bothered with the basement. To the right stood a furnace, hot water tank, and a holding tank for the well. Straight ahead, he saw an old bed, several broken chairs, a chest of drawers with the top drawer missing, and a pool table piled high with cardboard boxes. On the left was a washer and drier, a workbench with some tools scattered about, and two metal shelving units leaning precariously under the weight of more boxes.

He reached for one of the boxes from the top shelf of the first unit and placed it on the washer. Flipping open the top pieces that had been folded into one another, he found some Christmas decorations. There were strings of garland, a couple of packages of tinsel, a metal tree stand, and a few ornaments. Zappala hadn't seemed the type to bother with holiday decorations, and the condition of the contents of this box confirmed that opinion. Having folded the pieces of the top of the box back together, he replaced it on the shelf and grabbed another. He was probably wasting his time, but since he was already feeling grimy from being in the cellar, he thought he ought to take a peek at what the other boxes contained. Eventually, all of this stuff would be hauled off to the dump. The sooner the better as far as Bishop was concerned.

It was in the fourth box that he found something that complicated his understanding of Zappala. This box contained items from his childhood. As he began sifting through the contents, he recalled that his will had made clear that personal items were not to be given to the family. That was such an odd request. If there were old family photos or other remembrances, one would think that he would want his sister and her family to cherish them. There were hundreds of old photos, most of them in black and white. Most of the photos lacked any writing on the backs, so he had no clue as to who these people were. Some of the photos were undoubtedly of the coach as a boy growing up in Connecticut. One showed a scrawny boy of about six displaying the sand castle he had built for whoever was taking the picture. To his right was a dark-haired girl in her twenties pretending to be inspecting his work. There were also documents such as Zappala's birth certificate, some grade school report cards, expired driver's licenses, and other odds and ends.

The real find was a stack of letters still in their envelopes tied with a string. It appeared as though these letters had not been read in many years. The postmark of the letter on top of the stack was "Nov 17, 1965, Hartford, Connecticut." It was addressed to "Master Albert C. Zappala." The return address was "Domenico Santorini, Hartford VA Medical Center." Bishop pulled on the string, and the letters came loose. They were all addressed in the same manner, and all originated from the same place. He hesitated as he removed a thin, fragile piece of paper from the first envelope. He ended up reading for more than half an hour. All of them had been written by Zappala's father while he was a patient at that facility. One in particular stood out:

April 27

My dear Albert,

I received your letter of April 21st. You are getting to be quite a good writer. I am feeling better every day and hope to be able to return home soon. I know that living with Maria makes you very unhappy, but son, please try to be a good boy and do what she says. This is not an easy thing for Maria either. You must obey your sister. I am sure that she does what is best for you.

I do not want you to hate your mother. She will always be your Mother. Don't forget that. Even though you do not receive any letters from her, I am certain that she still loves you very much. You have to understand that she is not well. That is why she left. When you are older, you will understand better.

Keep up the good work in school. I am very proud of you.

All my love,

Father

From what he could piece together, Zappala's mother had left the family. It wasn't clear when that had happened. Reading between the lines, Bishop speculated that she might have run off with another man. The father became ill and sought medical treatment at a VA Hospital, leaving his young son with Maria, his older sister.

Just then, he was startled by the vibration of his cell phone. It was Stephanie. She was finishing up her grades. She was uncertain how to handle a particular student's grade, and she wanted his input on the matter. He told her that he would be glad to listen, but asked if he could call her back within the hour. She had no problem with that. His watch and his stomach told him that it was well past lunchtime. He decided to take the box of photos and letters with him. It just didn't seem right to toss them out with all of the junk. It was possible that he might find something else of interest if he took more time.

***

When he checked the fridge and the cupboards, he realized that he had forgotten to do any food shopping lately. Lunch turned out to be a peanut butter and jelly sandwich. With a cup of Earl Gray tea in hand, he went to the sunroom, sat down in his favorite chair, and put his feet up on the ottoman. Even though he had only been away overnight, it always felt good to be home. For years after Grace died, he had difficulty coping with the emptiness. He had considered selling the place and moving into an apartment in a new complex that had recently been built on the westside. He had even made an appointment to look at one, but then changed his mind. There were too many memories to leave behind. In addition, there were too many aspects of country life that he enjoyed too much. Sitting in the sunroom with its panoramic views of distant hills was one of them. As Wordsworth had written, "Let nature be your teacher."

  When he returned Stephanie's call, he learned the nature of her problem. One of her students in French III had an average of 64, and she wasn't sure if she should pass him or leave the grade as is. Then she added sheepishly, "He's one of the boys that was meowing and laughing at me that day in class."

  "You can't let that incident cloud your judgment," he replied emphatically. He shared with her some of his thoughts on the topic.

Grading was one of the toughest parts of teaching. Occasionally, a student or a parent would look at a particular grade as an assessment of the individual as a person. Nothing could, in fact, be further from the truth. Bishop took pains to make clear to his students that the grade given reflected only on the quality of the work completed, whether that be a single test or essay, a quarter mark, or even a final grade. He also knew that it was essential that the students could count on his fairness. Grades were based on performance, nothing else. He knew that he was perceived by many as a tough but fair grader. He could live with that. His message to Stephanie was that grades should be used to motivate and to reward students, not to punish. He apologized for his mini-lecture, and ended by adding, "Steph, you have to make this decision for yourself, and I don't even want to know what you decide to do. Personally, I would never give a 64. I don't think my grading skills are that precise," he said with a self-deprecating laugh.

She thanked him for sharing his perspective, and the conversation moved in another direction. Bishop was still trying to assimilate what he had learned on his visit to Madison. Complicating that was his discovery of Zappala's letters. He decided to share his recent discoveries with Steph, believing that verbalizing his thoughts would help clarify them. He told her about going to Madison and talking with Joel Lindstrom, the man who bought Zappala's home. He also recounted what Lily, the waitress, told him about her experiences with the coach as well as the sad story of Honesty Jones and the way that Edward Bostwick, the former principal at Madison, had handled the case.

Stephanie listened carefully. Then she said, "I can't believe that that creep was able to get away with what he did to that girl! And then he gets a job at Holy Trinity where he could potentially do the same thing!" It was a sentiment that Bishop shared. In fact, he planned to ask Sister Ann some pointed questions about exactly how much she knew about Zappala when she hired him. He realized, however, that asking the questions and getting truthful answers were two distinct things.

Bishop also told Stephanie about the letters he had stumbled upon in Zappala's cellar. He summarized what he had been able to piece together. As he did so, he had to admit to himself that he couldn't help but feel sorry for the boy who had received those letters.

"Did his father ever come back?" asked Stephanie as if hoping for a happy ending.

"Apparently not. The letters stop in December of 1966. I imagine that he died."

"What do you make of the references to obeying Maria?"

It was purely conjecture, but he explained that the young Zappala probably felt betrayed by his mother. He might have even blamed her for his father's illness. He seems to have been very unhappy living with Maria and her husband. Maria had been placed in a difficult situation. As the older sister, she had to care for her brother, but she was married with a child of her own. When the father died, Albert became her responsibility until he came of age.

"How does all of this relate to his murder?" Her question hit Bishop like a bucket of cold water thrown in his face. Solving that mystery was, after all, the reason for his visit to Madison in the first place. Was he really any closer to an answer? If anything, it added a few more people who might have wanted to kill Zappala. Was it realistic to think that any one of them would wait several years to seek out their vengeance?

"I'm not sure that it relates to it at all," he admitted. "I just think that it helps to explain a lot about the type of person that Zappala became.

The trauma of his mother's actions might have caused him to fear trusting or loving any woman. Maria's resentment of having to care for her brother in those days might explain why he refused to help her and her family save the bakery."

Steph added, "It would also explain why he didn't want any of his personal belongings to be given to them, wouldn't it?"

"Yes, I suppose he was still trying to hurt them in any way that he could since he had been hurt so much himself." Bishop suggested that that would explain why he had never married, and why he held women in such low regard.

"Mike, you can't possibly be trying to justify what he did to did that poor girl, Honesty Jones, because of these letters. Nothing could justify what he did!" She was clearly upset at even the suggestion that the coach was to be pitied.

"No, of course not. I'm not condoning his treatment of women. I'm simply trying to understand it."

Shifting topics once again, Stephanie asked, "Do you think whoever got into his house is also the person who murdered him?" With so much of his focus in the last day or two on Zappala's past, he had almost forgotten that the vandals were still unidentified. He hoped that Lieutenant Hodge might find some other explanation for the discovery of Chris's ID card at the scene.

"Actually, I don't. I think the murderer is much smarter than that."

***

He decided to call Lieutenant Hodge so that he could fill him in on his trip to Madison and on his discovery of the letters. Hodge listened as Bishop recapped his weekend excursion, only interrupting to ask for a clarification a few times. "I'm impressed with what you were able to find out, Mike. You would have made a good detective," he said with a laugh.

"I'm not so sure about that, but thanks. I don't know how you deal with all of the ugliness that you must encounter on a daily basis. I'm happy working with young people and maybe helping them learn to make the right choices so that you never have to deal with them down the road."

The growing respect that each had for the other had been largely unspoken up to that moment.

Hodge told Bishop that he thought the letters provided a different perspective on the man, but that he didn't believe they had any relevance in the investigation of his murder. He also admitted that he had never understood why Zappala would have left Madison after coaching so successfully there for so many years. Knowing the story of Honesty Jones answered that question for him. "I seriously doubt that she was the first," he added on a somber note.

Those words sent a chill through Bishop. How many others might there have been? How many more might there have been if he hadn't been murdered? His thoughts returned to Bostwick. How could that man live with himself knowing that he had not only covered up a criminal act, but that he had paved the way for more by helping him secure the job at Trinity? Bishop also couldn't escape the feeling that Bostwick had not told him everything he knew.

Before the conversation ended, the Lieutenant shared a thought that he had been mulling over in the last few days. Hearing about his troubled childhood just brought the thought to the fore. "You know, we've been looking at all of the people who might have a motive to kill the coach, from Rocco, to Doug Sanders, to Chris Delaney, to Delaney's father, among others. There is one person that had access to the cyanide that we haven't even mentioned."

Bishop had no idea where Hodge was going with this. "Who?" he asked, genuinely lost.

"Albert Zappala."

"You've got to be kidding, Lieutenant!" The idea that Zappala might have committed suicide would never have occurred to him. Zappala kill himself? It didn't seem possible. Not Zappala. He had never exhibited any of the warning signs, at least as far as he knew. Hadn't the medical examiner also ruled that out?

"I suppose that it's possible," Bishop admitted reluctantly. "But I do know one thing for sure."

"What's that?"

"He didn't come back to ransack his house!"

When Hodge stopped laughing, he said, "I have to agree with you on that one," and then he started laughing again.

Bishop's thoughts returned to the mysterious discovery of Chris Delaney's ID card in the investigation of the vandalism. "You don't really think that Chris did that, do you?"

"Well, I want to believe Chris, and finding his card there, in and of itself, is insufficient proof of his guilt. I just don't know." He seemed to be talking to himself more than he was to Bishop. The investigation had reached another dead end.

Chapter 23

As Bishop opened his classroom door the next morning, he couldn't escape the feeling that, despite all that he had learned over the weekend, he was no closer to figuring out who had murdered Zappala. He thought of Ahab and his pursuit of the white whale. His determination to find the answers to the mysteries of life had become an obsession, a monomania. Was he becoming obsessed in his search for answers? He vowed not to let that happen. He, unlike Ahab, could recognize his limitations. Perhaps the questions that nagged him would be answered when he least expected it.

Having flipped on the fluorescent lights, he noticed that someone had slipped a piece of paper under the door. He placed his bag on his desk and picked up the paper. The looseleaf sheet had been folded in thirds. Students occasionally handed in an assignment that way if they knew that they were going to miss his class later in the day. Something told him that this wasn't an assignment. He unfolded the paper and read,

Mr. Bishop, I need to talk to you after school today. Thanks. Aaron

All sorts of possibilities flooded his mind. Aaron had previously shared with him that he had overheard Chris Delaney's father threatening the coach. What could it be this time? Of course, Aaron's request might have nothing to do with Zappala. He folded the sheet, put it in his pocket, and resolved to put this out of his mind until the end of the day. He didn't want to turn into an Ahab. He had classes to teach.

As he went about the business of getting all of his books and folders out of his bag and setting up his laptop, he was aware of someone entering the room. "Can you tell me what I got on my report card?" Bishop looked up to find Jimmy Wagner waiting for an answer. With his baby face and short stature, Jimmy was an 11th grader who could be mistaken for a 9th grader. He was also a little short on social skills that Bishop had been

204

trying to develop in him. Bishop smiled as he spoke. "Good morning, Jimmy! How are you today? Did you say something to me?" He sometimes had to gently remind his students of the importance of politeness and of the need to make eye contact when speaking to someone.

Jimmy's face became flushed as he realized his mistake. "Sorry, Mr. Bishop. Good morning. Did you have a nice weekend?"

"Yes, I did, thank you," he replied, choosing to ignore the fact that he had been stung by a bee, gone into anaphylactic shock, and ended up in the emergency room. "What can I do for you, Jimmy?"

"I was wondering what I got in English this quarter?" He was strumming the coil of his spiral notebook as if it were a musical instrument.

"Well, as you know, the grades won't be officially available for viewing on the school's portal until Wednesday."

"Yes, but a lot of the other teachers are telling kids their grades," he pleaded.

"That may be true, Jimmy, but as I've said before, some other teachers may choose to do that even though they are advised not to." It irritated Bishop that so many teachers did, in fact, give out grades before the official release date. If teachers couldn't follow the rules, why should they expect students to do so? He then attempted to put his focus on grades into perspective. "Jimmy, how do you feel that you have done this quarter? You've seen all of your graded quizzes, tests, essays, etc."

"I think that I've done pretty good."

"Fairly well?"

"Fairly well, yes. I think that I've done fairly well." At least it wasn't too early in the morning for him to catch on to the gentle reminder to use proper grammar.

"Do you feel that your skills in reading, writing, and thinking have improved in the last ten weeks?"

"Yes, I think so," he said with some resignation, knowing the conclusion that his teacher was heading toward.

"Then, I would say that your grade should reflect that, and you needn't worry about it too much. After all, it's what you are learning that's important, not the specific number on your report card."

Jimmy thanked Bishop for his time, and as he left the room, Bishop imagined that he was still disappointed that he hadn't managed to learn his grade, and that he would hear a few "I told you so" remarks when he relayed to his friends how Bishop had responded.

***

Homeroom period was more than just a time to take morning attendance and to listen to announcements. The phone usually rang at least once or twice. A student might need to report to the main office or to the guidance office. One of the teachers might need to see a student for a moment. Since it was all part of the rhythm of the day, Bishop expected more of the same when he answered the phone, but on this occasion, the call was for him.

Terry Mortenson delivered the message succinctly. "Mike, Sister Ann wants to see you in her office right after second period."

It wasn't everyday that he was called down to her office. "Do you know what this is about?" There was a moment's hesitation. "No, I don't. All I know is that she wants to see you in her office. I've got another call coming in that I have to take. Bye now."

Someone had to have been listening to Terry making that call. Either Sister Ann or Sister Pat must have been standing close by. Bishop would have liked to have some idea of why he was being called down. Sister obviously didn't want to tip her hand. He fought the urge to get ahead of himself. Perhaps this had nothing to do with recent events. He would find out soon enough.

***

He walked in to Sister Ann's office at the appointed time. She greeted him with a curt, "Sit down, Michael," as she pointed to the hard-backed chair with which he was becoming much too familiar. She pressed one of the buttons on the phone on her desk, leaned toward the speaker, and said, "He's here." The heavy footsteps that he heard behind him confirmed his suspicion that Sister Pat had just been invited to join them. She closed the door with the flip of one hand as she grabbed a cushioned chair and dragged it across the carpet. She angled the chair so that she would be able to look at both the principal and Bishop. As she plopped into the chair, what air had been in the cushion was suddenly expelled, making a hissing sound. Bishop looked directly at Sister Ann who seemed to be deciding how to begin. Determined not to appear anxious, he sat in the silence, punctuated only by the belabored breathing of Sister Pat. Moving that chair perhaps had been her only exercise of the day.

Sister Ann finally spoke. In an accusatory tone, she said, "First thing this morning I had a phone call from Mr. Delaney." The anger in her tone intensified as she added, "He's threatening to sue the school!"

Bishop wasn't sure exactly how this related to him, and he wasn't about to ask. He wasn't going to ask what prompted the threat either. It was rather obvious that it had something to do with the meeting that had taken place in her office last Friday. Still, he wanted to hear what Sister would say. Sister Ann, however, was waiting for Bishop's response. Unable to contain herself, Sister Pat broke the stalemate. Gesticulating wildly, she shouted, "Don't you understand what this means? If he sues us, we'll be ruined! We'll have to close the school!"

Bishop was going to point out that Mr. Delaney had only threatened to sue the school. That didn't mean that he actually would. Even if he did, one would have to assume that the school would lose the case. Additionally, the judgment would have to be quite large to force the school in bankruptcy. Based on past experience, he knew that any appeal to logic would be disregarded. Hysterical overreaction was so much more satisfying. Bishop calmly looked at Sister Pat and offered, "Shouldn't you be telling this to the school's attorney? I'm afraid I don't have any legal bona fides."

Sister Pat gave him a befuddled look. As he suspected, the study of Latin had not been high on her list of academic pursuits. In an attempt to save her friend from embarrassment, Sister Ann interjected, "I'm not asking for legal advice, Michael."

"What exactly are you asking for, Sister?" Bishop knew that they hadn't called him in to a closed-door meeting to keep him abreast of the latest legal threats made against the school. They wanted something. They always did.

"I need you to call Mr. Delaney and convince him to drop this business of a lawsuit."

Sister Pat had recovered sufficiently to add a "That's right!" to Sister Ann's request.

Bishop had already decided that he would do no such thing, but he first sought a clear statement of the basis of Delaney's threat. Sister Pat hit her forehead with her open hand in frustration and blurted out, "For Pete's sake!" before Sister Ann could cut her off. "He's upset that we allowed Lieutenant Hodge to interrogate Chris without his parents and their lawyer being present."

"I don't think you have too much to worry about. Hodge explained to Chris that he didn't have to answer any questions if he didn't want to. In addition, Chris is eighteen and capable of making his own decisions."

"Well, that's not the way his father sees it, believe me," Sister said as she replayed the verbal lambasting she had received on that phone call. "That's why you have to talk to him."

"We all know that Mr. Delaney is all bluster. Now that he's made his threat, the best approach is simply to let him cool off."

"You're not going to call him?" Sister Pat asked in a tone of outrage and disbelief.

Bishop countered with an understated, "That's right, Sister." Before Sister Ann had a chance to dismiss him, he decided to ask a few questions of his own. Looking directly at the principal, he inquired, "Have you had a call from Andy White recently?"

"No. Why do you ask?" Sister Pat shifted her weight causing the chair's cushion to emit a rather unpleasant noise.

"Andy called me the other day to let me know that the Zappala family might contest the will."

She reacted as if she had been slapped in the face. "They can't do that! This school won't survive without that money!" Realizing that she had either overreacted or divulged information that was not for public consumption, she quickly added, "We could certainly use that money."

Her comments about the financial condition of the school gave Bishop cause for concern. Just how bad was it? Were they actually considering closing the school? If that were even a remote possibility, didn't the faculty, staff, students, and parents have a right to know? Something else occurred to him. "If they do challenge, they will contend that you exerted undue influence on Zappala to include the school in his will." He decided not to tell her that Andy had assured him that such challenges failed in a vast majority of cases. "Did you ever discuss his will with him?"

Sister Ann and Sister Pat exchanged a look that told Bishop that he had hit a nerve. The principal's face flushed, and she began to stumble over her words. "Well I might have ... I mean ... he said ... he asked me if he could ... help." Then, as she regained a bit of composure, she added, "But I never told him to leave his family with so little."

Bishop struggled to understand why Zappala would have even asked how he could help the school. Robert Penn Warren's *All The King's Men* came to mind. Willie Stark was a terrible man in many ways, but he wanted to build the best hospital in the state. He wanted the best care for his people, and he wanted everyone to have access to it. He thought that if he could accomplish that one goal without any corrupting influence, it would somehow redeem him for all his sins. Did it do that? No. Might Zappala have been like Willie in that regard? Giving almost all of his money to charity, including Trinity, might have been his way of buying redemption. Somehow, it didn't add up. There was a greatness to Willie completely lacking in Zappala. Giving money to help others? That wasn't his style. Unless he was paying someone off.

Suddenly, the pieces began to fall into place. "Sister, did you know why Zappala left Madison?" She looked as if she might become ill. He wouldn't have been surprised if she asked him to leave her office. Coming to her defense, Sister Pat said sharply, "You don't have to answer that question." However, it seemed to Bishop that she felt that she did have to answer. He thought of the ancient mariner in Coleridge's poem who admits, "I shot the Albatross," as he is compelled to retell the story of his sin. Sister Ann revealed that a few days after she had hired Zappala, she received a phone call from Mr. Bostwick, the principal at Madison, who shared with her the real reason that Zappala had left Madison. He apologized for not being truthful in his letter of recommendation.

Although Bishop had known Sister Ann for about twenty years, he was nonetheless shocked by her admission. "So you knew about Honesty Jones?"

"That's enough!" screamed Sister Pat. "Get out! Get out!"

Bishop stood up and stared at the principal. Grabbing a tissue from the box on her desk, she dabbed at her eyes. Her silence was an admission of guilt. He felt no pity for her, only outrage. "He could have done *that* to one of *our* girls," he said in disgust as he opened the door and left the room.

The halls were empty, but they wouldn't be for long. Classes would be out in a few minutes. As Bishop made his way back to his room, thoughts of the meeting that had just concluded flooded his mind. What the principal had done was morally reprehensible. He considered reporting her to the board of trustees. She should be removed from her position of leadership. Knowing that most of the board members had been handpicked by Sister Ann herself, he doubted that they would take such decisive action. She hadn't committed a crime, unless in her desire to receive Zappala's bequest, she had been involved in his early demise. He had to admit that that was fairly unlikely. There were more plausible perpetrators of that crime, with Rocco still at the top of the list. He muttered to himself that if the board did find out, they might sympathize with her dilemma. A million dollars was at stake.

Lost in his thoughts, he didn't notice that Terry had followed him upstairs. "Mike, are you all right?" she asked with a look of concern on her face.

"Yes, yes. I'm fine. Thank you."

"Sounds like it got pretty heated in there," she said, fishing for some information.

He wondered how many times Jack, the spymaster custodian, had managed to walk by that closed door.

"Nothing that I can discuss. I'm sure you understand," hoping to deter her from asking any more questions. Students thankfully began to emerge from their classrooms, providing him with a reason to end Terry's interrogation. He had decided not to divulge what he had learned to anyone other than Lieutenant Hodge.

***

A short time later Bishop found himself patrolling the noisy cafeteria with Ron who obviously knew that he had spent a long time in the principal's office. Unlike Terry, Ron didn't pry. While maintaining a watchful eye on the students, Ron told Bishop that Sister Ann had filled him in on Mr. Delaney's threat. Since she couldn't convince Bishop to make that call, she had ordered Ron to do so before the end of the day. Unfortunately, as part of the administrative team, Ron could not refuse as easily as Bishop had.

"I don't envy you that call." He didn't tell Ron that it was a call that Sister Ann had asked him to make. "You know how difficult some parents can be. Frankly, the more I know about the father, the more impressed I am with Chris. It couldn't be easy to live with that man and his expectations."

"That's another thing. Sister told me that Delaney is also blaming us for the fact that Chris hasn't received a scholarship."

Bishop wasn't surprised to realize that Sister Ann hadn't told him everything about that call. "His grades have slipped a bit, but his SAT scores are excellent. He's been involved in many school activities. I'm sure he received excellent recommendations from his teachers. I know I wrote a very strong letter for him."

"Apparently, it wasn't enough."

"What do you mean?"

"Delaney told her that the coaches who were scouting him so heavily have been calling one by one to tell Chris that he is not going to receive a scholarship."

"Did they say why?"

"According to Delaney, each comes up with a different excuse, but he believes that it all comes down to Trinity. It's our fault," mimicking the tone that Sister must have used.

"You know, Mr. Delaney might have been better off not telling her about the those calls from the coaches."

"Why?"

"Although his father blames the school, Chris might blame his coach whose recommendation would have been more important than anything in his formal application. Chris might have wanted to lash out at the coach in any way that he could." Ron agreed that Chris did have a temper as displayed in threatening Zappala in public and in his reaction at the dance.

Just then Mary Nickerson came into the cafeteria, walked up to Ron, and whispered a message in his ear. Apparently, Ron was needed elsewhere, and Mary had volunteered to fill in for him. Bishop smiled at Mary and told her that she didn't have to stay. He could handle it by himself. As he began to walk down the center aisle of the cafeteria, he surmised that Mary was not being exclusively altruistic in volunteering for café duty. Teachers didn't spend years of study and thousand of dollars in tuition so that they could watch students eat. Mary wanted to talk to him about something. Terry might have put her up to it, having failed herself to extract any details about the meeting earlier that morning.

Several 9th grade boys at the other end of the room were getting a bit too rowdy. He used that as an excuse to put some distance between himself and Mary. As he arrived at their table, it was clear that one of the boys was about to launch a tater tot as a missile directed at a group of 9th grade girls seated at the next table. A stern look from Bishop was all it took to prevent the attack. Inwardly, he smiled at the behavior of these young people. Year after year, the seating arrangements in the café were so predictable. The seniors always sat together on the same side, and freshmen instinctively knew not to sit there. The underclassmen, especially freshmen, sat by gender. More boys might be seated at one table than it could comfortably accommodate, but that was preferable to straying from the security of the group. Tossing an occasional tater tot or green pea at a group of the opposite sex was evidently some sort of rite of passage. It was his job to see that things didn't get out of hand. It also served to keep him and Mary at opposite ends of the café until the period ended.

Chapter 24

The remainder of the day had been something of a blur. He breathed a sigh of relief as the dismissal bell rang. He was hoping to make an uninterrupted escape to the parking lot just as Aaron Metcalf knocked sheepishly at the open door of Bishop's classroom.

"Of course. Come in, Aaron. Have a seat." With the revelations of that meeting with Sister Ann dominating his thoughts, he had completely forgotten about the folded piece of paper in his pocket. Aaron had wanted to see him after school. He got up from behind his desk, pulled a student desk around, and gestured for Aaron to sit down opposite him.

"Should I close the door?" Aaron asked.

"That won't be necessary. I've got a clear view of the hallway from here. If anyone stops by, we can quickly change the subject to English. Am I correct in assuming that you don't want to talk to me about English?"

"Yeah, that's right." His green canvas backpack, laden with heavy textbooks needed for that night's homework, made a thud as he dropped it on the floor. He fished out a pen from his jacket pocket even though he had no need for one and began to click it open and shut several times in rapid succession. Bishop understood that students, confronted with moments of high anxiety, were often unaware of this idiosyncrasy.

"Okay, Aaron. What's on your mind?"

Aaron, still subconsciously clicking his pen, began to explain that he had heard kids talking about the meeting held in Sister Ann's office last Friday. Apparently, Chris Delaney was telling his friends that Lieutenant Hodge had tried to accuse of him of vandalizing the coach's house. Aaron stopped several times when he heard someone passing in the hall. Each time, Bishop signaled that it was safe to continue. Metcalf said that lots of people thought that Chris did it because his ID card was found at the house.

"Chris didn't do it, Mr. Bishop," he announced as if he were telling him something he didn't already know.

"I agree with you, Aaron. I was at that meeting, and I can assure you that he had never been in possession of that card. Someone else had it, and the identity of that person is what the police need to find out." He spoke with finality as if this meeting was at an end.

"That's what I came to tell you."

"What do you mean, Aaron?"

He put the pen down on the desk, and twisted around to check that no one was near the door. Turning back to Bishop, he said softly, "I know who had that card."

"You do?" He wondered if this pimply-faced young man who seemed afraid of his own shadow could possibly have taken the card. How many times did the culprit turn out to be the one you would least expect?

The pause seemed interminable. "Well?" Bishop waited for his confession.

"Eric Munro," he said even more softly.

That wasn't the name he was expecting to hear. "Are you sure? How do you know that?" Aaron was startled. He dropped his pen on the floor and leaned down to grab it. Bishop realized that he would have to slow down and proceed at Aaron's pace. "Did you see or hear something?"

Aaron took him back to the day the ID cards were handed out. He had gone up to his homeroom early because he wanted a quiet place to do some homework.

"What homeroom are you in?"

"303." Metcalf looked at Bishop as if he had just asked a stupid question. He realized that it was, in fact, a stupid question. "Go on, please."

When he arrived at the room, the door was open as he had expected, but Miss Harris was not at her desk. Eric was standing at the desk looking through the stack of ID cards. Aaron froze where he was standing. At first, he thought that Eric was simply looking for his own card, wanting to take it so that no one would see his photo and make fun of it. Aaron watched as Eric removed one card and slipped it in his pocket. Before Eric turned around to leave the room, Aaron quickly walked away. Later, in homeroom, when Miss Harris handed out the ID cards, he was shocked when Eric received a card and Chris Delaney did not. Only Eric and Aaron knew why. Aaron said nothing. He figured that Eric was just pulling a prank since Eric and his crowd never got along with the jocks. Aaron assumed that he just wanted to have some fun showing Chris's ID photo to some of his friends and that he would leave it on the teacher's desk when no one was looking. After a few days, Aaron didn't give the incident much thought. Friday's meeting changed that.

"Am I going to have to tell Lieutenant Hodge? I really don't want Eric to know it was me."

"You may have to talk to him, but I'll talk to him first and try to keep your name out of it. Thanks for coming to me with this, Aaron. You did the right thing. Again." He smiled as Aaron slung his backpack over his shoulder and headed out the door. Bishop got up and straightened the desks. He wanted to talk to Ron about this latest development before he brought it to Hodge.

***

Although he hadn't noticed during his classes, the afternoon had turned unseasonably warm for early November. With his coat draped over his arm and his briefcase in hand, Bishop was eager to get home, change, and go for a walk before supper. He just had to make one quick stop to inform Ron of his conversation with Aaron. To get to Ron's office, he had to pass by Terry's desk. As she looked up from her typing, he gave her a wink and a smile. Without any change in expression, she looked down again at her computer screen. She was undoubtedly upset that her attempts to pump him for information had failed. He couldn't worry about that. She would get over it in a day or two.

  He thought about what he might say if he should bump into either Sister Ann or Sister Pat. Fortunately, their office doors were closed, and the lights were out. Perhaps they were in a meeting. Perhaps Sister Ann was in her room at the convent praying for forgiveness for her quid pro quo, her willingness to hire a known sexual predator in exchange for the promise of a large bequest. He should have used "quid pro quo" in that meeting so that he could have observed the befuddled expression on Sister Pat's face. A better guess was that Sister Ann wasn't praying. She was probably trying to figure out a way to get him to retire. Good luck with that.

  Sounds of laughter were coming from Ron's open office door. As he walked in, he heard one boy say, "No way!" and the other, "How did you do that?" Ron had just finished a display of one of his famous card tricks. He was smiling broadly as he swept up the cards from his desk into a neat stack. Seeing Bishop standing there, he told the boys, "That's enough for today, fellas. You go home and think about it. Come back tomorrow, and let me know if you figure it out."

Then he gestured to Bishop to have a seat as he tossed the stack of cards in his desk drawer. "Sorry about that. They've been after me to show them another trick." Bishop knew that Ron was doing more than just card tricks. It was a way for the boys to see him outside of his role as a disciplinarian. One of his strengths was his ability to build a rapport with the students. It had proven useful on more than one occasion when Ron needed information. They knew they could trust him.

"I'm glad you stopped in. I wanted to apologize for skipping out on café duty today. A couple of the kids were out in the parking lot without permission, and I had to grab them"

"Forget it. I understand. Mary stayed in your place."

"I'll have to remember to thank her for doing that," Ron said.

"I think she was hoping that I'd want to vent about my meeting this morning in Sister Ann's office, but I managed to escape," he said with a grin.

"As far as I can tell, that meeting has been topic number one all day."

Having decided to keep his knowledge of Sister Ann's lapse in judgment confidential for the moment, he switched topics. "How did that call to Mr. Delaney go?"

"Not as bad as I thought," he said as he tilted back in his chair and clasped his hands behind his head. "I'm used to dealing with angry parents. It comes with the territory. You know, he didn't even mention anything about suing the school. In fact, I'd say we had a pretty good conversation."

Bishop was relieved to hear that since his refusal to call had led the principal to force Ron into it. He suspected that the reason Delaney hadn't given him a hard time was the fact that Ron could be trusted to tell the truth. He had a willingness to listen and a reputation for fairness. Because

Sister Ann was deficient in these areas, she often drew out the worst in people. It was unfortunate that she chose to exclude Ron from her inner circle, relying instead on the embittered and mean-spirited Sister Pat.

He then briefed Ron on the conversation that he had just had with Aaron Metcalf without mentioning Aaron by name. Ron wanted to know if Bishop believed the young man whom he correctly guessed to be Aaron. Bishop pointed out that Aaron would have had no reason to lie since he was not under suspicion. Furthermore, it was highly unlikely that he was trying to protect Chris since he had been willing to come forward earlier with information about threatening remarks made by Chris's father. The incident between Eric and Chris at the dance also made it more likely that Eric would want to frame Chris for the vandalism by leaving Chris's ID card at the scene.

"That boy has been trouble since Day One. If he is responsible for that vandalism, he'll not only answer to the law. He'll be cleaning out his locker and looking for a new school." The anger in his voice was in sharp contrast to the playful tone of the man demonstrating card tricks moments earlier.

"Wait a minute, Ron. Let's not get ahead of ourselves." Bishop knew that it was unlikely that the principal would expel Eric even if he admitted his guilt. The incident had not occurred on school property or during the school day. More importantly, Eric's father was a very successful pediatrician in town, and he was a generous supporter of the school's fund drives. Sister Ann was unlikely to let that well go dry.

In convincing Ron that Aaron was telling the truth, Bishop began to have some doubts. Aaron and Chris weren't very close friends, but they were football teammates. There often was a special bond among the players. Could Aaron have made up the story of Chris's father threatening

Zappala as a way of deflecting the focus from Chris? Of course, others had heard Mr. Delaney make similar remarks, but Aaron wouldn't have known that. Could Aaron have lied about Eric taking the ID card to provide Chris an explanation of how his card could have been found at the coach's house? Could Aaron, knowing of the bad blood between Chris and Eric, intentionally be setting up Eric to take the fall for the vandalism? Bishop felt that he knew Aaron fairly well. He wasn't the type to lie, even for a friend. On both occasions that he had shared his knowledge with him, he had appeared genuinely upset and reluctant. Could that have been an act? Having dealt with so many students over the years, Bishop thought that he was a fairly good judge of character. If Aaron were lying, it would be an embarrassing error for Ron to accuse Eric of any wrongdoing. Embarrassing to say the least.

"I've got an idea," announced Bishop. He explained it to Ron. "Let's give him some rope and see if he hangs himself. That way we can keep Aaron's name out of this, too."

"Do you think I should bring Lieutenant Hodge in for this?"

"No, I think we have a better chance of getting at the truth if Eric doesn't feel threatened by the police."

"You're right. I'll call Eric down first thing tomorrow."

As Bishop left the assistant principal's office, he realized that even if his plan worked to perfection, it would not bring him any closer to the answers that he really wanted. Who had killed Zappala? And why?

Chapter 25

He had made the drive from school to home and from home to school so many times, it seemed as if the car drove itself. Now there was talk that self-driving cars would be a reality in the not-too-distant future. There had been so many technological advances in the last decade that Bishop felt that he had to run just to stay in place. There had been so many changes in education as well. He had been teaching long enough to know that many of the so-called changes were nothing more than fads. If you stayed around long enough, there would be changes to the changes, and you more or less ended up where you began. Despite all the theories about effective teaching, it all came down to two essentials: passion for the subject matter and common sense. He had known many teachers over the years who lacked one or both of those qualities. It was just a matter of time before they realized that teaching was not for them. Unfortunately, some didn't figure it out for years, and it was the students who suffered.

No notes had been slipped under his classroom door, so he thought that the day was off to a good start. One of his classes had been reading "Young Goodman Brown" by Nathaniel Hawthorne. It is a classic example of an allegory. Goodman Brown represents good, and the mysterious man he meets in the forest represents evil. The man dressed in dark clothes tries to convince Brown that the true nature of man is evil. When it is suggested that many of the people whom Goodman Brown most admires are in league with the devil including his father, grandfather, respected political and religious figures, and even his own wife, Faith, Goodman Brown continues to resist but lives the remainder of his life distrustful of others.

The class was struggling to understand the story. Jane raised her hand, and as she did so, her notebook slid off of her desk to the amusement of a few of her classmates. Not paying any attention to them, she grabbed the notebook, and placed it firmly on her desk. As if daring it to do that again, she kept an eye on that notebook as she raised her hand and asked, "Was he dreaming all that stuff or did it really happen?"

"What do you mean by 'stuff'?" Bishop asked, concerned with the tendency of his students to use words that didn't communicate precisely.

"Well, you know, all that business about the townspeople being secret sinners," replied Jane.

"This is a key point in understanding Hawthorne's theme. It's a very good question, Jane." He asked several students what they thought. Alex, whose artistic talents were prominently displayed in his open English notebook, pointed to evidence in the text suggesting that it had to have been a dream since Faith was still wearing the pink ribbon that supposedly Goodman Brown had found while in the forest. Andrea countered that it was entirely possible that many of the good people of Salem had committed sins that would align them with the devil. He waited until several other students had also offered their opinions before he got back into the discussion. "In the final analysis, does it really matter whether it was a dream or not?"

No one responded. He continued, "What really matters is that Goodman Brown *believed* that what he had witnessed had been real. It changed him for the rest of his life because he *let* it change him."

Andrea raised both hands to adjust the scrunchie holding her ponytail in place, and kept one raised to ask a question. "Do you mean that if we go around looking only at the evil man does, that is most likely all we will find?"

"That's what Hawthorne seems to be suggesting," he said, pleased with the way the class had responded. "And if we look for the good in man, that is what we will find as well," he added, sensing that the class now had come to a clearer understanding of Hawthorne's story. That seemed like a good place to end the discussion. He let the students work quietly on their next assignment for the last few minutes of the period. As he sat at his desk with a set of quizzes in front of him, he had a hard time concentrating on his grading. He kept thinking about their discussion of the question of good and evil. Someone among them, wearing a mask of innocence, was a liar, a thief, a vandal. Someone among them, wearing a mask of innocence, was a murderer. Bishop knew that he needed to find out who had committed these crimes before it permanently affected the way *he* looked at his fellow man.

***

It was fortunate that Bishop had not planned on using his prep period for any schoolwork. As he walked through the main office area to check his mail, Ron Jennings called him into his office.

As he sat down in one of the chairs often used by students sent down by a teacher for some infraction of the rules, he noticed that Ron had several cell phones on his desk. "Looks as if you've had a busy morning," he said as he gestured to the display of phones.

"I don't get these kids, sometimes," he said in a tone of exasperation. "They know that they're not supposed to use their phones during the school day. But does that stop them?" He answered his own question with an exaggerated, "Noooooo. They have to text a friend that they just talked to in the hall five minutes earlier. Or they're just posting a quick tweet." Students knew the consequences if they were caught using a phone. A teacher could confiscate it, and turn it in to Ron who could keep it for up to twenty-four hours, or until a parent came in to pick it up. The theory was that students would be judicious enough to avoid the inconvenience of losing the phone and having their parents involved. Of course, teenagers, like the rest of mankind, are not always judicious in their choices. Compounding the problem were the teachers who were compelled to pounce on every infraction. Bishop occasionally had to confiscate a phone that rang or vibrated during class, but instead of turning it in to Ron, he would often just hold it until the end of the day when the student could retrieve it. That was normally enough of a punishment to deter a repeat offense. Sister Pat, on the other hand, was among those who seemed to enjoy snatching phones from the guilty party. These were also the teachers who often took calls on their own phones during class time, failing to appreciate the inconsistency of their behavior.

Convinced that Ron had not asked him into his office to discuss cell phones, Bishop asked, "What did you want to talk to me about? Everything all right with you and Stephanie?" They were spending more and more of their time together, and they both seemed very happy.

"Yes, yes. Everything's fine. She's really looking forward to Thanksgiving at her parents' home." Steph had been kind enough to invite Bishop to join her and Ron and her parents for dinner. "I called you down to fill you in on my meeting with Eric." He got up to close his office door, then sat down again.

"When I called Eric down, he clearly had no idea what was coming," Ron explained. Getting to the truth of the matter wasn't always so easy, so he didn't always play by the rules. "When Eric was seated, I closed the door and tossed Chris Delaney's ID card on my desk. I had placed it in a clear, sealed pouch. I have to give you credit. Your plan worked so well I'm going to add that to my repertoire."

Bishop remained silent, somewhat embarrassed that he had so easily come up with the deception.

"I told him that I already knew how he had obtained the card, and how the card had been used. I told him that if he were to come clean with the whole story, I would try to convince Sister Ann not to expel him."

"Well?" said Bishop, waiting for the details.

"Let's put it this way, Mike. If there was a restroom in my office, Eric would have used it." They both burst into laughter. He went on to explain that Eric immediately confessed to taking the ID card from the desk of his homeroom teacher. It was just a prank. He intended to pass it around to some friends for laughs and then leave it someplace where Chris could find it. He said he actually forgot he had it after a few days and didn't remember it until the night of the Halloween dance. Ron continued, "I hadn't realized that Eric had briefly dated Bonnie King. He was still upset that she had dumped him for Chris. He also admitted that he and his friends had never gotten along with the football players since they felt that the jocks always got special treatment. After the incident at the dance, Eric and his friends were looking for a little revenge. They had a few beers, decided to go up to the coach's house, soap the windows, break a few things, and make it look like Chris had done it. Once they got up there, things got out of hand, and before long, they had trashed the place."

Jennings added that Eric had readily fingered his two accomplices who verified Eric's story when they were called to the office. He added that he was going to notify their parents and turn all three of them over to Lieutenant Hodge.

"One mystery solved, thanks to you."

Bishop replied, "One small mystery solved, thanks to Aaron. One big mystery to go," he said soberly.

"You're right, of course."

Then Bishop stunned Ron with a casual comment. "I'm not going to press charges against those boys."

Ron's mouth gaped open, "What?"

"Those boys told the truth."

"Only after Eric was tricked into it," Ron quickly countered.

Bishop continued, "As long as they and their parents are willing to pay for all of the damage, I see no point in giving them a criminal record. Have them do community service, and deal with the drinking as a violation of school rules. That's what I'd recommend, anyway."

***

The remainder of the day passed quickly. He was at the back of his room picking up a book that a student had left behind when someone knocked at the open door. For an instant, he thought it might be Aaron again, worrying if he would be required to speak to Lieutenant Hodge. Then he thought it might be Steph backing out of their scheduled meeting for coffee. Before he could entertain any more theories, he recognized the voice.

"Mr. Bishop? Got a minute?" asked Chris Delaney.

Even though he was hoping to have a chance to talk with Sister Ann before she left for the day, he said, "Sure. Have a seat." What he wanted to discuss with the principal could wait another day.

Bishop looked at the young man seated in front of him. He was fortunate in many ways. He was gifted academically and athletically. Combined with his outgoing personality, good looks, and ambitious nature, he was the type that one considered a "can't miss" for success in college and beyond. Yet, there was something troubling beneath the surface. He didn't react well to adversity, perhaps because he so rarely had had to deal with it. His parents, especially his father, had high expectations for him, and Chris didn't handle that pressure very well. His gut told him that Chris would be just fine.

"What's on your mind, Chris?"

"I heard about Eric. It's all over school that he confessed to using my ID to break into the coach's house. Why did he do it? Do you think he'll go to jail?"

Bishop was not about to tell Chris that he didn't plan on pressing charges. He also felt that concern about Eric's future was not what had prompted this visit. "To answer your second question first, Eric and his friends made a serious error in judgment, and I'm sure that there will be consequences. The truth has a way of catching up with people sooner or later." Bishop felt that this might be the opportunity he had been looking for to validate his belief in Chris's innocence in the murder of Zappala. "To answer your first question, let me ask you one."

"Okay," Chris said tentatively, not knowing where Bishop was going with this.

"Do you remember reading *The Scarlet Letter*?"

"Sure."

"Do you remember what drove Roger Chillingworth to revenge?"

"Yeah. He wanted to get even with Dimmesdale for having an affair with his wife."

"Yes. And what happened to Roger?"

"He destroyed himself because he went too far with his revenge."

Bishop now seized the opportunity. "That's right. His desire for revenge not only hurt Dimmesdale, but himself as well. I think that Eric still has strong feelings for Bonnie, and he wanted to get revenge on you for taking her away from him."

Chris shook his head in protest. "I didn't take her away from him. She made that decision on her own, and besides, she never really did like him that much."

"The point is that revenge is a powerful motivator, and someone wanted revenge against the coach so badly that a murder was committed. Do you think that your father could have hated him that much?"

The question stopped Chris for a moment. The discussion had jumped from literature to real life so quickly. "No, Mr. Bishop. You don't understand my dad. He may say stuff and get real mad, but he's never acted on his anger."

"I believe you, Chris. Now, what about you? Are you capable of acting on your anger? You had good reason to hate him when he offered to pay for Bonnie's silence and threatened to tell your parents."

Chris was so shocked and embarrassed that he said nothing at first. Then in a softer voice, he asked, "How did you find out about that?"

"That's not important now. What's important is what you said to him, and what you did about it."

"I admit I said some things I shouldn't have, but I never *did* anything to that man. I swear."

"Didn't you feel that you might have lost your chance at a Division I scholarship when he benched you in what turned out to be the last game he coached?"

"Mr. Bishop, I don't really care about scholarships. As a matter of fact, some coaches have called me, ready to make offers. I told them I wasn't interested."

Bishop was puzzled. "Why? Isn't that what you have worked so hard for during your four years here at Trinity?"

"I thought that was what I wanted, but it really was what my father wanted. Bonnie is going Claremont Community College next year, and I've decided that I'm going to go there too. It's really a good school, and…"

Bishop interrupted, "Your father is saying that the coaches don't want you, and he's blaming the school."

"How do you know that?"

"Again, it doesn't matter how I know. I just know. The question is which of you is telling the truth?"

"Listen, I finally got the courage to tell my parents about Bonnie and me. I told them that I wanted to go to Claremont. Needless to say, they weren't too happy, especially my dad, but they finally accepted my decision. Whatever he's saying about the coaches is just his way of protecting me, I guess. You know, he has to blame somebody."

"Yes, I know what you mean." Bishop felt that Chris was telling him the truth. He thanked him for stopping by and promised to keep their conversation confidential. As soon as Chris left, Bishop gathered his belongings, shut the lights, and locked the door. He was headed for Sister Ann's office. The last time that he had been there had been a watershed moment in their personal relationship. He would never forget her reprehensible decision to hire Zappala despite what she knew about him. He knew that she would never forget that he was aware of her hypocrisy. How she would react to the suggestion he was about to make was anyone's guess.

***

He stopped by Terry's desk on his way to her office. He wanted to be sure that Terry wasn't still upset with him for not answering her questions the other day. "Nice flowers," he said, gesturing to the vase filled with a dozen red roses set against a sprinkling of white baby's breath. "What's the occasion?"

"They are beautiful, aren't they? A guy I've been dating sent them for my birthday."

"Oh, my gosh! Is today your birthday?"

"All day," she said in response to his dumb question.

Bishop was a bit embarrassed that he had not remembered her birthday. Normally, he would have gotten her a card and included a gift certificate to a nice restaurant in the envelope. Other thoughts had preoccupied him. At least he hoped that that was the reason. The other possibility was that he was becoming forgetful in his old age. He quickly dismissed that idea since he felt that he was as sharp as ever in the classroom. "Well, I hope that you're having a wonderful day," he said, sensing that Terry harbored no anger from the other day.

"It will be even better when I can walk out that door in about fifteen more minutes," she said with a laugh.

In a hushed voice, he leaned over her desk and asked, "Where's the dynamic duo?"

Terry smiled knowing exactly what he meant and whispered, "Sister Ann's in her office, and Sister Pat left a while ago for a dentist's appointment. She has to have a filling replaced. That's all she's been yakking about all day. Apparently, she's afraid of needles."

Bishop easily visualized her playing up her appointment with anyone who would listen in an attempt to garner sympathy. Perhaps if she were a bit more charitable in her dealings with others, she wouldn't be so universally disliked.

After wishing Terry well again, he approached Sister Ann's office, determined to take advantage of Sister Pat's absence. Sister Ann was looking through the contents of one of her filing cabinet drawers. She had her back to the open door as Bishop knocked.

"Come in," she said pleasantly, unaware of who was standing there. As she turned around with a folder in her hands and realized whom she had invited in, the smile disappeared from her face. "Oh, it's you," she said disappointedly as she tossed the folder onto her desk.

Bishop quickly sought to reassure her that he was not there to continue their conversation from the other day. They obviously saw things differently, and nothing that either said to the other would change that. He told her that he wanted to talk to her as executor of Zappala's will. At that point, she asked him to be seated.

Not bothering with small talk, she sat down, took a sip of water from her cup, and placed her folded hands on the folder. "What about the will?"

Bishop cleared his throat and began. He knew that he was taking a shot in the dark, but he had to give it a try. "I've got an idea of how to stop the Santorini family from contesting the will."

Sister Ann reacted as if she had received a shot of adrenaline. "Really? How?"

Bishop reminded her that if they were to contest the will, she would be accused of exerting undue influence on the coach. It would be an embarrassing situation for her and for the school. There was a reasonable chance that the will would be invalidated, and that would mean that the school would lose the million dollars. A protracted legal battle might ensue. He watched as the possibility of losing all that money began to have the desired effect. "How can we stop them?" she asked.

Bishop proceeded to outline his plan. He had run his idea by Andy White, Zappala's attorney, who had said that it could be done if both of the interested parties were in agreement. Sister Ann initially balked at the suggestion, but Bishop had anticipated that. As he explained the advantages for the school, Sister Ann sat quietly. He could tell that she was running through various scenarios in her head. She clearly did not want to be questioned in court regarding the possibility of undue influence that she might have exerted on Zappala. She did not want the public to know what she had known about the coach when she hired him.

Bishop knew that he was taking a chance. Was he brokering a deal with a murderer? Could Sister Ann, with the encouragement of Sister Pat, have been greedy enough to arrange for Zappala's untimely demise? She might have even believed that eliminating that despicable man was somehow justified. On the other hand, Bishop still felt that it was more likely that Rocco had killed his uncle. How much of that feeling was based on his dislike for the man? Even if he were guilty, why should his mother, Maria, suffer any more than she already had? Either way, the motive was greed, and Bishop couldn't escape the feeling that the motive for Zappala's murder was to be found elsewhere.

Bishop convinced Sister Ann to consider his proposal. He reminded her that it was only a proposal at this point, and there were no guarantees that it would work even if she agreed to it. Before he left her office, he cautioned, "Please don't tell anyone about this." Before she had a chance to object, he looked right at her and said emphatically, "and that includes Sister Pat."

Not wanting Bishop to have the last word, Sister Ann waited until he had reached the door. "By the way, we have a meeting set up for tomorrow with Eric Munro's parents. I'm going to expel him," she said matter-of-factly.

"The final decision is yours, of course," Bishop responded. He had learned the value of diplomacy. "However, all three of those boys did admit to their mistakes. I'd hate to see Eric not be able to finish his senior year with us. I think that there's a better chance of him learning from his mistakes if he stays here under our guidance than if we just toss him out."

"Munro has been a problem in the past, and I want him out of this building."

Bishop was tempted to reply that she hadn't had a problem with allowing Zappala to walk the halls of Holy Trinity. He decided not to put that thought into words, hoping that she might see the inconsistency for herself. "I understand that, Sister. But the more I think about it, the more I can understand him too. He's really not a bad kid. A number of teachers have told me that. His problems seemed to start when Bonnie King broke up with him. Rejection is a bitter pill. I'm not condoning what he did. All I'm saying is that revenge is a powerful emotion. He made a mistake. I think he'll be okay."

"Well, I'll think about it," she replied as she picked up a pen and opened the folder on her desk.

Chapter 26

Before he left the parking lot, he called ahead for a pizza. Shortly after he and Grace had moved to the country, they had tried to have a pizza delivered. They called every pizza place in town only to receive the same response. "Pleasant Hill Road? Sorry, we don't deliver that far out." At that moment, they realized that they had moved exactly far enough from civilization.

He ordered a medium pizza with black olives, sausage, green peppers and extra cheese. Although he had ordered from all of the chain restaurants, he thought that Christy's Pizza on Jackson Street had the best pies. He liked the idea of supporting local businesses, and he liked the idea of not having to prepare a meal.

His order was just coming out of the oven as he arrived. The owner, Luigi Catania, was there to greet him. Luigi was about the same age as Bishop and showed no signs of slowing down. What was left of his gray hair was cut short. His smile revealed a full set of even teeth, likely not his own. He wiped his hands on his full-length white apron and greeted one of his long-time customers with a firm handshake. "Hey, Mr. Bishop, how you been?"

After hearing the latest news about Luigi's grandchildren, Bishop paid for his order, took the box, and inhaled the pleasing aroma of the freshly baked pizza. Just as he was about to leave, Luigi said, "It's too bad about Zappala, huh? He come in here a few times. I never like him too much."

Bishop was torn between wanting to get home so that he could dig into that pizza and his curiosity about what Luigi might say. His curiosity won. "Why is that?"

He shook his head at the memory. "He come in with young girl, about half his age. It no look right, you know?"

"Was it always the same girl?"

"No. Each time different."

He was reluctant to ask the next question, but he had to know. "Were they wearing uniforms?"

"How you mean?" asked a puzzled Luigi.

Bishop knew that kids from Holy Trinity patronized Christy's. He had bumped into students on occasion himself. "Like a school uniform?"

"Oh, that uniform. No. Not that."

Bishop thanked Luigi and got back in his car for the ride home. The pizza was still steaming in the box, but Bishop had suddenly lost his appetite. He was sickened by the thought that Zappala had taken advantage of other young women, or at least had tried to. He remembered the heartbreaking story told by Honesty Jones. Someone had made sure that Zappala would not harm anyone ever again. He was more determined than ever to find out the identity of that someone.

***

When Bishop got home, he put the pizza box in the fridge. Maybe he would feel hungry later. He knew that he had a few hours of grading ahead of him, but he needed to make one phone call. He went into the sunroom to enjoy the remaining daylight in this season of increasingly short days. With Prokofiev's "Sonata for Cello and Piano" playing softly in the background and a cup of hot green tea at his side, he punched in the numbers.

"Hello, Mrs. Santorini. This is Michael Bishop." He had to talk with Maria. He was convinced that she knew something that might be helpful in solving the mystery surrounding her brother's death. He had spent hours searching through the cartons of papers that had been taken from Zappala's home. He was certain that somewhere in all of those documents was a key fact that he had missed.

When she realized who was calling, the tone of her voice grew harsh.

"What you want? Why can't you leave me and my family alone?" She was obviously referring to the police questioning of her son's activity.

"I'm trying to help you, but…"

"Help?" she interrupted. "That's a joke. It's too late for help. Petrocelli, he don't think we can win that case. We're selling out. When my brother die and left all that money to strangers, he took our last chance with him. That bastard!" she added bitterly.

Despite what her lawyer was telling her, Bishop knew that they did have a good chance of challenging that will. If it were determined that Sister Ann had exerted undue influence, both Holy Trinity and the Santorini family could lose everything. The entire estate could go to charity. "Please listen to me, Mrs. Santorini. Don't sell your bakery. If you decide not to contest the will, I think that I can help you save your business." Bishop was taking a calculated risk in assuming that Sister Ann would agree to go along with his plan. If she didn't, Mrs. Santorini's decision wouldn't matter. However, if Sister Ann did the right thing, then it was essential that Maria cooperate.

"I can't explain all the details to you right now, but if you can just trust me, I know that I can help you."

"Well, I think about it," she grudgingly replied. He was getting that response a lot lately. At least she hadn't said no. From the letters that Zappala had kept, he had picked up bits and pieces of this family's difficult past. He decided to push for more.

"Your brother didn't just die, Mrs. Santorini. He was murdered. Wouldn't you like to find out who did it and why?"

"What difference does it make? He's dead. I'ma sure he deserve it."

Bishop was no longer surprised by this woman's bitterness. From the letters, it was clear that tensions had existed between them for many years. "What makes you so sure that he deserved to die?"

"What make me sure? I'll tell you why, meesta." Her anger had clearly freed her of any reluctance to talk. "My brother was murderer himself."

Bishop could barely summon the breath to ask, "What are you talking about?"

"A long time ago, he got a girl pregnant. He came running to my husband and me. He needed money so that girl could get an abortion and keep her quiet. He told us if anyone found out, he would lose his job. He begged us. He kill his own baby, and we help him do it!" As she told the story, the harshness in her voice was replaced by a soft sobbing.

His heart sank as he realized that there was another Honesty Jones. "Do you know the name of the girl?"

"No, no, never, and we didn't want to know. She was murderer too. He try to give us money back, but we didn't want his money."

"May I ask how much money you and your husband gave him?"

"Fifty thousand. It was all our savings."

Bishop finally understood why Zappala had written that amount into the will. It was not only to protect against a possible challenge to the will; he was repaying a loan. He was settling an account. He also understood why Zappala had been so adamant in refusing to help his sister save the family business. If they wouldn't accept his offers to repay that loan, he wouldn't give them one penny when they were in need. He was certain that Maria understood that as well. She knew her brother as well as anyone. She was only compelled to ask him for money out of desperation to save the business.

"I know this is difficult for you, Mrs. Santorini, but I need to ask a few more questions."

"What questions?"

"Do you remember when your brother came to you asking for the money?"

"Sure I remember like yesterday. He just had graduate from college."

"Then he was teaching at Madison?"

"No, no, not yet," Maria responded emphatically. "He was at a Catholic school. He was so afraid to be fired." Bishop had just assumed that Zappala had spent his whole career at Madison before coming to Holy Trinity.

"Do you remember where that school is located?"

"No. Somewhere in Connecticut. But I do remember the name of the school. Immaculate Heart. Imagine Albert with heart as black as sin teaching in a school with that name!" He recognized the irony, but he didn't find it unimaginable. After all, Zappala had also taught at Holy Trinity.

***

Bishop spent most of his Sunday at home. He had started the fireplace in the living room for the first time that season and settled on the sofa with the Sunday paper and a cup of green tea. A piano concerto by Scarlatti played in the background. The paper was twice its normal size, crammed with ads announcing Black Friday sales. He skimmed the news and skipped the ads, then tossed all of it on the coffee table. The holidays had become a difficult time of the year for him since he had lost Grace.

Her sudden death had shaken his world. He hadn't been sure that he would have the strength to move on. He did return to the classroom after the Christmas break that year. Although the emptiness never left him, he found that teaching allowed him to put the focus on others rather than on himself. How much longer he would teach was anyone's guess. Having been in education for over forty years, rumors of his retirement kicked up every spring. Sister Ann and Sister Pat probably prayed daily that Bishop, so often the thorn in their side, would call it a career. That thought alone gave him the incentive to keep going.

In an attempt to curb his reverie, he picked up his copy of *A Separate Peace* by John Knowles. The book never failed to have a significant impact on his students, and it had done so again recently. It told the story of two young men at a prep school during wartime. They were the best of friends, and yet also bitter enemies, at least as far as the narrator, Gene, was concerned. In a moment of unthinking maliciousness, Gene causes his friend, Finny, to fall from a tree. Ultimately, Finny dies, and Gene learns that the source of evil in the world exists within the human heart, including his own. Bishop's students always found the message sobering. It was a powerful lesson. Each one of us is capable of unspeakable hatred. Once evil is acknowledged, however, each one of us can choose good over evil.

As he thought about Gene's actions, he began to think about the killer approaching Zappala's home on that Sunday night. What could have driven that person to the decision to take his life? Regardless of Zappala's terrible flaws, how could anyone have laced his drink with poison? Who had assumed the right to be his judge and executioner? Shouldn't God punish and man forgive? Bishop thought it unlikely that the killer had ever killed before or would ever kill again. Just once. It seemed as though the murderer had committed the perfect crime. No witnesses. No fingerprints. Several suspects had motive, but nothing was proven. Would living with guilt be enough of a punishment? Was the perpetrator feeling the burden of guilt? Perhaps not.

***

After a quick brunch of scrambled eggs, rye toast, and tea, he decided that his yard needed one more mowing before winter. He changed into his work clothes, walked out to the barn, put some gas in his tractor, checked the oil, and started the engine. He had done this job so many times. Since the area that he mowed was probably the equivalent of several football fields, he knew that it would take a couple of hours out of his day. He didn't mind, though, as he found the simple task relaxing.

    As he mowed, he also mulched the dead leaves that had fallen from the many trees on his property. Shakespeare had described trees at this time of the year as "bare ruined Choirs." He felt the sadness that Shakespeare must have felt in acknowledging the end of the season. As he mowed the expanse of green for the final time that year, he felt a sense of finality regarding the Zappala affair.

    The culprits of the break in had been identified. They would accept their punishment. He had been correct in assuming that the vandalism had had nothing to do with the murder. It seemed likely that Mrs. Santorini would drop her challenge to the will, and he would be able to help her save the family business. It also seemed likely that Sister Ann would agree to his suggestion since Holy Trinity would gain needed funds, and her own scandalous behavior would remain a secret. The reason for the bitterness between brother and sister had been revealed. There seemed no point in pursuing what had happened at Immaculate Heart in the distant past. He could take comfort in the knowledge that there would be no more victims of Zappala's depravity. Bishop had to accept that the killer would likely never be found. As he had explained so many times to his students, works of literature did not always have a happy ending. It was true of life as well. It was time to refocus on his own life. In a few days, he would celebrate Thanksgiving with Ron, Stephanie, and her parents.

***

The atmosphere at Holy Trinity on the Monday and Tuesday before break was festive. Several dozen students had decided to take these two days off, extending their break from five days to nine. A few of Bishop's students had approached him in advance with a request for work that they would miss. Whether or not they actually would do the readings was another matter. Some of those early vacationers were already basking in the warmth of a Florida beach. A few planned to use the extra time for college visits. One was already posting photos of Paris on social media.

Of course, not everyone was in a good mood. One notable exception was Sister Pat who seemed to be perpetually in a bad mood. When she saw Bishop in the hall, she pounced. "What's wrong with you, Bishop? We get a confession and have a chance to nail those three thugs and you decide to let them go scot free!" The words exploded out of her mouth like punches as she made no attempt to hide her anger in front of students who were in the area. As long as she wasn't after them, they were smart enough to keep on walking.

Ron had already filled him in on the administrative meeting in which Sister Pat had advocated throwing all three of the boys out of the school. Sister Ann had decided to spare even the instigator, Eric Munro.

Undoubtedly, Sister Pat was still upset over one of her infrequent failures to influence the principal.

Bishop passed on his first reaction. After all, the students were watching, and he knew that he needed to be respectful and professional in his dealings with her. He calmly replied, "They are not going unpunished, Sister." Bishop explained that the boys had agreed to pay restitution for all costs associated with their actions. In addition, Eric and his two friends had agreed to perform fifty hours of community service and accepted the need for counseling for alcohol and anger management issues. In addition to that, they were placed on probation for the remainder of the school year. If they messed up again, they would be gone. If any of the students caught what he was saying, so much the better. The word needed to get out there that there were serious consequences for poor judgment and bad behavior.

Sister Pat remained unconvinced. She probably hadn't heard a thing that Bishop had just said. She jabbed the air as she pointed at him. "When those guys screw up again, and they will, it'll be because of you!" With that, she turned, and stomped off. In her haste, she accidentally bumped into a tiny 9th grade girl, sending her books flying. She didn't bother to turn around or to apologize. And she wondered why people didn't like her. Bishop helped the girl pick up her belongings and asked her if she was all right. She was more embarrassed than hurt. As he walked to his classroom, he was determined not to let Sister's negativity affect him. He preferred to think that those three young men could change for the better and that "nailing" them was the least likely way of effecting that change.

***

The end of each class brought the long-awaited holiday a bit closer. It was *the* topic of conversation.

Sister Pascala stopped him in the hall between classes. "Are you ready for break?" she asked with a broad grin. She looked better than she had in weeks. Thanks to the visit of Sister Wilhelmina in her dreams, she seemed to have moved past her feelings of guilt regarding the poison.

"No doubt about it," he responded enthusiastically. Knowing that most of the sisters spent Thanksgiving with their families, he asked, "What are your plans for the holiday?"

"One of my old chums, Sister Estelle, teaches at one of our schools in the City. We're going to see the Macy's Parade in person!"

"That's terrific! Maybe I'll see you on television!" It wasn't beyond the realm of possibility. Two elderly nuns still wearing the old habit might be an appealing shot for some cameraman. When she asked him what he had planned for Thanksgiving, he explained that although he felt a bit guilty about skipping his volunteer work serving meals at the shelter, Ron and Stephanie had convinced him to spend the day with them at her parents' home in Claremont.

"Don't feel guilty. You certainly deserve a break after what you've been through the last couple of months."

"We all do," replied Bishop, returning the sympathetic comment.

"Ron and Stephanie seem to growing quite close," she observed. "I'm happy for Ron. He's had a few tough breaks along the way. I don't know Stephanie very well, but she seems quite nice."

Bishop agreed with her assessment. He was happy for them as well.

"But," he added, "I'd feel even happier if the killer had been found. It doesn't look as though we'll ever find out."

"Michael, God works in mysterious ways. That answer may come when we least expect it."

"Yes, I guess you're right."

***

The students in his last period class were cooperative to the end. Bishop was from the old school in his belief that class time was not to be wasted. He was paid to teach, not to give study periods. The kids understood and respected that. With the sound of the bell marking the beginning of the first real break of the school year, cheers erupted from various places throughout the building. As his students stormed out of the classroom, many were kind enough to wish him a Happy Thanksgiving.

He stood at the door observing the bedlam in the halls. Lockers clanged as students rushed to pack what they needed for the upcoming days. Within minutes, only a few stragglers remained. As Bishop returned to his desk, Stephanie walked in.

"Whew," she said as she pretended to wipe sweat from her brow. "It was hard to keep a lid on things during that last period."

Since this was her first year teaching, she had a lot to learn. "Just wait until we get to Christmas break," he cautioned. Although he was teasing, there was also an element of truth in what he said.

Steph and Ron were driving to her parents' home on Wednesday. Bishop was joining them on Thursday. She had offered him the chance to stay over on Thursday night. Her parents' place could accommodate them all. Bishop had politely declined, explaining that his Aunt Katherine was in a nursing home in Brentwood which was about another hour's drive from her parents' home. He hadn't seen her in some time, and he planned to leave late on Thursday, drive up to his aunt's, get a motel, and then spend the next day with her. Katherine didn't have many visitors, and he knew that she would thoroughly enjoy his visit.

"I thought that you might want to come with us to do some Christmas shopping on Friday," said Stephanie.

"Shopping on Black Friday? You've got to be kidding!"

"Well, why don't you stop in again on your way back from Brentwood?"

"Thanks for offering, and I'd love to really, but I need a couple of days at home to get through all of the papers that have been coming in the last few days. I always manage to load myself down with paperwork over vacations."

"I know that some teachers are not going to touch a book during the entire break, and I plan on being one of them," Stephanie announced with some pride.

"I've always felt that if I expected my students to work over break, I could expect no less of myself." He didn't mean this as a rebuke; it was simply a statement of the way he felt.

"I've been working hard to get ahead so that I will really be able to enjoy this time with my family and with Ron."

"Listen, you don't owe me any explanations. I hear what you're saying."

Wanting to change the direction of the conversation, he asked once more what he should bring for dinner. Stephanie insisted that he needn't bring anything. He made a mental note to bring a couple of bottles of New York State wine, some French bread, and some Italian pastries. He would never think of arriving at the home of the Harris family empty-handed. What he did not realize was that he would leave late that night with far more than he had imagined.

Chapter 27

When Bishop headed down Pleasant Hill Road on Thanksgiving morning, the air was cool and crisp. He had brought with him several of his favorite CDs of Luciano Pavarotti to provide some accompaniment for the three-hour drive to Fairmont. Concentrating on the famous tenor's virtuosity always brought Bishop the serenity that had been in short supply during these last few months. The murder of his colleague who lived just up the road from him had turned his mundane existence into one filled with unexpected obligations, uncertainty, and frustration. Yet, he realized that he had much for which to be thankful. He had his health, and he had his teaching. He also had wonderful friends such as Ron and Stephanie who made sure that he would not have to spend the holiday alone.

"Welcome to Fairmont!" As he drove passed the sign, Bishop felt the electric anticipation of the new and unfamiliar. From everything that Stephanie had told him about her parents, he felt as if he knew them already. Her father, Brian, owned and operated a successful insurance agency in town with branch offices in several other towns. He considered his clients an extended family, and on more than one occasion, had forgiven policy payments for those having financial difficulties rather than let them lose their coverage. Steph had worked in her father's office after graduation before deciding that she wanted to pursue a degree in education. Her mother, June, was a kindergarten teacher who loved her work. It was through witnessing June's happiness that Steph had decided on a teaching career.

He had no trouble finding the home of her parents. It was a large, well-kept house on a quiet street in an affluent section of town. Bishop recognized Ron's car in the driveway and pulled in behind it. He approached the door with his hands full. He had wine, bread, pastries, and some fresh flowers that he had picked up on his way at one of the many stores open even on this special day. Stephanie opened the door before he had a chance to figure out how he was going to ring the bell. She was obviously helping out in the kitchen as her sunflower-filled apron attested.

"Oh, Mike! I'm so glad you're here! Please, come in." Her warm smile alone would have conveyed the same message had she not spoken at all. She helped him with the packages as she scolded him, "I told you that you didn't need to bring anything."

"I know I didn't *have* to. I just *wanted* to."

Steph put his coat in the closet, grabbed him by the arm, and led him into the living room to meet her parents. They were both sitting on a sofa watching the Macy's parade. Ron was stretched out on a recliner, looking very relaxed. They all stood to greet Bishop. Steph's parents were not at all what he had imagined them to be. Brian looked more like a security guard than an insurance executive. He was a large man, well over six feet tall, with blue eyes, and closely cropped grey hair. He grabbed Bishop's outstretched hand, shook it vigorously, and gave him a tap on the shoulder with his other hand. "Nice to meet you, Mr. Bishop. Steph has mentioned your name a number of times."

Whenever someone said this to Bishop, he assumed that it was a compliment. He realized, however, that he might be a topic of conversation for all the wrong reasons. "Nice to meet you as well. Please call me Mike."

June gave him a hug. She was a very attractive woman whose short blonde hair, blue eyes, and perfect proportions reminded him of a Hollywood actress whose name he couldn't remember. "I'm so glad you could come."

"Well, I'm happy to be here. Thanks for inviting me."

After shaking hands with Ron, they all sat down, Steph's parents on the sofa, Ron back on the recliner, Steph on an ottoman next to him, and Bishop on a loveseat that matched the sofa.

"That turkey smells wonderful," Bishop said as he inhaled the aroma emanating from the kitchen.

The Macy's parade was on television, and as he glanced at the screen, he remembered that Sister Pascala and her companion were in that mass of humanity somewhere. The camera focused on a giant Minnie Mouse floating down the street to the delight of the huge crowd there. It occurred to him that "giant Minnie" would be a good example to use when he wanted to explain the term "oxymoron" to his students.

***

He enjoyed the kind of Thanksgiving celebration that he had not experienced since Grace had passed away. The warmth and hospitality of the Harris family made him feel completely comfortable in their home. The dinner was truly a feast. The twenty-pound gobbler was cooked to perfection. Brian did the carving. June and Steph brought in bowls of gravy, stuffing, mashed potatoes, sweet potatoes, peas, and fresh cranberry sauce. There was also an enormous garden salad, and a basket filled with slices of French bread. Ron opened one of the bottles of wine that Bishop had brought and filled a glass for everyone. Since the dinner table looked like one straight out of a magazine, Steph took a picture of it. She also asked everyone to huddle together so that she could take a selfie of the group. The five of them ate and drank, talked and laughed, for a couple of hours. After dinner, Steph's parents insisted that they could handle the dishes. Steph and Ron decided to go for a walk around the neighborhood. They asked Bishop if he wanted to join them, but he declined. He thought that they should have some time alone. Dessert would be served on their return. He offered to help out in the kitchen, but June wouldn't hear of it. She urged him to make himself comfortable in the living room, and said that she and her husband would join him in a few minutes.

***

With a few moments to himself, Bishop glanced at the titles of some of the library books on the coffee table. One was on quilting. That was likely June's. There were several mysteries including one by Donna Leon, a mystery writer with whom he was familiar. Those could be either June's or Brian's. His thoughts drifted to Leon's books. Would Detective Guido Brunetti have figured out who had murdered Zappala? What detail had he missed that Brunetti would have noticed? He walked over to the mantle to get a closer look at one of the framed photos. He recognized the background as the famed Motif Number One in Rockport, Massachusetts. Brian was wearing a golf shirt, shorts, boat shoes, and a Red Sox baseball cap. June's outfit consisted of a blouse, shorts, sandals, and a wide-brimmed hat. Between them stood Stephanie, a good six inches shorter than either of her parents, wearing a tank top, short shorts, and sandals with her sunglasses pushed up over her thick, dark brown hair. Whoever had taken the photo had captured the happiness of all three. It was a wonderful photo, but there was something about it that bothered him although he couldn't say what it was.

Brian joined him in the living room. "I think I ate too much," he said as he patted his stomach, sat down, picked up the remote, and turned on the television.

"Me too," Bishop admitted.

"June is whipping up some cream for the pumpkin pie. By the time Steph and Ron get back, we should have some room for at least one piece." He then turned his attention to the football game that was tied early in the last quarter. The game was stopped as the officials were reviewing the tapes to determine if a receiver had managed to get both feet in bounds as he made a leaping catch in the end zone.

"He was in," Brian said before the replay was shown. "That was an incredible catch." The replay proved him right. They watched the next few plays with little comment. When the commercial break came, Brian turned to Bishop and said, "That was awful what happened to your football coach. Steph was quite shaken by the experience. She had only been at Trinity less than a month. Even though she hadn't said more that 'hello' to the man, it was quite unsettling. I'm sure it's been much more difficult for you."

"Yes, it's been tough. Unfortunately, I was the one that found him."

"So I hear. That must have been quite a shock. Do the authorities have any suspects?"

Bishop wasn't about to admit that Lieutenant Hodge and his men seemed to have hit a brick wall in their investigation. "I'm sure that they're still working on it. Apparently, several people had motive and opportunity, but there's not enough hard evidence to arrest anyone." He wanted to add "yet" but kept that to himself. Most likely, Steph had not told her father about her meeting with Zappala at the Blue Moon. She wouldn't have told Michael either if Sarah Humphries' comments had not prompted him to question her about it. Bishop made a few general remarks about the tragic event and was rescued when the seemingly endless string of commercials concluded and the game resumed.

Perhaps sensing the need to change the topic, Brian remarked that Ron seemed like a great guy. Bishop wholeheartedly agreed and added that he was highly regarded by students as well as the staff.

"Steph is happier than I've seen her in a long time. She loves her new job and her new apartment. And although she hasn't known him for very long, she seems to really like Ron, and you, of course," he added with a smile. "About the only one I hear her complain about is that other administrator … what's her name … Sister Pat."

Not wanting to speak ill of a colleague, Bishop simply said, "Well, she's not alone in that regard."

The front door opened and Ron and Stephanie came in. Steph said, "You should have come with us, Mike. That fresh air was so invigorating. I'm ready for dessert!" With that, she headed into the kitchen to help her mother, and Ron sat down to pick up on the game.

Soon, Steph and her mother emerged from the kitchen with desserts that would have been sufficient as meals in themselves. There was pumpkin pie, apple pie, ice cream, whipped cream, and the Italian pastries that Bishop had brought along. They chatted happily about everything and nothing over a second cup of coffee, or in Bishop's case, tea. When the dessert dishes were cleared, June went into another room to call her sister in Denver. The others sat at the dining room table and played a game of Scrabble. That seemed a safe bet for a guest who was an English teacher. As he played, he was reminded of another board game that he had enjoyed as a child in which a murder had been committed and the players had to figure out who did it. Was it the bald-headed man who used a rope? Was it the old woman who used a knife? Was it Chris Delaney? His father? Rocco Santorini? Doug Sanders? Russ Chandler? Sister Ann? Sister Pat? Was it someone else? At least in the game he remembered, there always was an answer.

The game ended as the duo of Bishop and Brian edged out Ron and Stephanie. She excused herself to make a few calls to some of her college friends, Ron headed for the sofa where he promptly dozed off, and Bishop and Brian decided to walk around the yard. The lawn and gardens had been expertly prepped for the coming winter. Bishop wondered whether the Harrises did their own yard work or hired professionals, but didn't ask. Brian pointed to a tree that was about as tall as his two-story home. The base had to be a foot in diameter, and its bare branches were perfectly shaped. "I planted that maple shortly after Steph arrived. I used to take a picture of her standing next to it every year."

Bishop said, "You and your wife must be very proud of your daughter."

"She's a wonderful young woman as I'm sure you've discovered for yourself. June and I were never able to have children of our own, but we were certainly blessed when Steph came into our lives. I can still remember the sense of absolute joy we felt as we drove up to Middleton to bring her home."

Bishop felt a sense of déjà vu, but he couldn't quite put his finger on what had triggered it. The two men continued to make their way around the yard, and then went back into the house. Ron, refreshed from his short nap, was entertaining Steph and her mother with one of his favorite stories. Bishop had heard the story many times of how Ron's picture ended up on the front page of the *Groveland Gazette*. It was the first day of fishing season and a school day. A reporter, doing a story from one of the hotspots along Cattleman's Creek, approached a teenaged angler. "Aren't you supposed to be in school, young man?" The lad looked at his watch and admitted that he should have been in Calculus class at Holy Trinity at that very moment. The reporter then asked, "How do you think school officials would react if they knew that you were out here fishing?"

Without any hesitation, the young man replied, "Well, I'm not sure, but the assistant principal is right over there," pointing to a man standing in the creek about ten yards away. "Why don't you just ask him?" Everyone had a good laugh including Ron himself.

Bishop looked at his watch and regretfully announced that it was time for him to get going. He had had a wonderful day and thanked the Harrises for their hospitality and Steph and Ron for inviting him to share in their celebration. June wanted him to take some leftovers, and it took several refusals for her to give up on the idea. He had made a reservation at a motel in Brentwood for the night so that he could spend some time with his Aunt Katherine on Friday before heading back to Groveland.

It took more than thirty minutes for him to actually leave as he said his goodbyes. This process moved from the house to the driveway. Finally, he started the engine, backed out of the driveway, tooted his horn and waved as all four of them watched. Bishop soon passed a sign that read "Leaving Fairmont." He was, however, not on the road to Brentwood. This road would take him to Middleton.

Chapter 28

When he was about ten miles north of Fairmont, he pulled into a rest stop. Once he had started driving, he realized what had been bothering him about the Harris family photo on the mantle. His theory was terribly disturbing to ponder, but he had to put it to the test. He had printed out a copy of his reservation for his stay in Brentwood. Since it was before 6:00 p.m., he was able to cancel his reservation without penalty. The second call was a bit more difficult.

"Hello, Michael. I wasn't expecting to hear from you until tomorrow," said Aunt Katherine. She was ninety-three years old, but her mind was still sharp. He hoped that he shared that gene with her.

"Well, that's why I'm calling."

"Is there anything wrong? You're not sick, are you?"

"No, no, nothing like that. Something came up that I need to take care of, so I won't be able to visit you tomorrow."

He could hear the disappointment in her voice. "That's all right, Michael. I understand."

"I'll definitely come up during the Christmas break."

They chatted for a few more minutes as she recounted for him the Thanksgiving Day dinner that she had shared with the other residents of the facility. She had transitioned from her own apartment to the nursing home rather easily. Although the home was pleasant and well run, it brought with it its own set of limitations. Bishop was determined to live in his own home as long as possible.

It was late when he pulled into the crowded parking lot of a Hampton Inn in Middleton. A young man at the desk greeted him. He was probably a college student working the night shift. At first, Bishop thought that he had a speech impediment, but he quickly realized that Jeff, which was the name on the tag that hung from his neck, had a post in his tongue. He couldn't imagine why anyone would want to do that to themselves, but to each his own.

He grabbed a cup of hot tea at the hospitality table set up for guests. He was pleasantly surprised that they had a variety of teas from which to choose including his favorite, Earl Grey. He carried his small overnight bag and the cup of tea up to his room.

He didn't expect to get much sleep, but he did need a place to shower and shave and to think. Stephanie had been adopted. That was what struck him about the family photo. Steph looked nothing like either one of her parents. Brian said that she had been born in Middleton. He didn't remember her ever telling him that. Middleton. There was something familiar about that as well, but he had drawn a blank as to what that something was. Then, as he settled in for his drive to Brentwood, he had remembered. When Maria Santorini had told him about the trouble her brother had gotten into in his first year of teaching, he had done a quick online search for schools with the name of Immaculate Heart in Connecticut. There were two, and one of them was located in Middleton. With that recognition, Bishop had pulled into the rest stop. The words of Othello came to mind: "To be once in doubt/ Is once to be resolved." Could he be on the verge of finding the missing piece of information that so far had eluded him? Was this another dead end? He needed to know the truth, however painful that might be.

***

He expected that the school would be closed on the day after Thanksgiving. The name of the current principal was on a piece of paper in his study at home. Although he was certain that he could have easily obtained that information on the Internet, he was unsure that it would be of any benefit. Whoever was the principal now was unlikely to have been the principal then. So what if he located the school where Zappala first taught? What would that prove? How would that knowledge bring him any closer to the identity of the killer? It was similar to his experience in Madison when he had found the house in which Zappala had lived. It was his conversation with Honesty Jones that had made the difference. Somehow he had to find someone who knew Zappala many years earlier. Perhaps he had overreacted when Stephanie's father had mentioned Middleton. What difference did it make if she had been born in the same town where Zappala had once worked? It was a small world as he was frequently reminded when he bumped into former students in airports or restaurants hundreds of miles from home.

Bishop decided that he would pass by the school building out of curiosity if nothing else. As he did, he noticed one car in the parking lot closest to the front entrance. Perhaps someone had had car trouble and was forced to leave the car there. Perhaps it belonged to a maintenance worker. He parked next to the car, a tan Nissan Altima, and tried the front door of the building. It was locked. He banged on the door a few times, not really expecting that his action would yield any result. As he made his way back to his car, the door opened and an older woman called out, "May I help you?"

"I hope so." Bishop introduced himself. When he told her that he was an English teacher at a Catholic school, she smiled. "So am I." He went on to explain that he was looking for information on a former faculty member at Immaculate Heart. "His name was Albert Zappala. He was a colleague of mine at Holy Trinity."

"I assume you are using the past tense for a reason?"

"You are quite right, Mrs.?"

"Bagley. Miss Edith Bagley. Why don't you come in, Mr. Bishop? It's a bit nippy out here."

Miss Bagley was wearing a deep blue dress accented with a string of pearls and what Bishop thought of as old-lady shoes, whose plain black leather and low heels were comfortable, if not very fashionable. Not a hair on her head was out of place. She seemed dressed for a day of teaching rather than a day off. Bishop was very much dressed down with his fleece sweatshirt, jeans, and sneakers. He hoped that Shakespeare's Polonius was wrong when he advised Laertes that "the apparel oft proclaims the man." Miss Bagley had stopped by the school to run off some papers that she needed first thing on Monday morning so they talked in the copy room. Bishop explained that Mr. Zappala had died a few months earlier, and that he had been appointed executor of the estate. He intentionally left out many details, but provided enough of a context to justify his visit.

"Zappala, you say? When was he here?"

"About twenty-five years ago."

"I started at the Heart in '78. Been here thirty-seven years," she announced with obvious pride. She was an English teacher also, which worked to Bishop's advantage. "Zappala. Zappala. The name sounded vaguely familiar when you first mentioned it, but there have been so many teachers who have come and gone over the years, it is hard to keep them all straight sometimes."

"I know exactly what you mean," he said sympathetically. "Sometimes I find myself looking at an old yearbook to jog my memory."

"A yearbook! That's the ticket! If I see a picture, I know I'll remember him." She was now on a mission herself. She left her copying work unfinished and invited Bishop to follow as she headed off to the library. On the way through the darkened halls, they talked about books and teaching. She mentioned that one of her classes was reading Joseph Conrad's *Heart of Darkness*. Bishop tried to dismiss the thought that he, like Marlow, was headed into the darkness to confront evil.

"Here we are," Miss Bagley announced as she gestured toward a long row of similarly shaped books on the shelf. "We have every copy of *The Emblem* from 1959 on. What year did you say it was?"

"Try 1985."

She pulled that volume from the shelf and began flipping through the pages. She found the faculty section. Her photo was on the first page of that section since the listings had been arranged alphabetically. "Would you look at that photo of me? My word. Where have the years gone?"

She passed the book to him, and he looked at the picture of an attractive young woman with a bright smile, and then he looked at Miss Bagley. "You haven't changed much at all, my dear!" She laughed as she accepted his compliment. Then he flipped to the last page of the faculty section and there he found Albert C. Zappala. His hair was black and rather long. He was much thinner than Bishop ever would have imagined. He looked perfectly normal except for the fact that he was not smiling. From what Maria Santorini had told him, Bishop felt that he knew why. He asked Miss Bagley if she remembered Zappala.

She took the book in both hands in order to examine it more closely. "I do remember him, now. Says here he taught Physical Education. Our paths probably didn't cross too often. I seem to recall that he got into some difficulty. Only stayed that one year. That's usually a sign of something serious. Normally, they give a new teacher a couple of years to grow into the job."

"Difficulty? What type of difficulty?"

"I really couldn't say. It would only be rumors, and I don't want to spread rumors about a man, even a man who's dead."

"Of course not. I understand." In fact, he felt that he probably already knew more about the difficulty than she did. He was ready to thank her for her time. He had gotten about as far with this as he was likely going to get.

Miss Bagley turned the pages of the faculty section, pausing to comment on some. "That's Marge Randolph. Poor woman got cancer. Passed away a few years ago. She was a wonderful Latin teacher." Turning another page, she gave a little chuckle. "That's George Mendoza. He was the assistant principal back then. Wonderful man. Wonderful sense of humor. Guess that's why he's lasted as long as he has." She handed the yearbook back to him, and, by force of habit, he simply leafed through the pages. There were all the standard photos of the students engaged in various school functions. Drama, basketball, dances, candids shot in the cafeteria. He glanced at some of the portraits of the seniors. Then he saw it. He strained in the light to get a better look. The name under the photo was Mary Gilbert. Bishop felt as if all the air had been sucked from his lungs. In the brief bio, he noted that Mary Gilbert had been a cheerleader. Perhaps she had been Zappala's first victim. She was most likely the first to become pregnant. Maria Santorini had been wrong. All these years she thought that her brother had used the money to pay for an abortion and for her silence. That must have been what Zappala told her. That must have been his intention. But the evidence was clear. Mary Gilbert had not had the abortion. She had given birth to a daughter that she gave up for adoption. He stared at the photo of Mary Gilbert. Her physical resemblance to someone that he knew was unmistakable. When he looked at the eyes and the smile of this beautiful young girl, he saw Stephanie Harris.

***

Bishop suddenly felt lightheaded. His heart was racing. "Would you mind if I sat down for a moment?"

"Not at all," she replied as she took a chair from the librarian's desk. "Are you all right, Mr. Bishop? Would you like a glass of water?"

"I'm fine, really," he said, hoping to disguise how terribly sick he did feel. "A glass of water sounds good. I think I might be a little dehydrated."

Miss Bagley returned in a moment with a paper cup filled with cold water and a small package of crackers. "I raided Eleanor's stash of goodies. I'm sure that she won't mind."

Bishop took a sip of the water, opened the package, and nibbled on a cracker. He assured Miss Bagley that he was feeling much better. The yearbook on his lap was still open to the page with the photo of Mary Gilbert.

"Miss Bagley, do you remember this girl?" He handed her the book as he pointed to the photo.

"Why do you ask?"

"Just curious. She looks very much like someone I know." If she didn't make a connection between Zappala and the girl, he wasn't about to suggest that one existed.

She looked at the name and the photo, thought about it for a moment, and slowly the painful memory returned. "Yes, I do remember Mary. She was a lovely girl, bright. Wanted to become a lawyer. She'd been accepted at Columbia, but she never went." Her voice trailed off to a whisper as she recalled the sad story.

"What happened?" he asked, hoping that Miss Bagley would feel comfortable enough to continue. He needed to be able to fill in the gaps in his own understanding of the past.

"It's a terrible thing, Mr. Bishop, but I'm sure you have witnessed this in your own experience as a teacher. Mary became pregnant in her senior year. Her parents wanted her to have an abortion, but she refused. She moved in with a girlfriend and finished out the year on home study."

"What about the father?"

"That's even sadder."

Bishop expected that she might now explain her earlier reference to Zappala's "difficulty." Instead, she turned the pages of the yearbook until she found the photo of Dennis Riordan with his big toothy smile and mop of blonde hair. "That's him," she said, tapping the page with her index finger. "Everyone knew that they had been dating. He must have been the father, but he insisted that he wasn't. He abandoned Mary when she needed him the most. He died in a motorcycle accident shortly after graduation."

Although she had stopped speaking, he sensed that she was considering whether or not she should say any more. He stood up as if he were ready to leave. "You've been so helpful, Miss Bagley. I truly appreciate your sharing this with me."

"There's one more thing."

"Yes?"

"Some people were convinced that it wasn't an accident. They said that Dennis had been so upset over what had happened that he might have…" She hesitated to put the rest into words.

"I understand," Bishop said softly. He actually understood more than Miss Bagley at this point. Dennis Riordan had insisted that he wasn't the father because he knew that he wasn't. He also would have felt betrayed by Mary who was pregnant by another man. He wondered if Zappala knew that he was responsible for the death of this young man, and if he knew, had he felt any remorse?

"Mr. Bishop? Are you sure that you are all right?"

He was so lost in his thoughts that he had for a moment forgotten that she was standing there. He assured her that he was fine and that she had been very kind to go to all this trouble for him. He had one more favor to ask. He wanted to make copies of a few pages. "I'll be happy to pay for them."

"Don't be silly. A few copies won't break the budget. Just give me the page numbers," she said, as she turned on the copier to let it warm up. With the copies he wanted in hand, they left the library, and she walked him back to the front entrance.

"It was very nice meeting you, Mr. Bishop. I hope you find what you are looking for." Bishop got into his car, waved to Miss Bagley, and drove away. He had no idea where he was going. He needed time to think. Could Mary Gilbert be the killer? She certainly would have had a motive. But why would she have waited so many years? How would she have obtained the poison? Perhaps she had hired someone to do the dirty work for her. He wondered if Stephanie knew about her birth mother. Had she been in contact with her? Could Steph have helped her by taking the poison from the science lab? He had no more idea where these thoughts were taking him than he did where this road was taking him. He kept thinking of more questions. Had Zappala recognized the similarities between Mary Gilbert and Stephanie Harris? He often told his students that it was more important to be able to ask the right questions than it was to know all the answers. Was he asking the right questions?

He pulled into a gas station and filled the tank. After getting back in the car, he reprogrammed his GPS. His destination was 156 Westlake Road. That was the address included in Mary Gilbert's yearbook bio. It was possible that her parents were still living there. Even if he found them, it was possible that they would not talk to him. He knew that he had to take that chance.

Chapter 29

Before he had a chance to thoroughly consider what he would say to the Gilberts, he found himself in front of their modest home. It was an old mobile home with a broken screen door. Toys were strewn about the yard, remaining where their owner had lost interest in them. As he knocked on the door, his heart was pounding. He was surprised when a man who looked to be about thirty years old appeared. He was holding a baby in one arm, and there was a toddler hanging on to his pant leg. "Whatever you're selling, I'm not interested. Sorry."

"I'm not selling anything. My name is Michael Bishop. Is this the residence of the Gilbert family?" He spoke rapidly fearing that the door was about to be shut in his face.

Before he could say anymore, the man replied, "Yeah, it was. My wife and I bought the place about six months ago." He was clearly interested in ending the conversation and turning his attention back to his own family. "The wife's out shopping, and I'm trying to hold down the fort here. Nice to have met you." He was ready to close the door on Bishop and the cold air that was streaming into his home.

"Wait, please. I'd really like to find the Gilberts. Do you know where they are now?"

"We bought the house from the estate of Mrs. Gilbert. She must have died about a year ago. I gather that she had been a widow living here alone for quite a while." The telephone rang. "Listen, I'm sorry, but I better pick that up."

"Yes, of course. Thanks. You've helped a great deal." He winked at the little one who immediately hid her face in her father's shoulder. He should have asked Miss Bagley where Mr. Mendoza lived when she had mentioned his name. He drove back to the school, but the Nissan was no longer in the parking lot. He pulled in to a convenient store just a block from the school. As he approached the counter, it occurred to him that in a small town where everyone knew practically everyone, the clerk might know Mr. Mendoza.

A young lady with streaks of purple in her long dark hair handed change and a receipt to the teenager in front of him. "Excuse me, miss. I'm looking for an old friend of mine. Would you happen to know a Mr. George Mendoza?" The woman, whose nametag simply read "Clarisse," quickly appraised Bishop and must have decided that although he was a stranger, he appeared harmless enough. She turned toward a back room and shouted, "Hey, Shirley, come out here for a sec." She turned back to Bishop and explained, "She's been here a lot longer than me. She might know." Another woman came up to the counter. She was wearing the same company uniform as Clarisse. "This guy is looking for a George …" She had forgotten the last name so Bishop finished her sentence by adding "Mendoza."

"Know him? As a matter of fact I do. He goes to the library across the street once a week and then he usually comes in here to pick up a few things. Did you teach at the Heart? You don't look familiar."

Bishop explained that he was a teacher, but not at the Heart. He came up with some vague story about having met him at a conference years earlier. "I'm only in town for the day. I thought I would try to look him up."

"He lives at the Tower Hill Nursing Home now. If you follow this road for about two miles, you'll see a sign for it. Take a right, and it's up the hill about a mile and a half." Bishop thanked her and left.

***

As he drove up the hill, he tried to imagine life in a nursing home. If the facility was well run, and if you had people who cared about you, it could feel like living at a country club; if you didn't, it could feel like a prison. If you didn't still have your wits about you, it probably didn't matter too much. At seventy, he was hoping that he would be able to live in his own home for another twenty years. Every time he thought about nursing homes, he recalled Eudora Welty's short story, "A Visit of Charity." A young girl named Marian is both frightened and enlightened during her surreal visit with two of the residents of the old ladies' home. That story always generated good class discussion as the students struggled to determine the meaning of the ending when Marian takes a big bite out an apple that she had hidden before entering the home.

He pulled into the entrance for the Tower Hill Nursing Home, and stopped in front of the gate that stretched across the driveway. A middle-aged man put down his magazine and leaned out of the doorway of the gatehouse. He greeted Bishop with a friendly smile. "Good morning, sir. Your name, please."

He hadn't expected to have to answer any questions to get in. "Michael Bishop."

He picked up his clipboard. "And who are you visiting today, Mr. Bishop?"

"George Mendoza."

He flipped through a few pages on the clipboard, and said, "I'm afraid I don't see your name on the guest list."

"Well, no, it wouldn't be there. I'm afraid I didn't call ahead. I just happened to be in the area, and I thought I would make a quick visit." He felt uncomfortable giving the impression that he and George were friends. At least what he had said was true.

The guard thought about it for a moment, then handed him the clipboard so that he could enter his name, the name of the person he was visiting, the license plate number of his car, and the time of day. As he handed the clipboard back, the gate began to lift. "Have a nice visit, Mr. Bishop. I'll call the front desk to let them know you're coming."

"Thank you," said Bishop as he put his car in gear and drove toward the building. He hadn't expected such elaborate security. Perhaps there had been some problem in the past, or perhaps they were just giving their residents peace of mind.

He was met at the entrance by another security guard. "You must be Mr. Bishop," he said as he pointed to another sign-in sheet.

"I believe Mr. Mendoza is in the Common Room watching television. Go through these doors, and it's the first room on your left."

Bishop found the room and stood outside the closed glass door for a moment. He could see a half a dozen old men sitting in front of a huge flat screen television. Despite the raised volume that made it possible to clearly hear the words of the anchor through the closed door, several of the gentlemen had nodded off. He gently opened the door. None of the residents seemed to notice, but an attendant who was seated in the back of the room quickly rose to meet him. "May I help you, sir?"

"Yes. I'm looking for George Mendoza. I was told at the desk that he was in here."

"That's him in the blue sweater. What's your name? I'll tell him you're here."

He gave the man his name, but before he could explain that Mendoza wouldn't know who he was, the attendant was tapping Mr. Mendoza on the shoulder and pointing to Bishop standing near the door, trying to look friendly. The old man grabbed his cane and made his way over to his visitor. He was wearing a cardigan sweater, a white shirt and baggy khaki-colored slacks. He shifted his cane to his left hand and reached out to shake Bishop's hand. "Bishop. Bishop. I don't recall any Bishops. Taught a Pope once. What year did you graduate?"

Bishop explained that he hadn't graduated from Immaculate Heart and that he currently taught at Holy Trinity in Groveland. He said that he was hoping to ask him a few questions about some people that he might have known. Mr. Mendoza looked a bit confused, but when Bishop mentioned that he had been talking to Edith Bagley earlier that day, he said, "Oh, you're a friend of Edith's. She's a wonderful lady. Why don't we go someplace where we can talk? That TV is so loud. They must think we're all deaf!" He led the way down the hall into a small visiting room. He offered Bishop a seat, and then slowly settled himself into a chair. "I bring guests in here all the time, that is when I have guests. They keep it a lot neater than I keep my room," he laughed.

Although he desperately wanted to get to the important questions, Bishop felt that it wise to spend a few minutes establishing a connection with this kindly old man. He tried to put thoughts of himself one day living in a place like this out of his mind.

"I understand that you are a regular at the library."

"I manage to escape this place once a week," he said with a grin. "Not that it's that bad, you understand. But I like to get out, you know. Go out to eat. Go to the library. I try to stay active. That's the secret, you know."

As the old man said those words, Bishop wondered if there was another secret that he knew and more importantly, if he would be willing to share it. After a few minutes, he decided that he had to approach the topic that had brought him here. He took the photocopies out of his jacket pocket, unfolded the one with Zappala on it, and handed it to Mendoza. While he stared at the paper, Bishop briefly told him about the unsolved murder of his colleague at Trinity. At the mention of Zappala's name, the old man shook his head. "Can't say that I feel sorry that he's dead. He committed the cardinal sin in teaching. Pardon the pun, Bishop."

"What's that?"

"You're a teacher yourself. You must know the most important rule." The old man waited for a response. Bishop realized that he was being quizzed by this retired educator, and that if he failed to give the correct answer, the lesson might be over.

"Never get too close to the students," he responded.

"Exactly!" Mendoza went on to explain the incident as if it were yesterday instead of decades ago. "I had forgotten some books that I needed for the weekend, so I went back to the office used by the male lay teachers. The door was locked, but I had a key. When I put on the light, I caught him 'in the act.' I should have killed him myself." His eyes became misty as he spoke. "Fr. Dowd, who was the principal then, hushed everything up. He didn't want any bad publicity for the school. Zappala 'resigned' at the end of the school year, and Dowd promised to give him a good letter of recommendation as long as he promised to move out of the area. I was Dowd's closest friend. I guess he had to confide in someone."

"Unbelievable!" Bishop said more to himself than to Mr. Mendoza. He recalled his conversation with Edward Bostwick, the principal at Madison, who had also let Zappala walk away after his encounter with Honesty Jones.

"Was the girl Mary Gilbert?"

"Yes. That's right. Only a few people knew that at the time."

"What happened to her?"

"She had been too frightened to tell her parents. When they found out that she was pregnant, they threw her out of the house. Their only child, and they threw her out! Most people thought that Riordan boy was the father. That was sad, too." He was shaking his head in disbelief.

"Do you know what happened to her?" asked Bishop, pushing the old man for more information.

"I heard that she gave up the baby and moved to New York City. Her life went downhill after that. She's dead now, you know. Fr. Dowd got transferred out to Minnesota a few years later after he was accused of molesting a boy. He died out there. Now Zappala's dead. That's the end of the story." The two men sat in silence for several moments.

Bishop stayed a while longer to talk with the old man. He apologized to Mendoza for asking him to recall a terrible chapter in his life, and he thanked him for his cooperation. The old man slowly made his way back to the Common Room, and Bishop signed out at the desk. It had taken less than thirty minutes for him to acquire the missing details that had eluded him for the last couple of months. However, for Bishop, it was not quite the end of the story. He still needed to confront the killer.

Chapter 30

As Bishop drove back to Groveland, he tried to come to terms with the fact that the woman who twenty-four hours earlier had seemed to have such a bright future was the person who had killed Albert C. Zappala, the man who was her biological father. The events of this day had given new meaning to the term, "Black Friday."

When he looked at the yearbook photo of Mary Gilbert, he knew that he was looking at the mother of Stephanie Harris. When Zappala saw Stephanie on the first day of the new school year, he must have realized that she was the child that Mary Gilbert had refused to abort, his child. He must have decided to tell Stephanie the truth when Jenny Forrest had interrupted them. What really transpired at the Blue Moon must have been far different from what Stephanie had told him. Bishop recalled her reluctance to talk about that meeting. He remembered her telling him that the coach had said she was "good looking." She said that Zappala had made some sort of inappropriate suggestion that had offended her deeply. That was exactly what Stephanie wanted him to think.

The more he thought about it, the more sense it made. She had thought her biological father had been killed in a motorcycle accident. To find out that he was still alive would have been a shock. To realize that the man who had ruined her mother's life was now a colleague that she would see regularly in the halls, at lunch, at meetings, and at parties would have been too much to accept. She must have wanted to kill him at that moment.

The idea that she was a coldblooded murderer sent chills throughout his body. He had prided himself as being a good judge of character. How could he have been so wrong about her? Poor Ron! He had no idea that his current happiness was about to end. Then he stopped himself. What was he thinking? He had discovered that Zappala was

Stephanie's real father. He had discovered that Mary Gilbert, Stephanie's real mother, had been Zappala's first victim. So what? Although that knowledge might have given her a motive to kill him, he had no proof that Stephanie had done anything wrong. Was he really any closer to bringing this saga to a conclusion?

***

Bishop arrived back at his home on Pleasant Hill Road at about ten that evening. Christmas lights illuminated many of the houses that he passed. He had not bothered with decorations for his own house since Grace's death. He had been looking forward to the holidays this year. Not any more.

Tired and hungry after his drive, he decided to have some soup. He opened a can of minestrone and heated its contents in the microwave. He sat out in the sunroom with only a reading lamp providing illumination. With a CD of Mozart's sonatas playing in the background, he sought illumination for the dilemma that he faced. How would he be able to determine if Stephanie had killed her own father? And if she were innocent, would the identity of the murderer ever be known? Every fiber of his being wanted to believe that Rocco had done it. He had admitted to being at his uncle's house that night, and he had the most to gain. When he went to bed a couple of hours later, he had decided on a strategy that might provide him the answers that he, like Melville's Ahab, so desperately sought.

***

On Saturday, Bishop made a few phone calls. One was to Stephanie. She sounded a bit surprised by his call. "I wasn't expecting to hear from you. Is everything all right?"

"Yes, yes. Everything's fine."

"How was your visit with your Aunt Katherine?"

Bishop responded without hesitation. "Very nice. She told me all about the Thanksgiving dinner that the staff had prepared for the residents. Then she gave me a rundown on all of the people who had called to wish her a Happy Thanksgiving. I took her to lunch at her favorite restaurant, and she insisted on paying the bill." He was mildly surprised at how easily he could fabricate a story. He asked Stephanie how her shopping went, and she excitedly listed a few of the best deals that she had snagged.

Bishop knew that he had to get to the purpose of the call. "Where's Ron?"

"He's helping my father clean the gutters. He really is such a sweet guy! Do you want to talk to him?"

"No, actually. I don't want Ron to hear this."

"Hear what?"

"Jason Moore wants me to write a blurb about Ron."

Stephanie said, "I don't understand."

Bishop reminded her that Jason was the moderator of *The Trinitarian*, the school's yearbook. The staff had voted to honor Ron by dedicating the yearbook to him. Since everyone knew that Ron and Michael were good friends, Jason wanted him to write a piece in which he explained what Ron means to Holy Trinity and why he is so deserving of this honor. Again, the fabrication came easily. Having recently looked through Immaculate Heart's *Emblem* gave him the inspiration for that fib.

"Oh, my God! Seriously? That's terrific!" She was as excited as if she had been the one selected.

"Of course, you can't tell him. Only a few people ever know the identity of the honoree until the yearbooks are presented in June. I'm counting on you to keep this hush hush."

Naturally, she promised that she would not tell a soul, but she asked him why he had told her about it in the first place. He explained that he had to turn in his comments on Monday morning so that the yearbook staff could meet one of their many deadlines, and he was hoping that she might be able to stop by his home on Sunday evening to give him some feedback on what he had written. She said that she would be glad to help, but that she had promised that she would pick up her landlady, Henrietta, at the airport.

"What time is her flight coming in?"

"9:10 p.m."

"That shouldn't be a problem. Why don't you stop by around eight? It shouldn't take more than a half an hour to polish up my statement. I already have a rough draft."

"Great! I'll see you then!"

Bishop was far less enthused by the prospect of their meeting. Nevertheless, he knew what he had to do. "Have a safe trip home." He concluded the call as quickly as possible. Tomorrow would come soon enough, and he wanted to be fully prepared.

Sleep was almost impossible as he played out a number of different scenarios of his upcoming conversation with Stephanie. What if she denied everything? He did not have one shred of evidence linking her directly to the murder. So what if she had concealed the fact that Zappala was her father? Given the circumstances, that was a reasonable course of action. Murder, however, was not.

***

When he awoke the next morning, it was still dark. Having tried unsuccessfully to fall back to sleep, he went into the bathroom to shave and shower. His mind was already in overdrive in anticipation of his meeting with Stephanie that evening. If his theory proved correct, it would result in pain for Stephanie, for her parents, for Ron, for the entire Holy Trinity community including himself. If he were wrong, he would suffer only the embarrassment of someone who had no business playing detective. Either way, Bishop knew that this would be a day that he would remember for a long time.

He brought his breakfast of rye toast and green tea out to the sunroom. Even though it was well past sunrise, it was still so dark that he had to turn on a lamp. A massive bank of dark clouds loomed above, matching his inner turmoil. He resolved to fill his day as much as possible with chores that he had been neglecting. He did several loads of laundry, ironed his shirts for the upcoming week, vacuumed the carpets upstairs and down, and did some grocery shopping. He also moved his tractor and a few boxes from the second bay of the garage.

As the hour approached, he found himself unable to concentrate on any serious reading and had kept busy by thumbing through stacks of magazines piled in a heap on the floor of his study. A recording of Bach's Brandenburg Concertos played softly in the background.

Since there was never much traffic on his road, he heard Stephanie's car as she pulled into the driveway. He waited at the front door as she got out of her car and approached the house. She was wearing a tan windbreaker and jeans that disappeared into her leather boots. When she saw him, her face lit up in a big smile. Bishop didn't think that he had ever seen her happier.

"Right on time! Come on in!" said Bishop as he took her jacket and placed it on a hanger in the hall closet. She was wearing a pink cable knit sweater that she had probably purchased during her Black Friday shopping spree.

"This is such exciting news about Ron. I really wanted to tell him, but I managed to control that impulse," she said with a laugh.

He invited Steph to make herself comfortable in the sunroom while he went into the kitchen to make some tea. When she offered to help, he insisted that it was unnecessary and that he could boil water and remove pastries from a box and put them on a serving dish as well as anyone.

Although he didn't have much of an appetite, he managed to eat half of a half moon and took a few sips from his cup of tea. They chatted for a few minutes about the Thanksgiving day that they had shared. She was so pleased that her parents liked Ron and vice versa. He was working up the courage to begin the conversation that was the real reason that he asked her to his home.

"Mike, why don't you let me see what you've written about Ron so far? I'll have to leave soon to meet Henrietta at the airport."

"I haven't written anything," he said as his discomfort increased.

"Isn't it due tomorrow? We better get to work on it right now."

"There's no need for that."

Steph was bewildered. "Why not?"

"Because Ron hasn't been nominated."

Steph's voice grew louder, fueled by her confusion. "But you told me that he was! Why would you tell me something like that if it wasn't true?"

He took a piece of paper out of his pocket, unfolded it, placed it on the table, and pushed it towards her. His hands were shaking a bit, and his heart was racing. He had no idea how she would react. "Do you know who this is?"

She glanced at the copy of the yearbook page containing the photo of Mary Gilbert. "No!" She shouted as she pushed the paper back towards him. Her face became flushed as she fought for control. She grabbed her purse and got up to leave. "I don't know what kind of a game you're playing, but I'm out."

Bishop had decided to use the strategy that Ron had employed so well in getting Eric Munro to confess to the vandalism.

"I'm not playing a game, Steph. I'm trying to help you. You can't live a lie. I know that this woman," as he pointed to the photo," was your mother. I know that Albert Zappala was your father. And I know that you poisoned him." There was a moment of silence as she considered her options. Then she exploded. "What? Are you out of your mind? My father died in a motorcycle accident."

"Dennis Riordan did die in a motorcycle accident, but he wasn't your father," Bishop said with as much calm as he could muster.

"How would you know about Dennis?" she shouted.

"When your dad mentioned that you had been born in Middleton, I decided to drive up that way."

"You never went to visit your aunt?"

"No."

"You liar! I trusted you! I thought you were my friend!" Her lips began to tremble, and he knew that tears would soon follow. Yet, it was necessary that he continue.

"I'm sorry that I had to deceive you, but it was the only way to get to the truth. When did you first realize that Riordan wasn't your father?"

She slumped back down into her chair. She had given up trying to pretend. "I knew when I saw my birth certificate. Instead of the name of the father, 'Unknown' had been typed in. Even if he denied that he was the father, I felt certain that my mother would have had his name recorded on the birth certificate if for no other reason than to try to obtain some child support. There had to have been another reason why she would have chosen not to identify the father. I never knew more than that until that day I met Zappala at the Blue Moon."

"Did he threaten you in some way?" Bishop hoped that this might be true. In that case, the horror of what she had done would be mitigated by self-defense. He was giving her a plausible way to explain her decision to take the life of another human being.

She dabbed at her eyes with a tissue. "It's funny. From my first day at Trinity, I noticed him staring at me. It was kind of creepy. We hardly ever spoke. Then that day in the lounge when no one was around, he asked me if I would meet him after practice to discuss the possibility of helping out with the cheerleaders. I didn't like the way he looked at me, but I was interested in the cheerleading position, so I agreed." She seemed relieved that she was going to be able to tell someone what had really happened.

"He didn't want to talk about cheerleading, did he?" Bishop asked sympathetically.

"He was late, and I was thinking about leaving when he walked in. He ordered a coffee. He just sat there looking at me and smiling. When I began to gather my things, he stopped me in my tracks by asking me if I had been born in Middleton. I sat back down. My whole body was shaking. I couldn't imagine how he might possibly know that. I didn't know it myself for a long time."

"What did you say?"

"I didn't say anything. I didn't know what he wanted. Then he said, 'You look just like your mother. It's goddamn amazing.' I was convinced that he had me mixed up with someone else. I told him that I really didn't look like my mother at all."

"How did he respond to that?"

"He laughed at first. Then he told me that he meant my real mother, Mary Gilbert." I couldn't imagine how he knew. I told him that I didn't know what he was talking about. He just laughed again as I started to cry. He reached into his bag and pulled out an old yearbook. He flipped through the pages until he found what he was looking for, and pushed it in front of me. I had never seen a picture of my mother. The resemblance was uncanny. I shoved the book back at him and said through my tears, 'You bastard! You're my father?'" Bishop handed Stephanie some tissues and held her hand as she struggled to continue. "I asked him how he could have treated my mother that way. You know what he said?"

"I can imagine."

"He talked about how she had wanted it as much as he had. He said, 'That Riordan kid was too nice. Not me.'" Had she a gun, she would have shot him right then. She said that she slapped him across the face, bolted from the bar, and drove back to her apartment. The whole experience had been worse than a nightmare. She went up to the attic to cry. She knew that Henrietta would not be able to hear her from there. It became quite chilly, and Steph opened a cedar chest hoping to find a blanket to wrap herself in.

"That's when I found the gun. I couldn't imagine Henrietta owning a gun, but then I remembered her telling me that her brother had often worried about her living alone and had given her something 'just in case.' I thought she had meant a baseball bat or something. Once I realized that there were also some bullets in a box, I started to think about how I could do it."

Bishop listened attentively giving her the opportunity to make a full confession.

"Then I realized that I couldn't just walk up to him at school and put a bullet in his head. I had to come up with another way to do it, one that would not cast suspicion on me."

"The cyanide?"

"Sister Pascala had asked me to cover her lab one day. One of the students had broken a beaker, and I went into the storeroom looking for a dustpan and broom. After the mess was cleaned up, I went back to the storeroom. That's when I noticed the key to the cabinet. I didn't know what I was looking for, but as soon as I saw that bottle with the skull and crossbones, I grabbed it and slipped it into my purse."

Of all the people that he had suspected of taking that poison from the lab, Stephanie was not one of them. Until he had seen the photos of Mary Gilbert and Albert Zappala in that yearbook, he would have said that she had no motive. Now he realized that she had the most powerful of motives, revenge. He thought of Milton's Satan who sought revenge against God by attempting to destroy Paradise, despite knowing that his revenge would ultimately "back on itself recoil."

Stephanie continued without prompting. "After that scene at the Blue Moon, I knew that in order to slip the poison into his drink, I was going to have to gain his trust. I told him that I wanted to learn more about my birth mother. I met him at a pizza place, but that didn't work out because there were too many people who had seen me there with him. That's when I got the idea of going to his house."

Listening to her tell her story so methodically sent a chill through Bishop. Had she stayed there to watch him die?

Then she smiled strangely. "You actually helped me, you know."

"What are you talking about?"

"Remember when you thought that Chris Delaney might have killed him after you had read his essay on *Moby Dick*?"

"Yes."

"I was observing your class the day you discussed Starbuck's decision not to kill Ahab when he had the chance. I decided that I wouldn't make the same mistake as Starbuck."

"However you might try to justify it, it's still murder, Steph."

"I did it for my mother!" she shot back. "And when you told me about Honesty Jones, I realized that I had done it for her as well."

"But Honesty Jones won't be going to jail, Steph."

"Neither will I," she said confidently. She glanced at her watch. "Look at the time! I have to get to the airport." Bishop froze as she reached into her purse. Was she carrying that revolver? Would she shoot a friend? After the first murder, would she hesitate to commit a second?

He felt his pulse quicken as he considered his options. Should he try to talk her out of it? Should he just grab for the gun and hope nobody got hurt? As she stood, she pointed directly at him.

"You can't prove a thing. It would be your word against mine." Her car keys jingled as she punched the air for emphasis. "I'll deny everything, Michael. I'll destroy your reputation if I have to."

"I don't think that will be necessary," said Lieutenant Hodge who was now standing in the doorway of the sunroom.

Stephanie stood there for a moment without saying a word. She seemed genuinely confused. Then she asked, "What are you doing here?"

"Mr. Bishop thought it might be a good idea if I dropped by."

"How long have you been here? I didn't hear a car pull up."

"He thought it best if I pulled my patrol car into the garage. I arrived before you did. I'm afraid that you'll have to come along with me, Miss Harris."

Stephanie turned towards Bishop in disbelief. "You set me up?" Before he had a chance to respond, she pounced on him as if she were Catwoman once again. With both fists flailing against him, she screamed, "I thought you were my friend!" As he fended off her blows, he said, "I'm sorry, Steph, I really am." Hodge grabbed her in a bear hug from behind. He waited a moment for her to calm down, got her seated again, and informed her of her rights. She sat there and began to sob.

After a few moments, she looked up at Bishop. There was no anger in her eyes.

"I need you to call my parents and tell them what happened. I know they'll be devastated, and I just can't face that right now. You'll know what to say."

He didn't have the faintest idea of how he would begin to tell those good people that their daughter had been arrested for murder. "Sure, I'll take care of it."

"And Henrietta. She's expecting me to pick her up at the airport tonight."

Bishop promised to be there in her place.

"And I'll need a lawyer."

"I'll call Andy White. He'll be able to recommend a good lawyer."

Stephanie sighed. "Even a good lawyer isn't going to be able to make this go away." She was right, of course. She had to be held accountable for her actions. Zappala was a twisted man who deserved punishment, but it was wrong to appoint herself his judge and executioner. And yet, he felt it entirely possible that her punishment would prove to be fairly lenient. She did have an otherwise impeccably clean record. The extraordinary emotional duress of discovering the identity of the man who had fathered her and abandoned her mother would likely evoke a sympathetic response from a jury. On balance she had been as much a victim of Zappala's immoral conduct as Zappala had been a victim of her desire for revenge.

Before Hodge escorted her into the garage for the ride to the station, Steph asked,

"Oh, Michael! Do you hate me? Do you think Ron will hate me?"

"No, of course not. I might hate what you did, but that doesn't mean that I hate you. I could never do that. I think that Ron will feel the same way."

"You know more about Zappala than anyone else. Will you explain to everyone what an evil man he was?"

"I'll tell his story and your story as best I can. That's all I can do."

"Ready to go, miss?" asked Hodge.

"Yes," she replied softly. He stood there and watched as she walked out the door. Although the circumstances were far different, it was the second time in his life that his world had been torn apart. Wanting to fill the silence, he put a CD into the player. The voice of Andrea Bocelli singing "Con Te Partiro" filled the room. "I'll go with you." How painful an irony that was.

He watched as Lieutenant Hodge backed his car out of the garage. Stephanie was in the back seat, with her head bowed. One poor decision had cost her her teaching career, her relationship with Ron, her freedom. He remembered the advice Atticus Finch had given to Scout in *To Kill A Mockingbird*. It was wrong to judge others; instead, we need to walk in their shoes. He got in his car and headed toward the airport to pick up

Henrietta Avery. She would be confused that Stephanie was not there to greet her; she would be even more disappointed when Bishop explained what had transpired in the few days since Steph had sent her on her way to visit her family for Thanksgiving. He played out the conversation in his mind several times as he drove to the airport. He would tell Miss Avery only as much as she needed to know. He would say nothing of the handgun that Stephanie had found in the attic.

Marion County Regional Airport was small enough that he didn't need to check for a gate arrival. All incoming passengers passed through the same waiting area. The flight had been delayed. The only book he had with him was his copy of Hawthorne's *The Scarlet Letter*. No sooner had he settled in to a wait of at least an hour in an uncomfortable airport lounge seat, than he heard someone say his name. It was not a voice he recognized.

"Mr. Bishop? Excuse me, are you Mr. Bishop?"

He looked up from his book and into the smiling face of a former student. This sort of thing happened all the time. The variable was whether or not he would remember the name of the student quickly enough. He stood up to shake her hand. She had been in his Advanced Placement class only a few years earlier. He could remember clearly what seat she had occupied in his classroom. All of a sudden it clicked.

"Kathleen Donovan! How nice to see you!"

"Are you still at Holy Trinity?"

"Why yes I am." Bishop was amused that many of his former students asked that question as if their graduation might lead him to retirement or at least a career change. Perhaps it was just their way of starting up a conversation with someone to whom they had not given a single thought after leaving school. "What are you doing these days?" It was obvious that she had been home on break, but he could not remember where she had decided to attend college.

"I'm at the University of Notre Dame, and I'm majoring in English," she said proudly.

"Good choice," said Bishop laughing. "Thinking of teaching?"

"Actually, I'm planning to go to law school."

"Also a good choice." He thought of Steph sitting in her cell and understood quite well the importance of a good lawyer.

They spent the next few minutes catching up. He asked her about the classes she was taking and how she liked dorm life. She wanted to know what was new at Trinity. She had heard about the death of the coach and expressed her regrets as if Zappala had been a member of Bishop's family. In a way, he realized, Zappala had been a member of his family, however unpleasant a thought that might be. Suddenly, Kathleen began to speak in a hushed tone even though no one was close enough to eavesdrop on their conversation.

"Do you remember my paper on Emily Dickinson?"

How typical this was of former students! Bishop had been pleased enough with himself for having remembered her name. Now she expected him to remember a particular paper that she had written. He hoped that she wasn't going to tell him that she still believed that she deserved a better mark than he had given her.

"A Dickinson paper?" he asked tentatively, hoping for some clue as to its significance.

"That was the paper that I foolishly cut and pasted from various sites on the Internet and handed in for a grade. You gave me a zero for plagiarizing." He certainly did remember that incident. Thankfully, the incidence of plagiarism in the papers that he read was quite low. Most students knew that it was better to write a poor paper and take the honest low grade than to cheat. Most "cut and paste" papers that he read were terrible anyway.

"Yes, I do remember now that you mention it."

"Well, I just wanted to thank you for setting me straight. You not only gave me a zero, but you insisted on a conference with my parents. I thought you'd hate me forever, but you didn't. In class and in the halls, you treated me just the same as before I made that stupid mistake. I just want you to know that meant a lot to me."

"People make mistakes, and they move on." As he said that to Kathleen, he realized that it was not just a line; it was what he believed. Zappala had made mistakes but refused to acknowledge them or learn from them. Until Stephanie arrived at his house that night, he had escaped punishment and therefore had never had the chance to experience forgiveness. Stephanie had made a terrible mistake, and she would be punished. And with her punishment, she also deserved forgiveness and the chance to rebuild her life. Just like Hester Prynne, he thought to himself.

Chapter 31

While he waited for Miss Avery's flight, Bishop decided to make a few calls. The first was to Andy White. He explained briefly the events of the last twenty-four hours that had led to the identification of Zappala's killer. There was little reaction from Andy. He was too busy running through several possibilities for a defense attorney. He recommended Johnson Deming. "He's one of the best."

"Expensive?"

"Yes, but when you're facing a murder charge, you don't look for a bargain rate," he said bluntly. "Listen, Mike. I know that you must be saddened by the way this turned out. From what you've told me, my guess is that she has a good chance of escaping a life sentence. She's young, attractive, and intelligent. She appears to have suffered a great deal from the actions of the coach. Most juries are not going to want to put her in jail and throw away the key."

"She killed a man, Andy. She shouldn't just walk away."

"I'm not saying she will. But I imagine that if Deming takes this case, he'll find even more dirt on Zappala, and the more the focus is on him, the better it will be for Stephanie." Andy offered to call Deming himself. "I'll call you tomorrow after I've talked with him."

Steph had wanted him to call her parents, and he would, but not just yet. He needed a bit more time to prepare for that sad task. Brian and June Harris were such wonderful people. He had so much enjoyed their hospitality only the other day. It would be difficult to deliver the devastating news about their daughter. Might they blame themselves for shielding Steph from the truth when she was a child? Did they know more than they had admitted? Might they blame him for his relentless pursuit of the mystery that led him to Middleton?

His next call was to Ron. Poor guy. Bishop hadn't seen Ron happier than he was in the last couple of months. Some guys just seemed to have bad luck with women, and Ron was one of them. In addition to the teacher who had run off with an old flame, several years ago, he had been engaged to a lovely young woman until Ron discovered that she was having an affair with her tennis coach. Everyone was hoping that this time would be different. Bishop kept the call short. Ron listened quietly as Bishop summarized what had happened. It would take a while before the reality sank in. Bishop promised to be there for him in the days ahead.

Informing Sister Ann was his next priority. He called the convent and was disappointed to learn that she was unavailable. That left him no choice but to speak to Sister Pat. "What do you want now, Bishop?"

No greeting. No warmth. This was her modus operandi. For a moment, he was tempted to use that Latin phrase since it would more than likely launch her into a frenzy, but he thought better of it. Instead, he explained to her that Stephanie had been arrested for the murder of Zappala and that Sister Ann needed to arrange for a long-term substitute for her classes. He had barely finished a sentence before she erupted. "Have you been drinking? Stephanie killed him? Oh, my God! Think of the bad press the school is going to get!"

He cut her off. "Think of Stephanie and her family!"

"Think of Stephanie?" she snapped. "She's a killer! She should rot in prison!" The extent to which this member of a religious order failed to demonstrate any feelings of Christian compassion truly was beyond his comprehension. Rather than trying to reason with her, he settled for giving her some practical advice. "Please tell Sister Ann that I think she should contact Helene Boulanger." Boulanger had retired after thirty-one years of teaching French at Holy Trinity. It was her retirement that had created the opening for Stephanie this year. Helene would have no problem filling in at least on a temporary basis.

"Boulanger? That woman was a head case. Why would we want her back?"

"Well, it was just a suggestion. I'm sure that you and Sister Ann will find a suitable replacement by tomorrow morning." That was as likely as Sister Pat teaching Latin.

***

Henrietta was one of the first passengers out of the gate. One of the flight attendants was guiding her into the waiting area with one hand while rolling her small travel bag with the other. She was understandably confused as to why Bishop was there to greet her instead of Stephanie. He promised to explain everything on the way to her house.

As he recounted the sequence of events leading up to her arrest earlier that evening, she listened with resignation. The old woman had undoubtedly dealt with bad news many times over the years. It didn't take the sting out of it, but it did provide some perspective.

"Who would have thought Stephanie capable of murder?" It was as much a question she was asking of herself as she was asking Bishop.

"I think every human heart is capable of great good and great evil. The challenge is choosing to do good and avoid evil." He had to believe that that was true.

***

As he turned the corner onto Glendale Avenue, Bishop encountered three police cruisers, a fire truck, an ambulance, and a few cars belonging to volunteers, all with their lights flashing in the night sky.

"Oh my," exclaimed Henrietta. "I think they're at my house!"

Bishop pulled his car to the curb. He told Henrietta to stay in the car until he could find out what was going on. Just as got out of his car, the ambulance took off, its siren blaring. There were some neighbors milling about, some in their pajamas, some talking in hushed voices, and others standing silently in the chill of the night air.

The house didn't seem to be on fire. Bishop was at a loss as to what was going on. He asked a few of the bystanders, but none of them had a clear idea of what had happened. A boy of about twelve whose eyes were filled with the excitement of the moment, stopped chewing gum long enough to report that he saw the EMTs taking someone out on a stretcher.

Then Bishop saw Lieutenant Hodge leaving Henrietta's house. His heart began to race even more than it had before. What would Hodge be doing here? He should have driven Stephanie straight to the police station. Had Stephanie escaped? He caught up to Hodge as he was about to get into his vehicle. Out of breath, Bishop managed to ask what had happened.

His friend looked quite shaken. He explained to Bishop that once they had left his house, Stephanie had requested that they pass by her apartment for a minute. Her contacts were really bothering her, and she wanted to pick up her eyeglasses. He didn't see any harm in that, although strictly speaking, it was against the book. He pulled his cruiser into the empty driveway. He waited in the kitchen while she went into the bathroom to remove her contacts. After a few minutes, he heard the toilet flush and water running in the sink. After another few moments, he became concerned. He could still hear the water running, but he didn't hear Stephanie moving around. He called her name as he began to fear that she might have tried to escape through the bathroom window.

Rushing to the bathroom, he found the door locked. He banged on the door, shouting her name. No response. Just the steady stream of the water running in the sink.

Using his shoulder, he rammed the door until he broke through. For some reason that he didn't quite grasp, the door opened only about ten to twelve inches until it met some resistance. He looked down to see what was preventing the door from opening all the way. Stephanie's body was sprawled on the floor, blocking his entrance. He immediately called in for assistance. Female down. Condition unknown.

Bishop tried to remain outwardly calm as he listened to Hodge recount what had happened.

He kept nudging the door until he had created enough space to enter. He checked for a pulse and was relieved to find one, although it was faint. As he scanned the area, a small brown bottle on the tank of the toilet caught his attention. It was open and empty. Without touching it, he knew what it was. The skull and crossbones said it all. Stephanie had taken a dose of the same poison that she had used to murder Zappala.

Bishop stood dumbfounded as Lieutenant Hodge got into his patrol car. He offered to give Bishop a ride to the hospital, but Bishop declined. Stephanie's landlady was waiting in his car. He needed to explain what had happened to her and make sure that she would be all right.

***

Since she couldn't return to her home until the authorities had finished their examination of the scene, her next-door neighbor, Trudy, also an elderly widow, invited her to stay the night. Once he had gotten her settled in, Bishop raced to the hospital. On the way there, he kept thinking of the question that Henrietta had repeated several times, "Why would she want to throw her life away? Why?" That was something only Stephanie could answer, if in fact, she survived.

When Bishop entered the ER lobby, he saw Lieutenant Hodge talking with one of the physicians on duty. Hodge waved him over and introduced him to Dr. Jayne Billings. She was probably no older than Stephanie. She greeted Bishop with a firm handshake and a comforting smile. She explained that it was fortunate that she was told of the probability of cyanide poisoning. Depending on the dose ingested, death could occur in a matter of minutes. Her own observation of an almond-like smell on the breath of the victim confirmed the diagnosis. Bishop suddenly flashed back to the strange odor that he had noticed when he had first discovered Zappala's body. Now he understood what that had meant. Dr. Billings immediately had pumped Stephanie's stomach to remove as much of the poison as possible. She then administered a dose of hydroxocobalamin to help cleanse the body of any remaining poison.

"We'll keep her here for a day or two for observation and for additional treatment of the antidote. We were lucky with this one. She should be fine."

"We'll also keep her on a suicide watch," added Hodge.

***

Bishop slept surprisingly well that night. Perhaps it was the relief of finally getting to the truth of Zappala's murder even if that truth had been so personally painful. He had delayed calling Stephanie's parents and that decision had proven fortuitous. Lieutenant Hodge had called them from the hospital to inform them of their daughter's admission to the hospital for an "overdose" of some kind. He assured them that Stephanie would be fine, but encouraged them to get here as quickly as possible. He would give them the complete picture then. Andy White had left a message on his phone informing him of Deming's belief that she had a 'very good chance' of receiving a lenient sentence in exchange for a guilty plea to a lesser charge of manslaughter.

***

Zappala's estate was soon settled. The Santorini family kept their bakery thanks to the deal that he had worked out with Sister Ann. Holy Trinity received half a million dollars to spend on needed upgrades. Bishop donated the remainder of the estate to PAVE, a national organization devoted to shattering the silence of sexual violence.

***

Like the wedding guest in "The Rime of the Ancient Mariner" by Coleridge, Michael Bishop woke the following morning, "a sadder but wiser man."